Heleen van Royen was born in Amsterdam in 1965. *The Happy Housewife*, her first novel, was a bestseller in Holland, and rights have been sold internationally.

D0862894

THE

Happy
Housewife

Heleen van Royen

Translated by
Liz Waters

A *Virago* Book

Published by Virago in 2001

First published by Uitgeverij Vassallucci, Amsterdam in 2000

Copyright © Heleen van Royen, 2000
Translation copyright © Liz Waters, 2000

A CIP catalogue record for this book
is available from the British Library.
ISBN 1 86049 900 7

Typeset in Perpetua by M Rules
Printed and bound in Great Britain
by Clays Ltd, St Ives plc

Virago
A division of
Little, Brown and Company (UK)
Brettenham House
Lancaster Place
London WC2E 7EN

This book is for you. While I was writing it I thought about you all the time. Maybe you've borrowed it, maybe someone gave it to you as a present, or maybe you bought it. I hope it was the latter. Anyway, now it's yours. You can do whatever you like with it. It's 82,574 words long. I'd really appreciate it if you'd read all of them. The story begins on page three.

chapter one

So here you are then, Lea. I've had to work pretty hard at it again, but that's all over now and we're all really happy with you, little mite.

'How long were you in solitary?' Beau van Kooten looked out of the window while he asked the question.

'I'm not exactly sure. A few hours, I think. They let me out in the morning.'

'They?'

'Yes, there were four of them. I hadn't seen anyone all night and suddenly there was a whole army at the door. In front was a man with a narrow beard, I heard later that he was the Head of Psychiatry.'

Van Kooten rubbed his chin. 'You mean Doctor Posthumous?'

'Him, yes. What a twat, that one. He started smooth-talking me like crazy as soon as he'd taken me out of the cell. Said what chaos it had been that night. And that the mayor had taken measures to have me admitted to hospital. I thought, sure, the mayor, he can't have had anything better to think about . . .'

'Doctor Posthumous is very highly thought of, Lea.'

'Oh yeah? Well, I saw him twice, apart from that he left everything to his assistant. She hadn't even finished qualifying, for God's sake.'

'I can hear a lot of anger in your voice.' Van Kooten looked me right in the eye. 'Why is that?'

'Because I shouldn't have been there. I was locked up against my will. Even when I got out of solitary confinement they didn't let me go home.'

He leaned back and crossed his arms. 'That was probably for your own good, don't you think?'

I bit my lip. Van Kooten was being so severe today. He'd been far nicer the first time. And this time round he hadn't even offered me a cup of coffee. Was he losing interest already?

'Like some coffee?'

Who says psychiatrists can't read your thoughts?

Van Kooten stood up and went over to his espresso machine. He came back with two steaming cups of coffee. 'One sweetener, wasn't it?'

To think he'd remembered that. I was ashamed I'd ever doubted him. This man obviously loved his patients.

Van Kooten nodded towards his computer. 'It's all in my iMac. I've developed a special little program. One touch of a key and it trots out the coffee and tea habits of my entire surgery.'

'Wow.'

'I thought about patenting it. But then it occurred to me that if all the others did it too, then there'd be nothing special about it any longer.'

I took a sip of coffee. It was a bit weak.

'Everyone wants to be unique, Lea. Unique and irreplaceable. You say you didn't belong in the psychiatric wing of a hospital. Shall I tell you a secret?' He put his cup down on the table.

I nodded briefly.

'You're not the only one! Every day I see people in my surgery who think they're normal and the rest of the world is mad. But every one of them has fallen apart somewhere along the line. You too.'

I looked down. 'Next you'll say I just have to accept it.'

'Exactly!' said Van Kooten enthusiastically. 'If you accept what's happened to you, you can come to terms with it. Then your anger will resolve itself.'

'And how do I do that?'

'What?'

'"Come to terms" with it. Open a drawer, throw all the shit in, shut the drawer – Bob's your uncle?'

'It's not quite as simple as that, of course. It's a process that can take months or even years, depending on the seriousness and extent of the trauma.' He gave me a searching look. 'But if you think you can get over it all by yourself, then be my guest.'

'No, of course not. I didn't mean to question your expertise. Without you I wouldn't know where to start . . .' Tears welled up in my eyes. 'I'm still so bloody unstable, sorry.'

Love means never having to say you're sorry.

'Don't mention it,' said my psychiatrist.

'The coffee is excellent, Mr van Kooten.'

'Great.' He cleared his throat. 'So I just need you to tell me one thing.'

I dabbed my eyes with a tissue.

'Do you want to get better?'

'Of course,' I said shyly.

'I want you to say it.'

'Sorry?'

'Say it. Out loud.'

'Now?'

Van Kooten nodded.

'I want to . . . er . . . I do want . . . to get better.'

My shrink brought his hands together with a clap. 'Wonderful! Shall we make an appointment for next time?'

chapter two

*Your full name is Helena Helma Maria. Helena comes
from a great-grandmother of your daddy's who was called
Helena Brood; Helena Brood was married to a certain
Pieter Cornelissen.*

I am a woman. I have given birth to a child.

My pregnancy lasted nine months and twelve days. After
nine months and twelve days Harry was a father and I was a
mother. From one day to the next we got life.

I have given birth to a son. I brought him into the world in
1998, although it might as well have been 1698. Midwifery in
the Netherlands hasn't changed to speak of since then. 'Natural
childbirth' hasn't gone out of fashion.

The word 'natural' makes my hair stand on end. I don't like
the natural world. I don't want to go there, I wouldn't want to
be seen dead in it.

The natural world is not a woman-friendly place. However
hard you try it's almost impossible to look attractive out there in

the open. It's the fault of the elements. The elements make me nervous.

If God had intended nature as something for women, he would have made women out of plastic. Actually, that wouldn't have been a bad idea. Plastic is great stuff. Half the things in my house are made of plastic. All my son's toys are plastic. I don't understand why plastic has such a bad image. It's indestructible. The elements can't destroy plastic and neither can my son. A comforting thought.

Machteld never asked me whether I wanted a natural birth. 'Your pregnancy's going so well you'll want to have it at home, right?' Machteld is my midwife.

Respectful of authority as I am I said 'Yes' right away. I swallowed whole the notion that there's a connection between an uncomplicated pregnancy and a problem-free birth. There are whole tribes of women who know otherwise, but what are tribes to me? I thought, this chick's done the training, if she says we can do it at home, then we'll do it at home.

Must have made Machteld happy, considering she gets some fifty guilders more for a home birth than for one in the hospital.

I didn't agree with her, by the way, that my pregnancy was going well. It wasn't going well at all. Being pregnant is dreadful. It's degrading. You look bad. Really bad. In nine months you lose everything you have going for you as far as proportions are concerned. Okay, those giant boobs are good, but your fat belly's more noticeable than the tits are. Suddenly there's not a man in sight who can see further than the end of his own nose. The workmen in the street never compliment you on your nice ass. The only people who watch you go by are women with that pathetic look in their eyes. They start telling you, without being asked, how radiant you look, and prodding your stomach with their fat, greedy fingers. 'Ooh, I think I can feel him kicking!'

I find that quite moving actually, that such a tiny child has the same impulse as me.

Usually the prodding bores don't have children themselves. They want to, but they can't find a prick mad enough to impregnate them, or they hang around half the week in hospitals with their cultivated eggs in Tupperware boxes, while their lawfully wedded imbeciles jerk themselves off in sterilised rooms with a copy of *Playboy* from 1988. If I ever had to stoop to that, I'd suck my Harry off myself. My aim is good, so I'd personally spit the resulting product into that lecherous petri dish, right onto the egg. Whatever I had left in my mouth I'd swallow, and I'd wipe the rest on my dress. I don't like immaculate conceptions, they only lead to trouble.

I hate those prodding motherly types, but I can't blame them. They haven't a clue what pregnancy is really like. If I try to tell them about all the ailments that make those forty weeks truly hellish they get angry. They'd give 'anything' to be able to have a baby. They'd greet every varicose vein with joy, stick pictures of their first haemorrhoids in the baby book and when their friends came round they'd raffle all the stitches that dropped out.

Motherhood is an incredible blow to your image.

This summer I went to a poolside party with Corine. Corine is my tennis partner. We were lying on sunbeds by the swimming pool. I had Harry Junior with me, because my Filipino girl had to go to the dentist.

Suddenly Danny Blind, my favourite soccer star, comes waltzing in. I thought I was going mad. Instinctively I plonked Junior onto Corine's lap.

She jolted out of her doze.

'Sorry, you have to take him for a moment. He's yours, okay?'

Corine sat up. Junior stared at her Jacky O sunglasses in amazement.

I quickly did my lipstick and rearranged my hair.

Corine yawned. 'Do I have to do anything with him?'

'Not so long as he's quiet. If he starts screaming just give him a lollipop. They're in my bag.'

I was running my eyes over Blind. God, what a luxuriant head of curls the guy had! That might be a good opening line. Should I ask him if they were real? And then run my hands through them nonchalantly. Pull his head towards me a bit. Closer and closer until our mouths were almost touching. 'I don't think that's a perm, Danny, and it seems you dress to the left. Do you know, I've never done it with an ambidextrous soccer player.' I'd lick my lips ultra slowly with the tip of my tongue. 'Shall we take a swim?' He'd nod and lead me to the water. I sat there, getting tremendously moist in my swimming costume. This was too good a chance to miss. Corine was discreet. Harry would never get to hear about it.

The host gave Danny a drink. I tried to make eye contact but he was too far away.

'Ah, what a sweetie!' I heard a woman's voice coo.

Fuck. I wasn't the only one with their eyes on Blind.

The voice came closer. 'How old is he?'

Fuck. She was standing right between Danny and me. 'He's your little boy, isn't he?'

Fuck, fuck and triple fuck.

'I don't need to ask really, he looks so much like you. Those eyes! What a handsome little man. You must be so proud. How was the birth?'

'Ugh.'

'Right, you don't get them for free, do you? But they give you so much in return. Don't they? I still remember the awful backache I had with my oldest . . . blah blah . . . middle one . . . blah blah . . . youngest . . . blah blah . . . so marvellous . . .'

Fuck, fuck, fuck with knobs on. It was a *mother*. A real one.

I'm allergic to real mothers. The chills run up and down my spine as soon as I lay eyes on one. Those fluffy pink Madonnas are experts at glossing over the truth. They describe squeezing an eight-pounder through your vagina as an almost orgasmic sensation that every woman simply has to experience. They go on about primal feelings and a bond with the earth and forget that they're just randy bitches who've fallen into a primeval trap. Stupid cunts. Give them three forceps deliveries and they'll still say that you forget the pain as soon as you hold the baby in your arms.

I haven't forgotten the pain. How can I when I could still feel it weeks later? I hurt all over, inside and out. I couldn't sit, stand or walk. It burned and stung like crazy. For the first time in my life my cunt wasn't out after sex. My head was of course, but my underparts simply refused. So did Harry, by the way. The asshole.

Real mothers are the worst thing that can happen to a child. They shouldn't be allowed to have children. They're sick. They're women who've given up being women. They're creatures who deliberately turn themselves into imbeciles so they can rediscover the world through the eyes of their offspring. Go away and play with yourself Mary and leave the kids alone. Keep your sick thoughts to yourself. And keep your hands off their Lego.

Real mothers think children are completely helpless. But that's exactly what they're not. Children are designed to survive and most of them manage it perfectly well. Unless they're unfortunate enough to have a mother who's a member of the good parenting brigade. Or worse still the breastfeeding mafia. Those are the kind of mummies who sometimes literally let their children waste away because they won't admit that their miserable tits give less milk than a can of Nutrilon.

I looked like an animal when I was pregnant. I can't quite think what it's called, but it's one of those things they try to push back out to sea when they get themselves stranded on the beach by accident. I retained so much water the neighbours complained about the sloshing noises.

The worst thing was that nothing fitted me anymore. My shoes, my rings, my bikinis, my suspender belts, my tops, my cylinder dresses; it got harder and harder to squeeze into them. After about six months I shut the wardrobe door. For the rest of my pregnancy I was severely depressed.

Natural childbirth is the worst thing that's ever happened to me. It was butchery. Not for the child, for me. It seems that's the idea.

I even went to prenatal yoga classes, for God's sake, to prepare for the big day. 'You do go to yoga, don't you?' Machteld had said.

I can still see myself sitting in that sweltering little room in the community centre, with sixteen other ladies. The yoga teacher was too lazy to provide a few decent chairs. We had to sit on thin mattresses which looked as though they might once have been purple. I thought, how many waters have broken on this mat? For the next lesson I brought my own. A plastic one, much more hygienic.

The teacher was actually quite nice, even if her clothes sense was seriously antediluvian. She talked a lot, in a slow, languid kind of way. ' . . . During labour you must become one with the universe. You must become one with your contractions and one with the unborn child inside you . . .'

All those pregnant cows, myself included, nodded obediently. No one asked how in God's name we were supposed to do that. It seemed a bit incestuous to me, becoming one with your unborn child. I'd rather become one with some strapping six-footer.

Maybe I fell asleep, but I think the teacher left out something rather important. Your little backside hole and your beloved slit can also become one during labour. That's called a total rupture.

chapter three

The name Helma comes from me, your own mother.

I am a happy housewife. I have everything my heart could desire. I don't need to work at all. Because work is something my husband does.

Harry's in real estate. I'm not sure what that is, but the money keeps rolling in. It's more than I can manage to spend, and that's saying something. A hard-working man is the best kind there is. He's never home, but the bills still get paid.

Before I forget, I love Harry. You don't often hear that these days. Most of the women I know go around complaining about their guy all day. God, how those twats can whinge! It never ceases to amaze me. In my fitness class there's a right Bambi; they ought to stick her on the Wailing Wall.

My Harry is a complete career junkie. He works eighty hours

a week, plays golf for twenty and the rest of the time he watches
television. I barely give a thought to Harry. It's no problem to
me that we're hardly ever together. Quite the opposite, it's a
blessing. The less I see of Harry the better.

People ask themselves, what's the secret of a happy marriage? I think the answer is simpler than they realise.

I used to bring Harry breakfast in bed every morning. The
alarm would go off at six thirty. I'd throw my silk dressing gown
on over my nightdress and put on a bit of mascara and lipstick,
because Harry doesn't like faces that look like bare backsides. I'd
press three oranges, make coffee and bake fresh croissants. We'd
have breakfast together. He always ate croissants while I had a
piece of fruit. He'd read *De Telegraaf* while I watched repeats of
'The Bold'. We talked as little as possible so as not to disturb the
peace and quiet.

In summer I liked our morning ritual best of all. Then I could
throw the doors open and we'd eat together in the sun on the
patio.

I often think back to those happy times.

My first husband was called Ed. He was a six-foot-six American
stud.

Ed was a very jealous type. He was always afraid I'd screw
someone else. So afraid that he gave it a go himself. Next day he
came home with an itchy dick and a bottle of pills. He said we
both had to take them, because the lady he'd shagged in his
Beetle hadn't been entirely kosher.

The pills ran out, the itch remained. Ed took me with him to
the doctor. He/she was in the middle of a sex change. He
looked like a woman, but still had a prick. Ed had received a

letter about it. Saying that Wim would be called Wilma from then on and asking whether he had a problem with that. Ed didn't mind. He did find it funny, though. I found it funny too. How was I to know Wilma was going to ask me to pull my trousers down and bend over? Wilma had the build of a docker and was wearing a light-yellow tent dress and pink lipstick. When I saw her freshly shaven hands pushing a hypodermic needle into Ed's right buttock I should have known my marriage was a hopeless undertaking.

All the same, I worked at it for another three years. Three interminable years in which I swung back and forth between heaven and hell at an incredible rate. I couldn't do without Ed, Ed couldn't do without the booze. When I pulled the door of our maisonette shut behind me for the last time, I felt on top of the world. I thought he would too. Ed had studied history in the Netherlands. His motto was, what's happened has happened, don't keep going on about it. I thought that was a great motto.

I did history at school. I found out that people rarely learn lessons from the past. If they've been through five years of misery, they complain about it for the rest of their lives. Take the Second World War. How many non-Jewish people here really had a hard time? Once they'd turned their backs on most of the Jews, including our dearly beloved Anne Frank, there was hardly a cloud on the horizon. All the same, Holland still harps on about it endlessly. As if we were all in the Resistance. As if we all lost half our families.

I hate the Second World War. Shut the fuck up about that shithead with the moustache. As if the rest of the world can wash its hands of all guilt. I was born in 1966. When I first broke wind, the camps had been shut for twenty years. Leave it alone. Don't go on at me about it. Do you really think I want to hear all the details? Why is it good to know how bad people are? Why is it good to know how stupid people are? Why is it good to know that millions of people have suffered and are still suffering – why is it good to have all that drilled into you? Why did I have to learn at school how much Zyklon B you need per train carriage?

When I was fifteen I was forced to look at videos about the concentration camps. My father worked in Germany during the Second World War. He had to do some sort of work on a railway. I never heard him talk about it. My father was a bastard but he wasn't a whinger. I have to give him that.

Ed was a bastard *and* a whinger. He didn't put his motto into practice. He still moans on and on about the fact that I left him. At parties he loves to reveal to everyone what a shrew I was. Which I was, of course. Or am. I mean, just like in a war, in every relationship there's always one person who does everything wrong, which makes the whole situation very clear and easy to understand, because everything the other person does is, in that case, therefore, accordingly and without any room for doubt at all, absolutely right.

Maybe it's time to say sorry. If the Pope can say *mea culpa*, then Lea can too. Sorry Ed, you were right. I shouldn't have sent out my mating call so quickly. ('Next!') The grass always looks greener on the other side of the fence.

Shall I tell you a secret? It *was* greener. And juicier, lusher. Longer and thicker. It was Harry's grass.

chapter four

You were born on a Tuesday morning at five to six. You weighed seven pounds five ounces. That's just perfect, you know. You had a terrible squint and your thumb went straight into your mouth, and so there you were. Your life had begun.

One day Harry came home from work and said, 'Darling, I want a child.'

I stopped arranging the flowers, wiped my hands on my apron and threw my arms round his neck. 'Oh darling, how lovely, did you watch Ivo Niehe last night as well? What do you think, should we start with one, or do you want to get two straight away?'

'What's Ivo Niehe got to do with our child?' Harry growled. He can be very jealous sometimes. He knows I've had a soft spot for Ivo for years. That *je ne sais quoi* of his is irresistible.

'Nothing of course,' I reassured him. 'He's just the presenter. I've been a bit naughty. I've made out a cheque already. You only have to sign it and we'll get a beautiful brown baby.'

'I don't want a brown baby.'

'Okay, then I'll ask for another colour. I'm sure that's possible. Would you rather have one of those adorable little slit-eyed ones?' I went to the fridge and got Harry a beer.

'Slit-eyed?' He sat down on the sofa.

'You know, my love, I've been thinking about it. It's a great idea. If you adopt a child you help all its brothers and sisters, parents and grandparents at the same time. The uncles and cousins probably get something out of it too. Wonderful, isn't it? It only costs a few guilders a month. Ivo says you can take it all off.'

Harry frowned. Perhaps I shouldn't have used the words 'Ivo' and 'take it all off' right after each other like that.

'Off your tax bill. I thought, if I can drum up the support of all the girls at the tennis club and we all get a child plus the half a tribe they throw in with it, it'll give Africa a tremendous boost.'

Harry sniffed.

'Okay then. I'll get all your friends at the golf club to join in as well. I'm sure Charles and Ted will be delighted when they hear it's for Foster Parents Plan. Apparently it's a very reputable organisation. According to Ivo.'

Harry burped.

I sat down next to him and tickled his neck. 'What do you think, shall we have it off right now?'

'No.'

My fingers froze. Harry had never refused me anything.

'No, I don't want all that Foster Parents Plan stuff. I want a real child.'

'What do you mean, a real child?'

'A baby. Yours and mine. Ours.'

I edged away from him. 'A baby, what do you want with a baby, for God's sake? You're never home.'

'You are.'

'Me?! The last thing I want is a baby. I'm completely happy the way I am. What a horrible thought, being shut up here all day with one of those screeching apes.'

Harry smiled. 'Wait till you hold the little one in your arms. Then you'll change your tune. I've seen women at work turn into completely different people when they have babies. Incredible. Even that prize bitch of a director went soft at the edges.' He gazed ahead dreamily.

'Harry! Don't you go expecting anything. I'll have to give it a lot of thought. Really a lot. And I can tell you right now that I'd want an au pair. One of those Filipino girls. I've heard they're wonderful. They never say a word and they do everything. Only you need to put a video camera in the baby's bedroom so you can check she isn't secretly torturing the baby. I saw a film about it on television, it was really awful. I couldn't sleep at all that night.'

'Of course my love, we'll arrange everything. Don't you go worrying about that. You'll get your Filipino girl.'

'And the hidden camera.'

'That too.' Harry looked satisfied. 'Go up and get your pills.' He said it that way of his that you just can't argue with.

Panting slightly I gave him the bubble strip.

'Let's see. It's Monday today.' Harry pressed a pill out of the strip, threw it in the air the way he usually throws peanuts, opened his mouth, caught the pill on his tongue and swallowed it. 'Hup! I could do with a few extra hormones.'

'Jesus Harry, I'm supposed to take that one this evening.'

'Don't be pathetic. Just take one from the other strip, right?'

I hadn't thought of that. I sighed with relief.

We went to bed early that evening. Harry wanted to screw me.

'Are you sure, darling? It's Monday. We did it the day before yesterday.'

'So? I'm allowed to ride my little woman whenever I please. Get used to it, Lea, soon I'll be making whoopee every night.' He tore my knickers to shreds. The brute.

I had a terrible fit of the giggles. 'Wait a minute, honey, wait a minute.' I crawled on hands and knees across the bed to the bedside table, while Harry pushed his dick into me from behind.

'Doggie-fashion. Great.' He bit my ear and growled softly into it.

I felt my way to my reserve strip and quickly squeezed out a pill. And then another. Just to make sure.

'If you stop taking those stupid pills I'll screw you every night, from the front and from behind,' Harry panted.

'Oh, Harry,' I moaned, 'do you mean that, do you really mean that?'

'I really mean it, Lea. And I'm about to come. Any moment now.'

'Oh, Harry, me too. And that's what I want. Every night . . .'

chapter five

We hope you'll be able to enjoy this life, that you'll be kind and devote a part of yourself to others, and always be able to see things from their point of view. Then your life will have been worthwhile.

Beau van Kooten has a permanent holiday tan. Beau van Kooten wears silk neckties. The first time I saw him, his outfit was smart-casual. A bit like Marco Bakker after the accident.* Nonchalant, but still well dressed. As for his age, I reckoned early forties to late sixties.

Van Kooten was recommended to me by Corine. Corine is my tennis partner.

We'd just finished a game of doubles with Vanessa and Milou, when I divulged to her that I'd walked out of my Community Mental Health Service treatment.

She understood immediately. 'That Mental Health Service is

---

* Dutch tenor who caused a fatal car crash.

no use to you at all. That's first aid for gibbering wrecks. I think
you should go and see Beau.'

'Bo?' I echoed.

'Beau van Kooten, haven't you heard of him? He's a world-
class shrink! Patty's with him, and Pia, and I think Loretta's
been seeing him for years. He's a darling, he really is.'

I felt something stir inside me. 'But do you think he'll take
me? I mean, does a man like that have time for me?' I looked
intently at Corine.

She put her sunglasses down on the table and took an unhur-
ried sip of her Bloody Mary. 'My dear, with Beau it's very
simple. You only need to wave your Gold Card.'

'You can't be serious.'

'Of course I am. And for appearance's sake you tell him
you're deeply depressed and feel you can't go on. Once you've
got your mascara to run, you're in.'

I'd never heard Corine talk like this before. I didn't dare ask
her if she'd ever consulted Beau herself.

She narrowed her eyes. 'Are you shocked now? Surely not,
are you?' She looked at her pastel blue nails with satisfaction.

Corine goes to Loes. I know that for sure because she got that
address from me. Loes is my manicuriste.

'Are you divorced yet?' Corine can ask things like that in
such a businesslike way.

'Not yet,' I said, hesitantly.

She sighed. 'I still don't understand why you want rid of
him. He gives you everything you need. Everything.'

'Do you have Beau's phone number?' I asked.

She suddenly started giggling. 'Don't you need a pee?' You
never knew where you were with Corine. She hopped so easily

from one subject to another, I sometimes had trouble keeping up.

'I don't need a pee, but I could have one if I wanted to,' I said truthfully. Any woman can produce urine at any time, if only a few drops.

'Then pop along to the toilet in the cafeteria for a moment. Use the one on the left. Pia's written his name and phone number next to the bin. With eyeliner. Max Factor. She's so cheap with things like that.'

I took a pen and my Filofax out of my bag and walked like a robot to the cafeteria. Sometimes you just have to jump in at the deep end.

Corine wasn't making it up. Only she'd forgotten to mention that Pia had drawn a swastika next to the bin too. Very neatly, which isn't easy with eyeliner. It also said

PIA HATES BEAU, ADOLF WAS A BETTER FUCK

I tried to ignore this announcement and took down the telephone number.

Beau van Kooten has a beautiful office. Wall to wall Jan des Bouvrie. A refreshing blend of styles.

The sitting area has a warm and comfy appearance, partly thanks to the authentic-looking open hearth. The desk, with its chrome fittings, makes a businesslike impression. There's nothing on it at all, apart from the computer. It's pretty unusual. It's transparent. Jan probably designed it especially for Beau.

Beau saw me staring. 'What do you think of my iMac? It's new. Nice toy, isn't it?'

I didn't know what an iMac was. It didn't look very cuddly to me. Unlike Van Kooten himself. Beau had a remarkably smooth chin.

'What do you shave with?'

'Sorry?'

I patted my mouth with my hand. 'I couldn't help noticing that your chin . . . I mean, my husband, my . . . er, almost-ex-husband, Harry, he has very sensitive skin and he hates shaving. So one time I bought him a hyper-modern shaver. A Ladyshave. Because of his sensitive skin, you understand, not because Harry's a lady, because Harry's . . .' My God, I sure was rabbiting on. I'd lost it completely. What on earth must Mr van Kooten think of me?

'Are you very nervous?' Beau van Kooten gave me a friendly nod.

God almighty, he can see right through me. Corine was right, this man is a very good psychiatrist.

'If you'd like to go and take a seat over there in the corner and relax, I'll be with you in a moment.'

Van Kooten was wearing a very elegant pair of glasses. The frames were so thin, you could hardly see that my new shrink wore glasses at all. He walked calmly over to his desk and got a gold-plated cigarette case out of the drawer. 'I hope you don't mind if I smoke?' he said.

'N-no, not at all,' I stammered. 'That's what dry cleaners are for, I always say.'

'It's a Marlboro Light, perhaps that helps too.'

I burst out laughing.

Van Kooten smiled. 'I'd like some coffee, how about you?' Without waiting for an answer, he went over to the espresso machine on the bar.

I wasn't sure, but I thought he was trying to distract me.

Before he started making coffee, he cleaned his glasses. With a Kleenex tissue. His whole practice seemed to have been sponsored by Kleenex, I could see boxes of tissues all over the place. Of course it was also possible that Des Bouvrie had done a deal with the Kleenex mob and forced Van Kooten to accept a large consignment. I thought that was very probably it. Van Kooten didn't look to me like the sort who would happily go scattering such ugly boxes about.

'May I hazard a guess? White coffee with one sweetener.'

Unbelievable. Right first time.

'Yes please,' I answered, beaming.

Having put the coffee down in front of me, Van Kooten looked at me with a serious expression. 'Your face looks so lovely when the sun breaks through for a moment. I see a lot of sadness in your eyes.'

I got a lump in my throat and quickly took a sip of coffee. Piping hot, just the way it ought to be.

Van Kooten tapped his nose with his index finger. 'Lea . . . May I call you Lea?'

'Of course, that's my name. At least, I'm really called Helena. Helena Helma Maria, born and bred in Amsterdam . . .' Oh boy, I was off again. I quickly shut my mouth.

'Helen of Troy,' he said solemnly. 'A magnificent woman. A war broke out over her, did you know that?'

I played dumb. I often do that with men. Not only with Harry, with intellectuals too. They find babyish women incredibly sexy. 'Oh yes, Mr van Kooten, terrible, wasn't it? Those pictures were heartbreaking. I really couldn't bear to watch. I paid up straight away when they gave out that bank number. I thought it was so good of all those stars to help out so unselfishly. Didn't you?'

Van Kooten smoothed his left eyebrow. 'Indeed, indeed. So, shall we make a start, Lea?'

I nodded.

Van Kooten stood up and went over to his desk.

I wasn't sure whether or not I should follow him.

'I want to say first of all that I never put anything down on paper. I have full confidence in this little chap.' He patted his iMac. 'I'm the psychiatrist, but this is my brain. And we're going to work with this brain.'

I nearly had kittens. 'You don't mean I . . .'

Van Kooten gave me a reassuring nod. 'We'll do it together. You and I. I'll come and sit next to you. I'll stay with you. But you're going to press the keys. That way you can make the best use of my brain.'

I wrung my hands. 'Do I really have to, Mr van Kooten, I'm a bit afraid of computers.'

'Great! Then that's the first fear I can help you overcome, Lea. Would you like to come and sit next to me?' He was already sitting at his desk, patting the empty chair beside him. Only now did I notice that there were two chairs on his side of the desk. The empty chair was in front of the iMac.

Hesitantly, I took my seat. The screen was blank.

'We'll start at the beginning,' said Van Kooten. 'Just turn on the computer.'

I found the largest key on the keyboard and pressed it.

Nothing happened. 'Is it broken? Have I broken it?! Oh heavens, I was afraid of that.'

Van Kooten put his hand on my shoulder. 'Below the screen there's an on/off switch, see? Why don't you have a go now?'

I sighed with relief and quickly pressed the button.

'That was a learning experience,' Van Kooten said. 'If something unexpected happens, you needn't panic straight away. First analyse the problem. Reduce it to its essentials, in this case the search for the right button. Don't just press any old key, look at the symbols. A circle with a vertical line in the middle of it is the universal on/off symbol. You'll find it on your vacuum cleaner and your coffee machine.'

'You really do understand everything, Mr van Kooten!'

He laughed modestly, but he was right. There are two large buttons on my vacuum cleaner. One for rolling up the lead, that's the one with a plug on it, and one with a vertical line inside a circle. I explained it only recently to my Filipino girl.

'If you concentrate on the essentials, in this case on finding the right symbol, then you'll be able to work out for yourself which button to press to bring the computer to life.'

'You make it sound so easy.'

'Most problems are easily solved, as long as you reduce them to their essentials. Believe me, that goes for all kinds of problems, big ones as well as little ones.'

I relaxed.

The screen had turned an ochre colour. There were tiny pictures all over it.

Van Kooten pointed to a little grey device lying on a small rectangular mat next to the computer.

'This is the mouse. Have you ever worked with a mouse?'

I shook my head.

'Just put your right hand on it.'

The mouse fitted my hand perfectly.

Van Kooten laid his hand on top of mine. A slim but power-ful male hand. Without a wedding ring. 'If you move the mouse, the little arrow on the screen moves too. You see?' Van Kooten pushed my hand to and fro. The little arrow on the screen fol-lowed our every move. 'If you want to do something, play a game for instance, or open a program, you move the mouse onto it – and click.'

It sounded simple enough.

'See that little drawing in the top left hand corner? Just go over to it, try to click on it.' Van Kooten let go of my hand.

I moved the arrow and clicked.

All kinds of things happened on the screen. I saw a rectangle appear, getting larger and larger.

'That's the way, Lea! You've just opened a program.'

'What now?'

'Now we're going to hook up to the Internet. Do you know what that is?'

'Not exactly. We do have it at home, though. Harry said we had to have it, because everyone else does.'

Van Kooten smiled. 'Has Harry explained to you what the Internet is?'

'No. Or perhaps he did. But I wasn't listening.'

'Do you know whether he has a home page?'

'What's that?'

'It's a page where you put text and pictures so that everyone who uses the Internet can see who you are.'

I giggled. 'I think Harry's got one, yes. He put a topless

photo of me into the computer once. He said the whole world would be able to see me in the nuddy.'

'Have you got the address of your home page?' Van Kooten got a notebook out of a drawer.

'Address? I'd have to ring Harry.'

'Don't bother. We'll come back to that.' Van Kooten put the notebook back. 'We're going to log on to the Internet now. You have to understand that millions of people all over the world have put information onto the Net. It can be in the form of photos, text or even sound. The second we log on, we'll have access to all that information.'

'Fantastic,' I said. I looked at my hand dreamily. When would he put his on top of mine again?

Van Kooten took charge of the mouse. He clicked a few times.

I heard a series of bleeps and then one long, piercing bleep.

'The connection goes via the telephone. Look, it's working. We're now on the Internet.

'Hey, that's you!' A large photo of Van Kooten appeared on the screen. He looked very distinguished, in a dark suit with a white shirt. The address of his practice and the phone number were written underneath the photo.

'This is my home page,' said Van Kooten proudly. 'I always start here. Look, there's the counter, I've had 1368 visits already.'

'Visits?'

'That's what you call it when people look at your page.'

'So now you're visiting yourself?'

'You could say that, yes.'

'Does that count too?'

'Yes. But that doesn't matter.'

'No, of course not.'

'Shall we surf a bit further?'

I nodded.

'Look, these are my bookmarks, the Internet addresses I visit regularly. By clicking, I can choose one.'

Van Kooten clicked, a moment later the screen went bright blue. On the left was a yellow strip. In the top right hand corner was a picture of a bust. It was a man's head. He looked a bit like the old Greek guy whose books Birgit was always reading. She used to have a poster of him above her bed. In my room I stuck the Bionic Man on the wall. That was *my* idea of a hunk.

'This is an excellent site,' said Van Kooten.

'A what?'

'A site is a place on the Internet. With the help of the Mental Health Site, quite a few of my patients have found a way out of the quagmire that is the human mind.'

'Wonderful. I didn't know it existed.'

'Don't expect it to perform miracles, Lea; you'll have to do most of the work yourself.'

'I was afraid of that.'

Van Kooten smiled. 'We'll manage it, if we work together. I'm convinced we will.'

If only he knew. He hadn't seen me in a straitjacket. Thank God. On the other hand, if he'd been there at that moment perhaps it wouldn't have come to that. He would have calmed me down. If anyone could have, it was him.

'Shall we?'

'Go ahead.'

'First you have to answer a series of simple questions. Then the computer will offer a diagnosis.'

Van Kooten clicked a few times. 'You have to fill in your name here. Just type it on the keyboard.'

It was a long time since I'd typed anything. I hunted like mad for the letters. 'You assume I can do anything, Mr van Kooten.'

'You can do a lot more than you think, Lea.'

With two fingers, and the tip of my tongue sticking out of my mouth, I filled in my name, Lea Meyer-Cornelissen.

'Your age there,' Van Kooten pointed.

I hesitated a moment. Could the computer check how old I really was? I put 29.

Van Kooten mumbled something about youth, beauty and flowers coming into bloom.

'Now what?'

'Now you just have to tick whether you're male or female.'

That was easy.

'Now the computer wants to know which disorder you're suffering from. Here's a list of possible disorders.'

I quickly ran through the list: eating disorders, personality disorders, mood disorders, schizophrenia . . .

'If you click that button at the bottom, the computer will take all the possibilities into account,' said Van Kooten helpfully.

Seven disorders for the price of one. What a feast. 'We can exclude some of them for a start,' I said.

'Such as?'

'Eating disorders, personality disorders.'

'Whoa, wait a minute, how do I know you don't have those?'

'I don't eat whole packs of butter, I still have periods, and I never throw up after a three-course meal.'

'Okay, you don't have an eating disorder.'

'And anyway, I'm not mad. And I certainly don't have schizo-phrenia.'

'No one is saying you're mad. But there is a reason why you're here.'

I looked away.

'I know you don't want to talk about it,' he said softly. 'That's why I'm trying to do this via the computer. To make it easier.'

'It's just that after Harry Junior was born I, how shall I put it, I got a bit confused . . .'

'I see.' That was all he said. No doubt he thought I'd fill the silence by giving him all the details of how I went off the rails.

'I was admitted to hospital.'

'Ah.'

'It was a compulsory hospitalisation.'

'I see.'

'They put me in a cell.'

I was expecting another 'Ah.' but he said, 'Oh no. Was that really necessary?'

'I haven't a clue. I read the report later, and it said I'd spent a few hours being cared for in the isolation ward. Well, I certainly wasn't being cared for, I was completely alone in there. No one came. No matter how often I rang the bell.'

'The bell?'

'There was a bell. At least, there was a push-button next to the door, I assume it was a bell. The first time, someone did come. A nurse, I imagine. She wasn't wearing a white coat, that was confusing, she had ordinary clothes on. She looked in through the little window for a moment, but she didn't open the door. I was locked in. After that I rang the bell a lot and for long periods, but she didn't come back.'

Van Kooten looked at his watch. 'I think we've done enough for today, don't you?' He stood up.

'I think so too.'

'Are you taking any medication?'

'Yes.'

'Do you have enough left?'

'Yes.'

'Good, then I'll see you next week.'

'Same time, same chick,' I tried.

Van Kooten opened the door. 'Bye, Lea.'

Shit.

As I was walking off along the corridor, Van Kooten fetched the next patient from the waiting room. I didn't dare turn round. I heard them greet each other enthusiastically. The woman had a high-pitched, kittenish laugh. No doubt she didn't have any kind of serious disorder. Actually, it was scandalous that she dared to take up his time, Beau's time.

My Beau.

chapter six

2nd March 1966

You don't look like your sister, so who do you look like?
Most people say grandpa Cornelissen, but I don't think so
at all. The first few days you were very good, you drank
greedily and soon got a taste for it.

Harry was painting my toenails when I felt something break. My
crotch became warm and damp.

'Harry, love. Don't be scared. I think my waters have just
broken.'

'Jushhh . . .' He did an impression of old Queen Juliana trying
to hush hostile crowds at her daughter's coronation.

'Yes, just a few seconds ago. What a good thing we put these
waterproof covers on the sofa cushions.'

Harry started on the big toe of my right foot. 'Mind you, I
still don't understand why you had to do all the cushions, chairs
included. My mother got very sweaty, sitting on plastic. What
was that about your waters?'

'They've broken.'

'What does that mean, exactly?'

'That amniotic fluid is seeping into my vagina.'

'Bloody hell, why didn't you say so in the first place.' Harry screwed the top back on the nail varnish. 'Should I go and get a towel?'

'No, darling, I'm wearing a panty liner. Finish off my right foot, would you?'

Harry unscrewed the bottle again. 'Are you sure? Shouldn't you ring the doctor first?'

'I'll do that shortly. A first labour can last for days. I don't want Machteld to see me with only half my nails pink.'

Harry picked up my foot, adjusted the wads of cotton wool and carried on. 'Good grief, Lea, is this really it?'

'Yes, my love. Watch out, you're dripping.'

Once the nail varnish was dry, I rang Machteld to tell her my waters had broken.

'Great. What colour is it?'

I wondered how she knew. 'Salmon pink,' I said, hesitantly.

'Salmon pink amniotic fluid?!'

'Oh, the fluid. I don't know what colour that is.'

'Take a look, would you. If it's brown, it's not good.'

'Brown, how could it be brown? Harry's white.'

Machteld sighed. 'If it's brown, it means the baby has defecated in it. If he has, then he's in trouble and you'll have to go to the hospital.'

'But I can have it at home, can't I? You said so.'

'In theory, yes, but not if you have meconium in your waters.' What long words she was using all of a sudden. She was being so shrewish, I didn't think she was being very nice to me at all.

'I'll look. Just a minute. I'll put you down on your back,

Machteld.' I went to the toilet and looked in my trousers. I ran straight back to Machteld. I whispered into the phone so as not to alarm Harry. 'It's terrible, Machteld, there's blood in it. The child's bleeding. We have to go to the hospital right away.'

'No, a little blood is normal. It's because of the mucous plug.'

'The mucous plug?'

'The plug that's been keeping your cervix closed. That's come out now too.'

I'd been going around with a mucous plug inside me for nine months without knowing it. 'How does it go from here?'

'I really can't tell. We're waiting for the contractions now. Ring me once you're getting them every five minutes, not until then.' She hung up.

I went and sat next to Harry on the sofa. 'We have to wait for the contractions, Machteld says.'

'And what do we do in the meantime?'

'Nothing, just wait.'

'Feel anything yet?'

'No.'

'Do you know what I feel like?' said Harry twenty minutes later, while I was leafing through *Libelle*. 'A bit of porn.'

I looked up, surprised.

'We haven't done that for ages. You know, just a little porn movie. We'll do your favourite, the Tyrolean.'

I smiled. It certainly had been a long time.

Harry tilted his head to one side. '*Bitte?*'

'Fine, darling, put it on. I'll get something to drink. I think there are some Chipitos left, would you like some?

He nodded and rubbed his hands with pleasure.

We quickly got into the story.

Bambi's Birthday is about an Austrian waitress. She works in a *Bierstube*. One day a large group of noisy men comes into the place. They're wearing *Lederhosen* and they've just been doing something together. It's not clear exactly what, but it's something that makes men cheerful, agitated and thirsty.

The waitress brings them big heavy glasses of beer, and she's good at it, she carries six at a time on her tray. While she does this, the men reach their hands up inside her skirt. They make comments about Bambi's breasts, which are round and full; she's laced them up in a tight little bodice. One of the men pulls the lace and undoes it, so that her breasts roll out.

I'm really quite jealous of Bambi, to think that all this happens to her while she's at work. When I was younger, I worked as a cashier at the A&P and that kind of thing never happened there.

After a while the men take her outside with them into the woods. Bambi lies down on the ground giggling. The men all get a turn with her. One after another they all put their Waldhorns between Bambi's Alps.

By this point Harry had got Big Harry out of his trousers.

'Oh honey, I want you,' I said.

'Not now, Lea.'

'You've been saying that for months.'

'It's not good for the little one, I'm sure it isn't.'

'Machteld says it can't do any harm.'

'I don't care. I'm not doing it.'

'Then do the little trick.'

'Do it yourself.' Harry was barely looking at me. He sat there pulling away at Big Harry.

I stroked myself with my fingertips. I moaned softly.

Harry growled.

Then came the scene we both really like. A man with a red beard takes the waitress from behind, while another man puts his dick into her mouth. The rest of the men stand around them, jerking off.

I moaned. I was almost there.

I moaned louder.

I screamed.

I screamed my head off.

'Jesus, Lea, you sure are horny. Is it *that* nice?'

'Nooo!'

'No need to shout. I was only asking.'

I panted. It was a while before I could answer. 'I had a contraction. It hurt like hell.'

'So you didn't come?'

'No, I didn't come. Goddammit, Harry, I had a contraction.'

Harry still had half an eye on the video. The man with the red beard came all over Bambi's back. 'But my love, I'm almost there. It'll go down if I stop now.'

'I'll give you five minutes.'

While Harry emptied his barrel, I paced up and down the room. That contraction was viciously painful.

'Sorry, I just had to finish the job.' Harry was busy wiping himself with a handkerchief.

'Okay, okay. Now turn off the TV.'

'You look very pale. Are you sure you're alright?'

'Not really. I've got cramps. I think there's another contraction coming.'

I'd hardly said it when it came. I grabbed hold of a chair.

'Oh, this hurts. Oh, it hurts so much! Oh, Harry, I have to do something, to work with it. I have to puff.

Harry had come to stand next to me, he was rubbing my back. 'Puff then, darling.'

'I don't know the song any more,' I said, half crying. 'There's a little song you have to do it to, a nursery rhyme.'

'*One potato, two potato?*'

I shook my head.

'*This little piggie went to market?*'

I shook my head wildly.

'*Twinkle, twinkle, little star?*'

I took a deep sigh. The contraction was over. 'No, not that one either.'

'How does it go?'

'Fuck.'

'I think you should call Machteld. Those contractions were very close together. You can ask about the song right away too.'

I rang Machteld. The midwife was annoyed, because I'd only had two contractions. The next one came while I was talking to her. 'Machteld, here's Harry for you.'

Moaning, I got through the contraction. The official term in the Netherlands is 'absorb', but that was completely out of the question in my case. There was no way I wanted to absorb that insane amount of pain.

I heard Harry say something about Humpty Dumpty.

Oh yes, that was it. First take a deep breath, puff it out to the rhythm of *Humpty-Dumpty-sat-on-the-wall*, and then suck in another breath.

I tried it. It had seemed so easy during yoga lessons. But then you didn't feel anything else. You just sat there puffing away in a vacuum. Now the last thing I wanted to do was puff. I didn't want this pain, I didn't want to puff. I wanted it to stop, that was all I wanted.

Harry had put the phone down. 'We have to ring back in an hour. If it's still going the way it is now, she'll come over.'

'Gosh, how wonderful. How tremendously decent of Machteld.'

Harry took off his watch and put it on the table. He took a pen and a piece of paper out of the dresser. 'No need to panic. I'll keep a precise record of the contractions.'

'I'm not panicking. I'm angry. It fucking hurts, you know?'

'Yes I know, my love, that's nature. It's part of the process.'

I wanted to hit Harry. *Nature!*

The contractions got well under way. Every two minutes I almost died of pain. Sometimes the gap was a little longer. If it was, then the next contraction hurt so much that I wanted to throw vases across the room.

'God in heaven, Harry, this isn't normal. Call Machteld and tell her she has to come right away.'

Harry rang.

Seventeen contractions later, Machteld arrived. She walked calmly into the room. She was carrying a sort of stool. 'What a long way out you live. I went the wrong way twice.'

'Doesn't matter, Machteld. Do you want something to drink?' asked Harry.

'Just a glass of Spa.'

'One mineral water. On its way. What's that you're carrying?'

'A bar stool. Lea can sit on it while she's giving birth.'

'*Sit?* Shouldn't she do it lying down? I've drunk four crates of beer to get that bed raised to the right height.'

Machteld laughed. 'She's allowed to lie down too. But it's easier to push if you're sitting up. It's logical, you sit on the toilet too. Have you ever defecated lying down?'

Harry thought about it and shook his head. 'No, that was a very long time ago.'

'Pushing is like shitting. If you sit upright, gravity works in your favour.'

'Of course,' said Harry. He went over to the living room bar.

Then Machteld turned to me. 'How's it going?'

'Badly. Have you got any anaesthetic with you?'

'Oh come on, Lea, we've only just started. Shall I take a look and see how far you've got?' She wore her hair in a ponytail. She had glasses on. It struck me that she looked a good bit fatter than the last time I saw her.

Machteld stroked her stomach, smiling. 'Can you see it? Another seven weeks. Irene is on cloud nine.'

I couldn't reply, because there was another contraction coming.

Harry gave Machteld her Spa water. 'Boy oh boy, two pregnant women in my house. If you start getting contractions too, then I've got a problem.

Slowly, I recovered. 'Irene? She works at your practice too, doesn't she?'

Machteld nodded. 'Yes, and we live together. This child will have two mothers.'

Suddenly I felt sick. Very sick. I ran to the toilet and threw up. Right after that I had another contraction. I clung to the wall and puffed. 'Hump-ty-Dump-ty's-a-fuck-ing-beast.'

Machteld was sitting on the sofa when I got back to the living room. Harry was standing next to the dresser.

Machteld put her Spa to one side. 'Did you have to vomit? That's perfectly normal. Your body is emptying itself before labour really begins. You may get diarrhoea too.'

'Yippee.'

'Just lie down here for a moment and I'll examine you.' She pointed to the chaise longue.

God almighty, this was it. I'd been dreading this moment. And now I'd found out that Machteld did it with women. Could it be she enjoyed performing this kind of intimate examination too?

Machteld put on a rubber glove. 'Have you got a birthing mattress?'

'Sorry?'

'You have to lie on something, your waters have broken, right?'

'Oh yes. I've bought one, yes.'

At one of the check-ups, Machteld had given me a list of all the things I'd need for a home delivery. I'd left the room feeling thoroughly perplexed. Where on earth was I supposed to get sterile gauze and a navel clamp, for heaven's sake? What were 'chocks'? Why couldn't Machteld bring her own stuff with her? Or did she only do that for disadvantaged families?

'Did you get a list like this?' I asked a very pregnant floral-print dress in the waiting room.

She nodded. She'd got everything from the pharmacy. The chocks were to raise your bed with, so that Machteld could get at you more easily. You could get them from the Home Delivery Service. If you were a member, anyway. 'But you can always use crates.'

'Crates?'

'Yes, ordinary empty crates. Heineken or Amstel, makes no difference.'

I took off my maternity leggings and lay down on the chaise longue. Harry got the birthing mattress. It was square, about fifty by fifty centimetres. The top side was made of an absorbent material, it looked like a disposable nappy, only thinner. The underside was green plastic.

'Lift up your bottom.' Expertly, Machteld pushed the little mattress underneath me. 'And now take off your knickers.'

I wormed my way out of my underwear. My sanitary towel was heavy with amniotic fluid. There was even more blood in it than before. I folded up the knickers, so that Machteld wouldn't have to sit staring at my excretions, and laid the whole lot on the floor.

I parted my legs.

'A little wider, please.'

Machteld stuck her hands between my legs. She pushed two fingers into my vagina.

'Wait a second, Machteld, there's another contraction coming.' I wasn't bluffing.

Machteld took her hand away.

I rolled onto my stomach and curled up in a ball. No one had told me this level of pain existed. I moaned.

'Easy does it. Breathe nice and easy. That's the way. You're doing well.' Machteld whispered and stroked my back with her hand. It was the gloveless hand. She'd obviously done it before. 'Now turn over on your back again,' she said, when the contraction was over.

I parted my knees without protest. If Machteld had to give me a vaginal examination, then so be it. I looked around for Harry's support. He'd gone.

'Tilt your bottom up.'

I shut my eyes.

Machteld's fingers slid back inside. 'It may hurt for a moment. I'm going to feel how far open your cervix is.'

Machteld groped around deep inside me.

'Try to relax, Lea.' That soft voice again.

I couldn't see how I was supposed to relax. It hurt. I stared at the ceiling. My husband had vanished without a trace. My pelvis was angled upwards. A pregnant lesbian was feeling my cervix. I'd felt better.

'So.' Her fingers slid out.

I lowered my hips and relaxed.

'Three centimetres.' Machteld took off her glove.

'Three?! Three centimetres?'

Machteld emptied her glass. 'Yes, my dear, it's your first.' She got a wooden trumpet out of her bag. 'I'll just listen to its little heart.' The trumpet was placed on my stomach. Machteld put her ear to it. 'Wonderful. Really wonderful. The baby's doing fine.'

*

Harry came into the room.

'Where were you?'

'I thought I heard the fax machine. How's it going?'

'Getting nowhere fast. Only three centimetres dilation.'

'You're right, it's not going very fast at all. What now?' Harry looked at Machteld enquiringly.

'If it goes on like this she'll give birth tonight, and at any rate by tomorrow morning. I'm going home to eat. If things suddenly start to speed up, you can call me.'

I had a contraction.

'Do you really have to go home?' asked Harry, while I squeezed a cushion to death.

'There's no sense in staying. I can't do anything for her.' She put the ear trumpet back in her bag.

'And what if I go and get a Chinese? I have to eat too and I don't think Lea's going to be all that keen on cooking this evening. Ha ha ha!'

She'll never agree to that, I thought, she wants to go back to her own little love nest. With Irene on her pink cloud nine.

'Not a bad idea,' said Machteld, 'Irene's eating at her mother's this evening, so as far as that's concerned . . .'

Harry's face brightened. 'Great. I don't like eating alone. What do you want? An egg roll? Fried rice? Fuyong hai?'

'Just get me some shark's fin soup and fried rice.'

'You won't be wanting anything, right?' Harry asked me.

'Well . . .'

'You definitely mustn't have a Chinese,' Machteld said firmly. 'Much too much fat. You'll have problems giving birth if you do. You're only allowed easily digestible food. A dextrose tablet. Or a cracker with jam.'

Harry stuck his wallet into his hip pocket. 'I'm off then. Mind the fort, Machteld?'

He came back more than an hour later.

Machteld had made three phone calls by then. Irene would feed the cats and her mother-in-law's arthritis was a bit better. Patient A from H shouldn't worry about her swollen ankles. It was safe for G to drive home from a birthday party. With one contraction every half-hour that wasn't a problem.

Harry was carrying two plastic bags. The smell alone made me feel sick as a dog.

I ordered the pair of them to go and eat in the kitchen.

'Are all women unbearable when they're about to give birth?' asked Harry as they walked down the hall.

I didn't catch Machteld's reply.

I sat down on the chaise longue and looked at the clock. The next contraction didn't come for twelve minutes – four points on the Lea scale. Up to then, the Lea scale had a maximum reading of ten.

I went to the kitchen.

Harry was just breaking off a piece of prawn cracker for Machteld.

'Hey, listen, is it normal for the contractions to come and go?'

'What do you mean?' asked Machteld with her mouth full.

'Well, they don't hurt so much. And there's more time in between.'

She took a sip of Spa. 'How much more time?'

'Every fifteen minutes.'

'What a pity, my dear. You were going along so well.'

Harry heaped some more rice onto his plate and poured a generous amount of satay sauce over it. 'You want more too?'

'Yes please. I haven't had such good satay in ages,' said Machteld.

Harry nodded, 'What did I tell you? Good Chinese take-aways like that are thin on the ground. It's a bit of a drive, but it's worth it.'

'Shall we call the child Tong Fa, then?' I asked.

'Don't be silly, Lea.'

'Silly?! This really is the limit! You drive all the way to Tong Fa while I lie here being tortured to death. Lun Tin is just around the corner, for God's sake. But no, the satay from Lun Tin isn't good enough for His Lordship. The very idea. Only the best is good enough for Mr Meyer.'

Harry remained icily calm. 'Machteld said it would be perfectly alright to go out for a bit. She said it would take a while yet.'

Machteld nodded.

The cow. 'As soon as you left, the contractions got weaker. Thanks a lot, Harry.' I stalked out of the kitchen. I couldn't face them any more. And anyhow, I could feel a contraction coming.

After the satay incident Machteld went home. She said she was going to get some sleep and I should try to rest too. If I thought things were starting to get a move on, I could ring.

chapter seven

12th March 1966

We postponed the baptism until I could be there too. It was held this afternoon. You didn't cry, you slept very peacefully. You peeped out once or twice through half-closed eyelids. When the water was poured over your head you cheekily wiped it away with your little hands.

After I'd seen Machteld out, I went to find Harry. He was sitting on the toilet in the bathroom.

'I'm sorry I lost my temper just now.'

'That's alright.'

'These contractions are driving me crazy. Everything hurts. My back, my stomach. Machteld was sitting here having a nice Chinese with you, but apart from that she wasn't doing anything.'

'There's nothing she can do, Lea. No one can do anything.'

I gripped the sink for support and puffed my way through another contraction.

Harry rubbed his stomach. 'It isn't easy for me either, Lea.'

'That,' I panted, 'is not what I want to hear right now. I want you to stay with me. Support me. Not go off to check your fax traffic or set out in search of the best satay in the county.'

'I guess I won't be able to call in at the office tomorrow?'

'No, you can't call in at the office tomorrow. I'm terribly sorry. I'll do my best tonight, but I don't think I'll be able to finish up in time.'

'Okay, okay, I'll call the guys in a while.'

'Very good.'

He stood up, wiped himself and pulled the flush. When he'd pulled up his trousers he came and stood next to me. He put his arms around me. My stomach got in the way. I hated that stomach. The baby moved. It was still alive. Bully for him.

Harry stroked my hair. 'Hang on in there, girl. I'll stay with you.'

The contractions came and went. All evening. For convention's sake, I went to bed at nine thirty.

At ten thirty, Machteld's prophesy came to pass. I got diarrhoea. After three intensive sessions on the toilet I was thoroughly purged.

The contractions came and went. All night long. My husband left a little after twelve to sleep in the spare bedroom. He didn't see any point in witnessing every millimetre of my dilation live. I tossed and turned and puffed. At four I got up. I went to Harry's study and took down the Guinness Book of Records. What was the maximum amount of time labour could last? I couldn't find anything about that. The fact that a man from New Guinea had ear lobes seventeen centimetres long which he could tie under his chin was something I nevertheless regarded as a noteworthy piece of general knowledge.

*

At six o'clock I got up once and for all. There was one term that had acquired unexpectedly positive connotations during the night. I called Machteld. She sounded sleepy.

'Hello, Machteld speaking.'

'Machteld, it's Lea Meyer. I want a Caesarean section.'

There was silence for a moment. 'How did it go last night?'

'Badly. I've had enough, I want to get it over with. As quickly as possible.'

'When was it your contractions started?'

'Yesterday afternoon, at about four.'

'So it's been less than twenty-four hours?' She yawned. 'Listen, Lea, it's better to let nature take its course. It's such a pity to intervene if your body can manage by itself.'

Nature. 'I don't think my body can manage by itself. It's never done it before. It simply doesn't know how.'

'That's what all women think. Believe me, you're more than capable of giving birth. How are the contractions going?'

'Off and on. About every seven or eight minutes.'

'You still don't feel the urge to start pushing?'

'No.'

'Good. I'll come round some time this morning. If it suddenly starts to go really quickly, you should call me.'

I put the phone down and staggered to the spare bedroom.

'Harry! You have to get up.'

He was startled. 'Am I a father?'

'No.'

Harry looked at the alarm clock. 'Lea, it's only ten past six.'

'Well, so what?'

'I don't have to go to work. Couldn't you have let me sleep a bit longer?'

'No. You've been asleep all night. I haven't slept a wink. Machteld will be here soon. She's going to start grubbing about inside me again. I want you to be up.'

He threw back the duvet. 'Okay, okay. How are you doing?'

'How do I look?'

'Honestly?'

'Yes.'

'Fat. Pale. Dark rings. Pissed off.'

'Have I ever told you that I profoundly and intensely hate you, Mr Meyer?'

Harry pulled me down onto the guest bed and pinched my bottom. 'My naughty little droopy drawers. Today you're going to be a mother.'

When Machteld arrived at eleven thirty, the birthing mattress was lying ready for her on the chaise longue. I suspected there was no amniotic fluid left, as I was hardly leaking at all any more.

Yes, Machteld would like a cup of tea.

Harry sat down, I lay down.

Tilt your hips, spread your legs, fingers in, I was starting to get used to it.

'How did it go this morning?'

'Not too bad. Irregular contractions. Sometimes nothing for half an hour, then two within ten minutes.'

Machteld took her fingers out.

'Well, how much?'

'Four centimetres.'

'Four? That's impossible. I've been in pain all night. Feel it again.'

'I've had a good feel. It's not progressing very well. I'll just have a listen to the heartbeat.'

Machteld put her ear to the ear trumpet. 'Sounds like the little one is pretty happy in there.'

'That's the problem. He's too happy in there.'

Harry came in with the tea. 'And?'

'Four centimetres. If it goes on like this we'll have a child by the end of next week.' I hauled myself upright.

'Come on, Lea, don't be so negative.' That was Machteld again.

'What did you say? Don't be so negative! Are you the one who's been lying here puffing away for four lousy centimetres? We're not getting anywhere, Machteld, that's what I've been telling you all along. I'm not the bar-stool type. I want a Caesarean section. Just a nice little incision under the bikini-line and it's all over.'

Machteld pulled off her gloves. She put the ear trumpet back in her bag. 'A Caesarean is a very intrusive medical procedure. It's an operation . . .'

'Great, I can't wait to get under the anaesthetic.'

'You can have an injection in your spine, you know. Then you'll be conscious when the baby comes out.'

'Thanks but no thanks; I only want to see the child when I've been neatly sewn shut.'

Machteld shook her head impatiently. 'Listen, Lea, at this point there's no reason at all why you should be given a Caesarean section. None at all. It's a pity the dilation isn't progressing, but it's nothing to worry about. I suggest we see how it goes for a bit longer. If the contractions don't get going again soon, we'll go to the hospital to have you induced.'

'Induced? What's that?' asked Harry. He put the tray down on the coffee table.

'It means that Lea would be given a drip with a medication that stimulates contractions.'

I felt a contraction coming. Not a heavy one. I pretended I was stifling a sneeze.

Machteld fell for it.

'I don't think it would be a bad idea to go to the hospital. It's been going on for so long already,' said Harry.

'There's absolutely no reason to make any hasty decisions. The child is doing fine. Lea's doing fine. A journey to the hospital might disrupt the process. I suggest we stay here for a bit, so that I can see how powerful the contractions are, and then decide what to do after that.'

'Can you live with that, Lea?'

'Yes, fine.'

'Good,' said Machteld. 'We can have a nice quiet cup of tea, then.' She got a wad of obscure bits of paper out of her bag and started making notes.

Harry rang the office.

We drank our tea.

I had a few contractions, but I gritted my teeth manfully. I wanted to get out. Out of the house. My Laura Ashley interior was getting in the way of a successful delivery, that much was clear. I just couldn't get into the mood. White coats were what I needed to see. Nurses running to and fro. Professionals who would mop my brow.

Every fifteen minutes, Machteld asked how it was going.

I mumbled something about slight cramps.

After an hour and a half Machteld said, 'It does look as

though the contractions have stopped.' She sounded disappointed.

I was relieved. Action at last.

Machteld rang the hospital. When she put the phone down
she asked, 'Have you got your suitcase ready?'

Oh yes, the suitcase.

When you have a child you have to have so many things ready,
it's unbelievable. The stuff you need for a home delivery, the
stuff you'll need if you end up in the hospital after all, and then
all the stuff for the newborn itself: from cradle to cot, from
Maxi-Cosi to Maxi-Taxi, from rompers to toughened glassware,
from baby sheets to baby blankets. Then there are all the things
you absolutely must not have ready: no second-hand cot mattress for fear of cot death; no duvet for fear of cot death; no
cushions for fear of cot death; no thickly lined cradle for fear of
cot death – and no playpen with bars a baby could fit its head
through.

My wickerwork travelling bag full of hospital-delivery-
necessities was standing in the hall.

'Shall I carry it for you, darling?' asked Harry.

'I can manage. You go and get the car out of the garage.'

'My car's on the corner, shall I go in front?' asked Machteld.

'Okey-dokey,' said Harry – probably the only man in Western
Europe who still uses that expression.

I had a contraction and tried as discreetly as possible to support myself against the wall. I squeezed the handle of the bag
with my right hand.

'See you in a bit,' said Machteld.

Harry drove the car round to the front. He got out and

helped me in. Harry remains a gentleman under all circumstances.

We drove to the gate. There was Machteld in her Fiat Panda. She waved merrily and set off. We followed her. Machteld's right-hand brake light wasn't working. I'd have to mention it to her later.

The sky was semi-overcast. My neighbour was walking along the street with her Jack Russell. The hairdresser's was still shut because of a death in the family. I'd have been happy to switch places with them. A dog is nice, and you can get over a death in the family.

'That woman's going an awfully long way round,' Harry grumbled.

Not long after that the hospital loomed up ahead of us.

chapter eight

We went to the clinic this morning. You weigh ten pounds five ounces now. That's very good. You did cry a lot, especially when you got your smallpox injection. It's not pleasant, little child, but it is necessary. If you ever want to emigrate, you'll have had the jab already.

I want to say something about breasts. I've got two of them. The left one is slightly smaller than the right. I like my breasts. There's nothing so reassuring as a quick glance down the valley of ecstasy. The valley is almost as exciting as the breasts themselves.

Other women have breasts too. I prefer to call them 'tits'. I like looking at tits. Bare tits, tits in micro-bikinis and of course drooping tits and fake tits. Fake tits are great. Impact-resistant, wrinkle-free, with the nipple exactly where it belongs, in the middle and not dangling somewhere underneath. Fake tits drive me crazy. To tell the truth all tits drive me crazy.

Priscilla, a girl who works in Harry's office, what a pair of knockers she has!

Last summer we held a barbecue, to celebrate our new driveway. Harry invited Priscilla. She wore a white cotton top which her nipples poked right through. As if they wanted to make contact with me, I swear.

After four glasses of white wine, Priscilla said, 'Lea, you keep staring at my tits.'

'I can't help it, they keep looking at me.' Now that she'd brought up the subject, I found the nerve to ask her, 'Are they real?'

She straightened her back so that they stuck out even more. 'Of course they're real. Mother Nature did her best. Where were you when she was handing them out? Right at the front, for the try-out cups?' She laughed loudly.

Suddenly everyone was looking at my breasts.

'I'm a 34B,' I whispered.

'You? A B cup? Impossible. My dear, I've worked in lingerie. Nine out of ten women go home with a B cup, when four of them need an A cup and another three a C. Take it from me, you're an A. It doesn't matter, you know, some men get a real kick out of little champagne glasses like that – they say more than a handful's a waste.'

Harry put his half-litre can of Heineken down on the grass, went and stood behind me and massaged my breasts. At least, so he thought. He was mainly massaging the filling of my Wonderbra. 'What's this I hear, do your boobs really fit into champagne glasses? Shall we try?'

'Not now, darling.'

'Have you ever tried the pencil trick?' asked Priscilla.

'No,' I lied. I went bright scarlet.

*

I hardly ever lie. I just can't. It's because of my mother. The last time I told an outright lie was when I was five. My mother took me with her to the greengrocer's. There was a box of Donald Duck chewing gum in a rack next to the till. My sister and I were never allowed to have sweets. Sweets were bad. The Donald Duck chewing gum looked jolly and innocent though. There were Disney characters on the colourful wrappers. They cost five cents each. Without anyone noticing, I took a piece of gum. It was Uncle Scrooge. While my mother was being served, I took the wrapper off and quickly stuck it in my mouth.

A few minutes after we got home, my mother called me over to her. 'What have you got in your mouth?'

'Chewing gum.'

'Where did you get it?'

'I got it from a lady.'

'Which lady?'

'The lady downstairs.'

'You're lying.'

There was a woman downstairs washing the windows, but she hadn't offered me any sweets.

'No Mum, it's really true.'

'You mustn't lie to your mother.'

'I'm not lying, Mum, honest I'm not.'

It went on like that for a while. My mother was convinced I was fibbing and I stuck firmly to my story.

She took me to the bedroom. She picked up the carpet beater. 'Where did you get that chewing gum?'

'I got given it. By that lady. I didn't steal it.'

She sat on the bed and put me over her knee. Then she

smacked me on the bottom with the carpet beater. I don't know how many times. 'Where did you get that chewing gum?'

'Got given it.' I think I was crying a bit by then. But I didn't want to give in. I wanted her to believe me.

She didn't. She pulled down my trousers and my knickers and hit me again. Probably not any harder than the first time, but now it hurt a lot more. I put my hands over my bottom to protect it, but that hurt too, and my mother kept pushing my hands away.

Tears running down my cheeks, I admitted I'd lied. Only then did she stop hitting me.

I looked up cautiously.

Her grim expression softened. 'You must never tell lies, Lea. And certainly not to your mother.'

I had done the pencil trick. I did it every week, but even if I'd stuck a whole pencil case underneath them it wouldn't have helped; since I'd given birth, my two little maids had hung their heads.

I ought to have known what I was in for. I could have read all about it in *Childbirth & After*.

Childbirth & After is the Bible for pregnant women. Every pregnant woman gets it pressed into her hand at some point. It's written by Jetske, Else, Hilda, Lilet, Aafke, Margot, Miriam and Hetty. Need I say more? It's full of nauseating passages about everything that 'happens to your body' and the 'emotional changes' you go through when you're expecting a baby. It's larded with black and white photos from the Seventies. They show frightful-looking women with glasses, feathercut hair and no make-up. They're wearing check maternity dresses. They display their big round stomachs whether there's any reason to or not. Some of them are already After, and are pressing the little creatures against their naked boobs. Not sexy.

The book ends with the childbirth stories of all the contributors – called 'This is what it was like for us' – in which, by the way, one of the babies dies. A baby called Jesse. He was a Down's syndrome baby. His mother writes about it as sentimentally as possible. She calls him Jesse Miracle Heart. I wouldn't call half a heart a miracle heart. For ten pages the mother gives a minute-by-minute account of her dying baby. She has visions of a gurgling toddler in a field wearing a jumper of a thousand colours. She floats with him across a meadow while he breathes his last breath. Then she sings for him and carries him around for a while longer. She leaves the hospital with an empty carrycot, her husband Juul, son Jisk and friend Ysk. With names like that you're asking for trouble.

My copy of *Childbirth & After* was fourth-hand. There were blotches and smudges all over the pages about Jesse. My predecessors were great vats of hormones that started leaking as soon as they read this. Well, not me. It cheered me up no end. It could all have been so much worse, after all. You could go through that whole song and dance only to find out you'd been conned. That wasn't going to happen to me. No way was I going to give birth to a mong! Harry had wangled me an amniocentesis in Belgium. There they don't begrudge the under-36s a healthy child.

Childbirth & After devotes just one paragraph to breasts. With a diagram. It shows six breasts, in profile. The breast of a child, a pubescent girl, an adult woman, a pregnant woman, a breast-feeding woman and a post-menopausal woman. This last breast, which you couldn't really call a breast at all any more, made Corine and me fall about laughing. Corine is my tennis partner.

'Imagine walking around with two envelopes like that!' she hiccuped.

How was I to know? How was I to know it would happen to me? That your tits can get a lot emptier after you've spawned than they were before. I didn't need to wait for the menopause. It happened to me of its own accord. I've never understood why it had to happen to me. To me, when I've always taken such good care of my prow. To me, whose mother is an E cup. And whose mother-in-law went through the menopause fifty years ago but still fills a D cup. Her fleshy bosom is covered in liver spots and wrinkles, but she can still work up a fine-looking décolleté out of it. And she does, too. God only knows who she thinks she's doing it for – my father-in-law stopped looking in her direction a long time ago – but she does.

There's one thing *Childbirth & After* doesn't lie about, though; your nipples get darker when you're pregnant. I was horrified when I read that. They were right. They go brown and they stay brown. For the rest of your life. Harry calls them my 'negro nipples'.

I miss my little pink buttons.

I miss my pert little maidens. I miss them every day.

chapter nine

*The smallpox vaccination didn't give you a fever, but you
have been crying a lot, at night too. The gland under your
right arm is a bit swollen, fat and round, because of the
jab. It hurts, but we have to let it go down of its own
accord.*

I was sitting in a wheelchair. Harry was pushing.

'Straight on all the way down to the end of the corridor and
then turn left.' Machteld pointed.

'Where are you going to give birth, by the way?' I asked.

'We haven't quite resolved that one yet. Irene wants me to do
it in hospital. For safety's sake. But I dream of a large bath with
lots of candles and the family all around.'

'Family?'

'Well, our mothers at any rate. So that the baby can bond
with all the generations right from the start. I read something
the other week about giving birth surrounded by dolphins. They
say it's a very intense experience.'

Harry nodded. 'I ran into a dolphin recently who'd fainted

during one of those sessions. Couldn't stand the sight of blood. Ha ha ha!'

Machteld didn't react. 'Here it is.' She pushed open a heavy door.

We went in.

The room was large and white. There was a bed with stirrups. This was actually starting to look like a real childbirth.

Machteld showed us how to dim the lights. 'You can put the radio on if you like. I'll go and get you a drip. Back in a moment.'

'Are you still having many contractions?' asked Harry when Machteld had gone.

'I had one just then. But no more of those strong ones.'

Machteld came back. She had a blonde nurse with her who wheeled the drip into the room.

'Hello, I'm Anita,' she said. She shook hands with Harry and me. 'I'm going to help with the birth.'

I looked around behind her. 'Where's the doctor?'

Anita nodded towards Machteld.

'There won't be a doctor,' Machteld explained. 'I'm still doing the birth. An obstetrician will only come along if intervention is needed. We're going to connect you up to the drip now. That'll make sure the contractions get going again.' She pointed to the bed. 'You should lie down now.'

I took off my shoes and my trousers and climbed onto the bed.

Anita took my arm and looked for an appropriate vein.

Harry looked on, intrigued. 'It's really amazing what they can do,' he said. 'They inject you with something and you start having contractions.'

Anita smiled. 'Are you comfortable?' she asked.

'Yes, thanks.' I leaned back.

Harry went to get some coffee. Anita got a few things ready for the birth. Machteld went and sat at a small table and got out her paperwork again.

The drip did what it was supposed to do. Forty-five minutes later I was having whopping great contractions.

Harry, Machteld and Anita looked very satisfied to see me wracked with pain every few minutes.

'It's really starting now, right?' Harry asked Machteld.

'Definitely. If the dilation goes well, there'll be three of you in a few hours from now.'

Harry opened his bag and got out his video camera.

'Are you going to film it? Darling, how nice! I thought you'd only brought the camera.'

Harry frowned. 'Have you got your make-up with you?'

'In my sponge bag, why? I put my make-up on this morning.'

'You look very pale.' Harry got the bag out of my case. 'Perhaps you should touch it up a bit.'

I looked in the mirror. Harry was right, I looked terrible. I smeared on a bit of liquid make-up. While I was working on the rouge – suck in your cheeks and brush it lightly over the cheekbones – I had a contraction. I gripped the brush hard until it was over. Then I put on a bit of mascara and lip-stick.

Harry turned on the camera. 'What's going through your mind at this time, Mrs Meyer?'

'Mainly contractions,' I giggled.

'And how did that come about?'

'Well, my husband – Harry Meyer, you know him I'm sure – got me pregnant and I became very fat and—'

'Extremely unpleasant,' Harry suggested.

'Not at all! It was hard, but it's almost over now.'

Harry turned the camera on Anita. 'And who might you be?'

Anita blushed.

Harry slowly slid the lens down the length of her body. 'Name! Age! Vital statistics!' Behind the camera, Harry likes to imagine he's Paul Verhoeven.

Machteld was rearranging her ponytail.

Anita said shyly that her name was Van Dam and she was twenty-three years old.

I had a contraction.

Harry immediately pointed the camera at me. He went on in a whisper. 'We are witnessing a unique biological process. Lea is dilating. From her grimace you can see that it's not easy. Look, she's puffing. Puffing is a special way of breathing that the human female uses only during contractions. Contractions are powerful cramps. They can be very painful. Thanks to the contractions—'

'Shut the fuck up.'

Harry took a step back. 'The woman is now clearly in labour. She makes thumping motions in my direction. I have to seek safety for myself and the camera. End of take one.'

'You okay?' asked Anita. She offered me a damp flannel.

I dabbed my forehead gratefully. I'd hardly recovered when the next one came. Moaning, I curled up in a ball. Machteld was standing next to the bed. I grabbed her arm. 'Machteld, it hurts so much. Oh, it hurts so much!' Was that weepy, whining voice mine?

Machteld pulled my hands away. 'Don't! You're pinching me.' She beckoned Harry over. 'Take it out on your husband.'

Harry picked up the flannel that had slid down onto the sheet. He wanted to lay it on my forehead.

I knocked his hand away. 'Not now, idiot.'

Harry held the flannel in the air, uncertainly.

I gave a deep sigh. The contraction was over.

'Do you want the flannel now?' asked Harry.

'No.'

'Shall I massage your back?'

'No.'

'Is there anything else I can do for you?'

'No. You've done enough. Thank you very much.'

'Do you want me to go away?'

'No.'

He shrugged and looked at Machteld with an I'm-doing-my-best-you-can-see-that-can't-you expression.'

I could barely tolerate Harry being there. But I wouldn't let him leave. He had to see what I was having to go through to bring his child into the world.

'Do you mind if I film?' asked Harry.

The next contraction came rolling in. I concentrated. Another of those dreadful fuckers. Fourteen on the Lea scale. Why had no one told me about this? I wanted to cry but I couldn't. It hurt too much. I hoped I'd faint. Pass out. Until it was all over. 'Machteld,' I whispered, 'I want an anaesthetic.'

Machteld shook her head. 'That's not necessary, Lea. You're doing fine. Really, you're doing wonderfully well.'

'I'm not doing well. I'm dying. Give me something. Give me something for the pain.'

'I can't give you anything.'

'Yes you can. I want laughing gas. Or a narcotic. Or both.'

'Out of the question. You'll have to push soon, and I want you to be fully conscious.'

'I beg you.' I'd never begged anyone for anything in my life. Machteld was the first.

It left her cold. She was unshakeable.

'Grit your teeth, my love,' said Harry, 'you're on the last lap now.'

I wanted to kill him. He was asking for total verbal annihilation. It was no good. I had another contraction. And another. Then there was a series of five in the Unbearable category. I tried various positions: on hands and knees, on my side, on my back, bicycling with my legs in the air. It didn't make any difference.

Anita looked sympathetically at me.

Harry went increasingly quiet.

Machteld pulled on her gloves. 'I'm going to examine you.' She pulled off my knickers.

I spread my legs. *Go on then, Machteld, go ahead. Pull the child out while you're at it, would you?*

Machteld's fingers in my cunt. I'd miss them when it was over. *How wide now, darling, how's it coming along?*

'Eight centimetres.' Machteld nodded at me. 'What did I tell you?'

Anita and Harry looked at each other and laughed.

I hated them. There was no reason at all to be optimistic. Two more centimetres. God knows how many more contractions. Here came yet another one.

Hump-ty-Dump-ty-sat-on-the-wall.

When the contraction was over, Harry took my hand.

'Alright, my love? It's terrible to see you in so much pain.'

'Do you know what I don't get?' I said, panting. 'What kind of madman calls an embryo Humpty Dumpty? And why is he always sitting on the fucking wall?'

'*Humpty-Dumpty-had-a-great-fall*,' Anita contributed.

'The last few centimetres can go very quickly,' said Machteld. 'Soon you'll have to push.'

'Can't we take a break for a moment? I'm thirsty.'

Anita fetched a plastic cup of water.

'Do you feel the urge to push yet?' asked Machteld after twenty minutes.

'I don't think so.'

'I'll have a feel.' Machteld knew the way. 'You're almost completely dilated. There's just a little lip. I'll be able to massage that away. Relax, Lea.'

Harry zoomed in while Machteld carried on with her internal business.

'When the next contraction comes you can start to push. Do you feel the urge to?'

'No. I'm tired.' The only urge I had was to stand up, leave the hospital and never come back.

'Chin up,' said Harry, 'you're on the last lap now.'

'If you say that just *one* more time!'

I had a contraction.

'Pull up your knees,' Machteld directed, 'and push.'

My legs shook. I sucked in a lungful of air and pushed. 'It hurts,' I said angrily.

'Hold on tight so you can put your back into it,' said Machteld. 'Push right through the pain.'

It was easy for her to talk. I didn't have any choice. I gulped for air and pushed again. There was no end to the contraction. I started puffing again.

'Listen, Lea,' said Machteld, 'you're supposed to use the whole contraction. You wasted the last part of that one. Keep pushing until it's over.'

I hate it when people tell me what to do. They were my contractions, not hers; I'd decide for myself how much use I wanted to make of them.

Anita gave me a fresh flannel. 'Have you brought the baby clothes with you?' she asked.

I pointed to my bag. I'd put a white Babygro in there. There were blue rabbits on it. I mustn't forget to tell the baby that real rabbits are white, brown, or piebald. 'Oh yes, Machteld, your right brake light is broken.'

Another contraction. I pushed with all my strength. The child simply had to come out now.

'Is anything happening yet?' I asked when it was over.

'I can't see anything yet,' said Harry, putting the camera down.

'Maybe we should try the bar-stool,' suggested Machteld.

The pressure in my lower body increased. 'There's another one coming!' I shouted. That got everyone's attention immediately.

Harry snatched the camera from the table.

I adopted my favourite position and took a deep breath.

Machteld looked into my crotch.

Harry got down on his knees for the best shot.

Nothing happened. I lowered my legs again. 'Sorry, false alarm.' Slightly embarrassed, I took a sip of water. 'Could I have some dextrose?' I asked.

Without a word, Harry handed me the roll. I'd bought it specially for the birth. It was on Machteld's list. Next to the navel clamp.

'Do you want to get onto the stool?' asked Machteld.

I looked at Harry. He was already walking across the delivery room with the bar stool. 'If you sit over here, I'll have enough light.'

Before I could get out of bed I had another contraction. I pushed like a maniac.

'Quick!' Machteld said to Harry. 'You can see its hair.'

Sighing, I lay back on the pillows.

'Gone again already,' said Harry, disappointed. And to me, 'it's shut up tight again.'

'But we're really making headway now,' said Machteld. An ill-judged remark.

With difficulty, I rolled out of bed. Anita squeezed the drip. I lowered myself onto the bar stool. It looked like a little stepladder for the kitchen, but with a large hole at the front.

'Could you move a bit further to the left?' Harry asked, opening one of the curtains.

I shuffled along on the stool. 'This thing's so low.'

'Just give it a try,' said Machteld. 'It works, you'll see. Harry, would you go and sit behind Lea? Then you can support her.'

'How am I supposed to film?'

'Shall I do the filming for a bit?' Anita suggested.

Harry looked at her doubtfully. 'This is a very expensive camera, my girl. I don't just go passing it around to anybody.'

'Don't whinge, Harry, give the girl the camera.'

'Have you ever used a video camera before?'

Anita nodded.

'Look, here's the record button. And this is the zoom func-
tion. If you look through this little window here you can see
exactly how the picture is framed . . .'

Anita calmly took the camera from him. 'Have you got a
fresh battery? This one's almost empty.'

'What do you mean?'

'The battery light's flashing. Didn't you notice?'

'No. It must have only just started,' Harry mumbled.

While Harry rummaged in his bag, I had a contraction. As no
one was watching, I puffed it discreetly away. A moment's
respite.

Then things started to get serious.

Harry came and sat behind me.

Machteld crouched down, with some difficulty. 'Just push,'
she said, at random. Her fat stomach was obscuring her view of
my epicentre.

'Shouldn't you put a pillow underneath? When it comes out
it'll hit its head on the ground.'

'No need, I'll catch it,' said Machteld.

Zealously I pushed and pushed. The child didn't seem all that
impressed by Machteld's beloved gravitational effect. All we
got to see was a little tuft of hair.

Machteld had brought out a mirror. 'Look, Lea, this'll
encourage you. You'll be able to see what you're doing it for.'

I looked. My cunt was round as a ball. The whole lot was
stretched and swollen. My new-style labia reminded me of
the ear lobes of that man from New Guinea. There was blood
sticking to them. I ought to have shaved. If I pushed with all
my might, I could see a little opening with a dark, wet dot of
hair the size of a quarter. That was all. Was that why I'd bought

half the stock of Prénatal? A matchbox would have been enough.

The little dot disappeared as soon as I stopped pushing; it simply got shoved back in, and then the gate shut behind it. That didn't surprise me. My sluicegate was designed for one-way traffic. No one had ever left that passageway of their own free will.

I pushed on, with half an eye on the mirror. I pushed while Harry massaged my back. Anita brought me flannel after flannel. The dextrose was in great demand among all those present, but whatever else happened, no child was born. The quarter didn't want to turn into a guilder.

Machteld listened to the heartbeat. 'He's doing well, but it's taking too long. Go and lie on the bed again and I'll give you a bit of a hand.'

I had no idea what she meant until I saw the scissors.

'One snip is enough, you'll see. You won't feel a thing, I'll do it during a contraction.'

My heart thumped in my chest. Machteld wanted to cut me open. I didn't like the idea. I didn't agree with her. With which organisation could I register a complaint? I looked pleadingly at Harry.

'Come on. Machteld knows what she's doing.'

Trembling, I lay down on the bed.

I had a contraction. There was no escaping. I spread my legs. Machteld moved in with the scissors. Cold steel against my warm pussy. She squeezed the scissors firmly, as if she was cutting through cardboard.

'Ow, ow, bloody hell!'

'It's done already, calm down. You can push now.'

Push yourself, you damned hag! Did I say that or only think it?

I pushed.

I pushed, because I wanted it to be over.

I didn't want that child inside my body any longer. It had to come out. Hop it. On your own two feet.

I longed for a plop, but no plop came.

Machteld looked worried. She waited for a few more contractions, she kept on listening to the baby's heart. Harry and Anita kept encouraging me, but the conviction had gone out of it. It seemed as if everyone in the delivery room had suddenly realised that, for now at least, the child wasn't planning to show its face.

'There must be something wrong,' mumbled Machteld. 'Perhaps it's in the wrong position . . . Something may have gone wrong with the rotation . . .'

'Can't you try another cut?'

'HARRY!'

'Maybe it would help, and then Machteld can turn him round inside you.'

Machteld shook her head.

'Listen, guys,' I said hoarsely, 'let's get it over with. I've said it right from the start. Give me a Caesarean. Cut me open, sew me shut.'

Machteld shook her head. 'That's not up to me.' She turned towards Anita. 'Is there an obstetrician around?'

'I think Dr Kallenbach's on duty. I'll go and see.' Anita left.

'It's a pity, but I can't do anything more for you. I'm going to hand you over to Dr Kallenbach,' said Machteld.

I leaned back on the pillows. Finally a real doctor at my bedside. Maybe everything would be alright after all

chapter ten

You get one dessertspoonful of orange juice a day and five bottles of infant cereal.

Harry was pacing along the walls of the delivery room.

'What are you doing, love?'

'I'm looking for a socket for my battery-charger. This thing goes down so fast. I'll be flat again in no time.'

The door opened. Anita came in. Followed by a man who was holding the door open for her. He was wearing a white coat. When he got closer, I had palpitations. George Clooney! My gynaecologist was the spitting image of that marvellous creature on *ER*. The same bedroom eyes. The same dark eyebrows. It was unbelievable. Did God exist after all?

Clooney shook my hand.

'Mrs Meyer, I'm Maurice Kallenbach, how are you feeling?'

I suddenly realised that I wasn't wearing any knickers and that my vagina had been cut open. I crossed my legs as best I could and laughed a toothy laugh. What a good thing I'd put on my make-up. 'Call me Lea. I feel so old otherwise.'

Harry came and stood next to the bed.

Kallenbach shook his hand.

'Your face is familiar,' said Harry.

Kallenbach stroked his chin thoughtfully. 'Yes, that's just what I was thinking.'

I didn't understand it at all. As far as I could remember, there wasn't anyone in the cast of *ER* who looked at all like Harry. I'd have noticed if there had been.

Suddenly Kallenbach waved his forefinger. 'The Kennemer!'

'Ah, of course, I've seen you there so many times. I didn't recognise you in that coat.'

I sighed. The Kennemer Golf and Country Club. Maurice was a golfer. Something of a disappointment. I preferred to imagine him in a small canoe racing down a raging river. But perhaps it was just that he played golf on the side.

While Machteld brought Kallenbach up to speed, I had a contraction.

'Go on, push,' said Anita.

I looked at Maurice out of the corner of my eye and pushed. He came and stood next to the bed. He laid his hand on mine for a moment. Was his really so cool, or was it that mine was warm? Next he went to the foot of the bed and looked between my legs. He pulled on a pair of gloves.

Without saying anything, he inserted his fingers into me. 'Keep pushing,' he said.

I did.

He took his hand out when the contraction was over and

told Anita to get the vacuum extractor. 'We're going to apply a little more force,' he explained.

Waggling her hips, Anita approached. With a professional smile she rotated the suction cap.

Harry reacted like a prizewinner on *Wheel of Fortune*. He zoomed in on the apparatus, fascinated. 'Nice piece of equipment,' he said to Kallenbach appreciatively.

'Yes, I've dragged a lot of little Haarlemmers onto the shore with this.'

They laughed.

'I want you to put your feet in the stirrups. Slide your bottom a bit further forward,' said the doctor. 'Are you having a contraction yet?' He held the scissors in his right hand.

The contraction came and Kallenbach snipped. It hurt, but I didn't dare scream. I didn't want him to think I was common.

'Legs a little wider,' said Kallenbach. He pushed the suction cap inside me. 'At the next contraction, press,' he said to Anita.

Anita nodded. She came and stood next to the bed.

The contraction came.

Anita bent down over me and started pressing my stomach very hard.

'Push!' Kallenbach shouted.

Harry took a wide-angle shot from the door.

I felt something slurp inside. And then a plop. The extractor flew out.

Kallenbach swore and thrust the suction cap back in.

Anita kept pressing down, I pushed and again there was that plopping sound.

Kallenbach frowned. 'The head's probably too distended already. The cap can't grip.'

Anita took her weight off my stomach.

Machteld listened to the heart. 'He's doing okay.'

'I want to try one more time,' said Kallenbach.

No one wondered what I wanted. No one listened to my heart. No one gave a shit whether I was doing okay.

Kallenbach shoved the suction cap roughly back inside. 'Push!' he commanded. He signalled to Anita, who threw herself onto my stomach like a lunatic.

Tears came to my eyes. My passion for a man had never cooled so quickly.

'Got it,' said Kallenbach triumphantly.

I pushed.

The vacuum extractor sucked.

Plop.

The suction cap flew off. I felt it. At the same time I noticed a familiar smell. A shit smell. It was my shit. Or rather, my diarrhoea. It dripped down my buttocks. It stank tremendously.

'Anita,' Kallenbach said simply.

He could smell it too. Of course. Everyone could smell it. And everyone could see it.

The twenty-three-year old blonde wiped my arse clean without further ado.

'We're not getting anywhere,' said Kallenbach. 'We'll try something else. Do you mind if a few of my colleagues come to watch?'

'Sorry?' I could hardly hear what he was saying. Everything hurt. My stomach, my cunt. My whole body was shaking.

'Two assistants. It's instructive for them.'

At that moment there was a cautious knock at the door. A young man wearing National Health Service glasses appeared on stage. He had spiky hair. He was wearing a lumberjack shirt under his white coat.

He looked inquiringly at Dr Kallenbach.

The latter gestured to him to come in.

The young man was followed by a young Asiatic woman. Her long black hair was tied in a tight bun.

Kallenbach spoke to the two of them in a whisper. They listened to him with earnest expressions on their faces and looked shyly at me from time to time.

Harry came and stood next to me. 'Doing alright?'

'No. Get me out of here. I want to go home.'

'Hang on in there, my love, it's for our child.'

'For *your* child, you mean. You're the one who wanted it so badly.'

'Lea, please. Not here.'

Kallenbach came over to the bed with his entourage.

'I don't want it,' I said.

He raised his eyebrows.

'I don't want those characters in here.'

Machteld took Kallenbach's side. 'Lea, it's important for assistants to see as many births as possible. Especially if there are complications.'

'Invite them to your own labour then. Or get them to watch *Real World*.' I shut my eyes. I heard mumbling and when I opened my eyes again, Jack and Jill had gone.

Kallenbach had also gone.

'I'll give you some anaesthetic now,' said Anita. She was holding a hypodermic needle.

'What? Am I getting a Caesarean?'

Anita didn't answer. 'Just open your legs.' She stuck the needle between my legs. I felt it go in. Deeper and deeper. She got a second syringe. Another vicious long injection.

Kallenbach came back with two women and a young man in his wake.

I opened my mouth.

He was ahead of me. 'They're nurses. They're here to help me. Clear?'

The man – 'Hi, I'm Koen' – had a metal instrument with him. It looked like a kitchen utensil from a family of giants.

With my last reserves of strength I hauled myself upright. I pulled my legs out of the stirrups. 'That's it, I'm going home. Nice of you to come. Cheers, thank you and goodbye.'

'Calmly, Lea.' Harry. He pushed me back, while I tried to get out of the bed.

'See that thing? Do you know what Kallenbach's going to do with it?'

'He's about to tell us, aren't you Maurice?'

Kallenbach crossed his arms. 'Lea, the baby has to come out right now. I don't have any choice. It's taking too long.'

'Those forceps are far too big. I don't know what you're used to, but mine is small and tight. And it's staying that way.'

'Let me just listen to the heart again.' Machteld.

Reluctantly, I let her do as she pleased.

'The heartbeat is getting weaker. He's in distress.'

'Gosh, what a coincidence.'

'Lea,' Harry sounded shocked, 'our child is in danger. Our child is now the main concern. You agree, don't you?'

'Our child could have been born twenty-four hours ago! If *she*'d let me have a Caesarean!' I pointed furiously at Machteld.

'Enough,' said Kallenbach curtly. 'Put your legs back in the stirrups. The sooner you do, the sooner it's over.' He picked up the scissors.

I thought I'd gone mad. 'Are you going to cut me again, that's the umpteenth time, for God's sake. What's it gonna be, the star of Bethlehem?'

Anita walked over and shut the door.

The other nurses were quiet as mice.

'Would you rather tear?' Kallenbach had no compassion. He didn't even wait for a contraction.

He snipped.

He snipped again.

Koen passed him the forceps.

Harry went very pale.

I prodded him. 'The camera!'

'Are you sure?' he said, doubtfully.

'Get the camera and film those forceps!' *Evidence.*

'I put the forceps in one blade at a time,' Kallenbach told Harry.

I tried to think of the lower half of my body as unconnected to the upper half. I didn't succeed. I thought about my mother, who hadn't torn at all while giving birth to her three children. *You have to dab it with wet cotton wool. That's what they did with me. Keep it wet, keep it wet all the time, then it's not a problem.*

Then came the pain. My crotch was pulled open. The first blade of the forceps had to go in.

I heard someone scream. Very high and very loud.

My insides were being ripped open. Piece by piece.

'Now I'm putting the forceps around the baby's head . . .'

'Close them!' I screamed. I meant it. I didn't mind if he crushed the head. He could squeeze it to a pulp and drag it out of me.

Kallenbach put his foot against the end of the bed. 'Push!' he shouted.

Two nurses dived onto my stomach.

Kallenbach tugged at the forceps.

Again the smell of shit. A sewerage stink filled the delivery room. Unexpected triumph. Now I was more than happy that they could all smell it.

A second furious tug from Kallenbach.

The forceps shot out of my body. There was something sticking to them. It was blue and bloody. It wasn't moving.

I shut my eyes.

It was dead.

I was alive.

It was for the best.

It was him or me – and he'd lost.

chapter eleven

*I've stopped giving you orange juice. You detest it so much,
I can't get it down you. When you're bigger I'll try
again. Very soon it'll be summer; then you'll get enough
vitamin C.*

I wanted to speak to Harry, but no sound came out. I wanted to
tell him that I didn't want a funeral. They could throw it away.
We'd go home. We'd forget this whole episode as quickly as possible and buy a goldfish.

Someone laid the child on my stomach.

I wanted to push it off.

Frightened, I looked around to catch Harry's eye.

He didn't notice. He was standing next to the bed looking at
the baby. He had a look in his eyes that I'd never seen before.

'Your son is doing well,' said Machteld.

Cautiously I peered at the creature on my stomach. It was a
horrible shock. It was deformed. Its head was long and purple.
The marks of the forceps stood out on its face. There were deep
grooves down both its temples. 'It's terrible,' I whispered. 'A

child like that won't have a life worth living. For God's sake give it an injection.'

'Everything will be fine,' said Kallenbach. 'It'll all clear up in a few days.'

Pull the other one.

'When the next contraction comes, you can push one more time for the placenta.' Kallenbach signalled to the nurse.

She moved the little creature a bit higher up me and started pressing my stomach.

The pain was so bad and so unexpected that I passed out. The light slowly faded. It was heavenly.

'Lea, Lea!' I heard from far away. Machteld was slapping my cheek. 'Are you still with us? One more push.'

Leave me alone, get away from me.

'Come on, Lea, then it really will be over.' Harry.

I felt something like a contraction and pushed.

'That's the way,' said Kallenbach. He lifted up a fleshy, bloody clot. 'Your son lived on this.'

I turned my head away.

'What are you going to call him?' asked Anita, who was putting a wristband on the baby.

'Harry,' said Harry quickly, 'Harry Junior. Just like me.'

Anita smiled. 'Nice. You hardly ever hear of boys being named after their fathers these days.'

'Do you want to cut the umbilical cord?' Kallenbach asked Harry.

'Of course!' He glowed with pride and handed the video camera to Anita.

Harry Junior made squeaking noises.

'Is that normal?' Harry asked, concerned.

It was normal.

Kallenbach gave Harry a pair of scissors.

Harry hesitated. 'Will he feel it?'

'Not at all,' Maurice reassured him, smiling.

With the tip of his tongue poking out through his lips, Harry cut his son loose from the placenta.

Then Machteld took the baby and wrapped him in a cloth. 'I'll take him with me for a moment,' she told me. 'So the paediatrician can have a look at him.'

That was fine by me. The freak could do with a check-up.

'A little more painkiller, Anita,' said Kallenbach, 'then I can put in the stitches.'

Oh God, now that. 'Can't you sedate me for this?' I asked. I was shaking like mad. I was hot and cold by turns. It hurt just thinking about myself down there.

'No need, it won't take a moment,' said Kallenbach curtly.

Anita injected the painkiller.

Kallenbach went off and came back with a darning needle and various kinds of thread. Thoughtfully, he examined the damage. He called the nurses over. With his finger he pointed out what needed to be done. 'The soluble stitches go here, and I'll put the main sutures there.'

I was getting used to people looking into my crotch without even glancing at me first.

Kallenbach got a stool and sat down. He threaded the needle and stuck it into my flesh. He pulled the thread through my cunt and jabbed it in again.

Harry came and stood next to me. 'Hang on, Lea, it's almost over.'

I grabbed the top of his shirt and dragged him towards me. 'You're right. It's over. I'm going to ask Maurice if he'll sew it shut completely. You're never getting in there again. And nothing's ever going to come out of there again. Understood?'

Harry didn't answer.

'Can you fix that for the wife of your golfing companion, Maurice? Like with female circumcision; sew the whole lot shut and just leave a little hole to pee through. Perfect!'

No one spoke.

Kallenbach cleared his throat and went on sewing.

'Got a good view, ladies?' I asked the nurses. 'This is what you look like after giving birth. Ripped to shreds. Isn't it wonderful?'

'Lea, don't make such a fuss,' said Harry.

'Excuse me? Excuse me for a moment. It's all very well for you to talk. Your prick's still in one piece. And no doubt Maurice's is too.'

The nurses looked at the floor.

'Lea! Shut up!' Harry was angry.

'Enjoy it, Maurice. Go down on your wife tonight and whatever you do don't think about me.'

'If she goes on like this, you can find another doctor to finish the job,' Kallenbach told my husband sternly.

'Congratulations, he's in fine shape.' Machteld came in. She was wheeling a little transparent container in front of her. There was a small bundle lying in it. 'A bouncing baby boy, nearly eight pounds. Would you like to clean him up and put some clothes on him, Anita?'

Harry walked over to the container. He stroked Junior's hair. 'Be careful, won't you?'

'Of course, Mr Meyer. And congratulations.'

'Thank you.'

'You too, Mrs Meyer.'

Harry knelt down next to my bed. 'Hear that? You did a great job. We've got a beautiful, healthy son. We'll have to be patient for a little bit longer, but tomorrow we can all go home. The three of us.'

I could hardly speak. Kallenbach had started on the main sutures. 'And . . . how's it supposed to go then . . . with us?'

'What do you mean?'

'With the two of us. The little trick, the big trick, you know what I mean.'

'That'll be fine. Soon you'll be good as new.'

'And – ow! – until then?'

'Until then Junior will keep you happy. Guess what? My father's bought him a tiny pair of Nike trainers.'

'Nice.'

'Can't you just see us in the park, Dad, Junior and me?' Harry chuckled. 'This boy's going to be so spoilt . . .!'

'Mm.'

Harry's prattle was distracting. That was the only reason I put up with it.

'Shit! I haven't even called them. I promised I would.' He took his phone out of the inside pocket of his jacket. 'Hello Mum, it's me. You're a grandmother.'

' . . .'

'It's a boy. Called Harry. Everything went fine. Great, isn't it?'

' . . .'

'Wait a moment, Mum.' He put his hand over the mouthpiece.

'Will it take long?' he asked Kallenbach, who was working next to my anus.

'A few minutes.'

'They'd really like to come by, Lea. They've tried to reach us a few times already today. They're completely over the moon.' He looked pleadingly at me.

I sighed.

'That's fine, Mum, do come over. Don't let Dad drive too fast, okay?' Harry rang off.

'Would you ring my mother too?'

'Of course.'

'Ask her if she'll come over.'

Perhaps I'll feel less lonely with her here.

Kallenbach had finished. At last. 'Most of the stitches will come out by themselves. The rest have to be removed in a week's time.

'Will I have to come to the hospital for that?'

'No, the midwife will do it.'

'When can I go home?'

'If all goes well, tomorrow morning. The nurse will wash you now. Then you'll be taken to your room. My colleague, Dr Dijkstra, will come and see you tomorrow morning.' Kallenbach gave me his hand. 'I'll be off then. Congratulations on the birth of your son.' He shook Harry's hand and gave him a pat on the back. 'All the best, old boy. And good luck.'

'Thanks for everything. Do you have my card?' asked Harry.

Kallenbach shook his head.

Harry fished a business card out of his pocket and gave it to him.

Kallenbach left.

I tried lying on my side, but I couldn't. 'When's my mother coming?'

'She's not coming.' Harry picked his camera up from the table and started filming Junior.

'Why not?'

'She said she didn't know the way.' My mother never drives anywhere if she doesn't know the route; she gets into a panic if there's a diversion.

'But couldn't she take a taxi?'

'That's what I said.' He was walking backwards.

Anita watched, smiling.

'Have you called a cab yet?'

'No need. She said she'd come round tomorrow. Once we get home.'

For the first time since Junior was born, tears burned behind my eyes.

'I'll go to the main entrance, Mum and Dad will be there any minute.'

'Shall I freshen you up?' asked Anita.

'Yes please.' I looked away. *She mustn't see me crying.*

'Doesn't he look lovely, lying there? What a little doll. And your husband's so pleased with him. I've never seen such a proud father!'

chapter twelve

We've put two little toy pussycats in your crib, and you always give them a very friendly laugh when we put you in there. You laugh a lot when you've just had a good feed, and so prettily.

'Con-gra-tu-la-tions!' Mama Meyer flew into the room first. She had an enormous bunch of roses in her arms. Loose roses, without any paper or Cellophane, not even a piece of string around them. She dumped the whole lot onto my bed. 'Aren't they beautiful? They're from our garden. Don't come any fresher.'

'Thanks very much. Could you find a vase, Harry?'

'You could always sit on them. Then it'd be a bed of roses!' Papa Meyer roared with laughter.

I put the roses to one side and opened my arms.

Papa Meyer put his arm around my shoulders for a moment. 'Congratulations. You had a hard time of it, I hear . . .'

'It's always hard, everyone knows that,' said my mother-in-law. 'Oh my goodness, is that the baby?' She walked around my bed and thrust her face down into Harry's plastic box. 'He's so small! And so crumpled . . .'

'It's because of the forceps,' said Harry. He picked the roses up off the bed.

Mummy-in-law started talking like a retard to Junior. 'Hello little man, this is your grandma. Did they pull you out with forceps? Couldn't your mother do it by herself? Or didn't you want to come out into the big, bad world? It's alright. You'll be just fine. Won't he?' This last question was directed at me.

'Dr Kallenbach says he will.'

'Did Kallenbach do the birth?'

'Yes.'

'Oh, but he's a fantastic gynaecologist! You were very lucky to get him. He did my fibroids. Sweet man he is. And so handsome too.'

'Lea's very tired,' said Harry. He winked at one of the nurses and gave her the roses. 'You can't stay long.'

'Of course not. But we had to see him. Our first grandson. Give them the Nikes, dear,' said Mama.

Papa Meyer handed over the little trainers.

Harry took them. He held them over the plastic container, 'Look, Harry, these are from Granny and Grandpa. What do you say to Granny and Grandpa?'

Junior didn't say anything. He didn't even bother to open his eyes.

'Thank you Granny and Grampa,' said Harry in a little piping voice.

Less than two hours old, and Junior was already having an

amazing effect on his surroundings. People spontaneously metamorphosed into semi-imbeciles.

Harry saw his parents out.

He came back to tell me he was going home. With a sigh, he came and sat on the edge of my bed. 'Do you know, I'm completely exhausted. My back hurts, I've got a headache.'

'Poor darling.'

He went over to Harry Junior. 'Bye bye, my little laddie. Daddy's going to get some sleep. Daddy's going to beddy-byes.'

'Hey, talk normally to that child.'

'Hear that, Harry? Mummy's a little bit cross with Daddy. Mummy has to go to sleepy-pies too.'

'Mummy can't go to sleepy-pies, because Junior keeps whining.'

'I've asked the sister about that. She says he's probably got a headache, from the forceps.' Harry looked concerned.

I had an idea. 'Hey, my love, couldn't you take Junior home with you now?'

'Why?'

'Why d'you think? I'm completely shattered. This is my last chance of a quiet night.'

'I really don't know.'

I rang the bell.

A few seconds later, a nurse put her head round the door.

'Can my husband take our baby home with him now?'

The nurse came in. She looked surprised. 'That's not the usual practice. He can lie next to you tonight, we won't have to take him to the special-care nursery.'

'That's exactly the problem. He's making such a racket there's no way I'll be able to sleep.'

'Then I suggest we do take him to the nursery. He's had a difficult time, it's better if he doesn't have to travel just now.'

Harry gathered his video things together and took elaborate leave of Junior. I got a fleeting kiss.

'Is he going to the nursery right away?' I asked the nurse when Harry had gone.

'If that's what you want.'

'Yes please.'

She gave me a quizzical look.

'It's been a heavy day,' I explained. 'A forceps delivery.'

'I know. What a letdown, eh?'

'Rather, yes.'

'My sister had one too, she said it was psychological, that you don't want to let the child go, my sister got torn in all directions, eighteen stitches she had, I've got two children, but they just popped out, no cut, no tear, nothing at all . . .' She looked into Harry's plastic box and rearranged the sheets. '. . . I reported the second one myself, the registrar couldn't believe his eyes, but well, with my sister it was a whole different matter, she had to sit on an inflatable rubber ring for weeks . . .'

The rubber ring wasn't on Machteld's list. I was sure of that.

'. . . then it went wrong with one of the stitches too, they were all supposed to come out, but the midwife missed one, it got all infected, it was terrible, the pus dripped out of it, you have to watch out for that you know, that they take out all the stitches, how many have you got?'

'Well, I haven't cou—'

'—I'd ask someone if I were you, my sister had so much trouble on account of it . . .' She wheeled Harry's container away from my bedside. 'Say goodbye to Mummy.'

Junior moaned.

'Have you got a sleeping pill perhaps?' My body was a wreck, but my mind was clear. Clear as day. All I could think about was Machteld, and Kallenbach.

Machteld's burrowing fingers. Machteld with the scissors. Kallenbach with the scissors. Kallenbach with the extractor. Kallenbach with the forceps. Kallenbach with the needle . . .

'Of course. I'll bring you one shortly.'

At last I was alone. I shut my eyes.

Such peace.

The door opened. A bed was wheeled in. In it lay a woman with a blissful look in her eyes. A second nurse wheeled a transparent container into the room.

Fuck. Why haven't I got a single room? I specifically asked Harry for one.

The woman raised her hand.

I nodded politely.

The baby in the container started to cry.

The nurse came up to me. 'Where's your little son?' she asked.

'One of your colleagues took him to the nursery. I've had a difficult birth, I want to sleep now.'

'This lady has just given birth too. She'd love to keep her little daughter with her. Do you have a problem with that?'

'Actually I do, yes.' It came out before I had time to think.

'If you really do object, then we'll take this baby to the nursery too.'

The woman looked imploringly in my direction.

I ignored her. 'I'm sorry,' I said to the nurse, 'but before long that child will be bawling the night away.'

'If that's what you want.'

The nurse went to the other bed to deliver the bad news. The woman started to cry. I would have liked to roll over, but I lay there as if turned to stone, watching the scene unfold. The mother took her daughter out of the plastic box and held her close. She stroked her hair and kissed her all over.

Eventually the nurse took the child from her and laid it back in the container. The nurses left, they took the baby with them.

I cleared my throat. 'I'm sorry. I had an extremely difficult labour.'

The woman swallowed awkwardly. 'The sister told me, yes.'

'How did yours go?' It didn't interest me one jot, but I wanted her to stop crying.

'Viola was born at home. The placenta didn't come out properly. It was incomplete. So I still had to come to hospital. For a curettage.'

'Oh, what a shame.'

'Yes, I needed an anaesthetic for the curettage. I was scared to death. Fortunately it's all turned out fine, I can go home tomorrow.'

The nurse came in with my pill. 'Do you want a sleeping tablet too?' she asked Viola's mother.

'No, I don't like pills.'

I took the pill gratefully. The stitches were pulling and burning. The sooner I lost consciousness the better.

Viola's mother turned her back to me. She picked up the phone next to her bed and started making calls. One friend after another had to be told how wonderfully well the birth had gone and what a peach of a baby Viola was. 'She's got such a pretty little face. So perfect. And she has those sweet little fingers that look like prawns, with the tiniest little nails. Her eyes are blue and every now and then she gives me an inquisitive look, as if she's thinking, are you my mother, then? It's a real miracle. I never realised it would be so wonderful . . .'

I turned onto my side. How quickly would the pill take effect? I could silently sing a song to myself. I used to do that sometimes as a child.

> *Sleep softly, little Lea, sleep softly*
> *The angels are watching over you*

It didn't help. Perhaps I ought to play 'If-I-could-wish-for-anything-at-all'. When I was seven, it was my favourite falling-asleep game. I would lie on my back in my foldaway bed with my eyes shut and imagine I had supernatural powers.

First I used to wish that all the sick people would get better. Then that all the dead people would come back to life. I realised that this would have far-reaching consequences, so I adapted the wish to mean that only those who'd died prematurely (in an accident or a war, or from disease) would come alive again. The blind would be able to see, of course – whether they wanted to or not – and the deaf hear. Cripples would be able to walk again, the poor would become rich; in other words, life would be one big party for everyone. As for my own wishes – a Barbie doll, riding lessons – I usually didn't get that far. I dozed off before then.

If I could wish for anything at all, I'd wish I'd never given birth. It was a pure, simple wish.

chapter thirteen

You're a sweet little girl and I hope we'll all be able to have a good and enjoyable life together. Your sister dotes on you, Birgit would like to cuddle you all day long.

I had a happy childhood.

My mother was a housewife. She often had a headache. My father had an office job. Besides that, he devoted himself to the preservation of the black-fringed water beetle. He did a lot of things most fathers don't do. And most of the things that fathers generally do, he didn't. Such as earning a lot of money. Loving me. Or watching *Studio Sport* on Sundays.

My father died when I was thirteen. It's almost twenty years ago, but I still remember exactly how it went.

It was a normal Saturday morning. My sister Birgit and I were still in bed. I was dozing, Birgit was in a semi-coma. She'd spent the previous few nights with three Germans she'd picked up on holiday.

The intercom rang. My mother answered it and said, 'Fine, do come up.'

Inquisitive, I got out of bed. I put my slippers on. Then the doorbell went. As I was coming out of my room, my mother opened the front door. I went down the stairs. I stopped halfway down.

Two police officers were standing just inside the door, a man and a woman. I saw my mother pull her housecoat tighter around her in an effort to cover her breasts. The woman said they had bad news and that my mother had better sit down. They walked one after the other to the living room, my mother leading the way. They all sat down. My mother sat in her usual chair, the police officers next to each other on the sofa. The man did the talking. I understood that my father was dead.

I went back upstairs, to Birgit's room.

If you wanted to put Birgit into a bad mood really fast, you only had to wake her up on a Saturday morning when she hadn't asked you to. I didn't hesitate for a second, I shook her by the shoulder and told her that Daddy was dead. She was wide awake immediately. We looked at each other. A gleam came into our eyes.

'So he's dead then?' Birgit said.

'Dead as a doornail,' I said, 'move over.'

I climbed into bed with her. She wouldn't normally have dreamed of letting me do that, but today everything was different.

'We'll have to bury him,' she said.

I nodded.

'And there'll have to be a death notice in the paper.'

That was also true. I cleared my throat. 'With great pleasure . . .' I couldn't finish the sentence, I had to laugh at my own joke.

Birgit started to giggle too.

'With great pleasure . . .' I tried again.

'And gratitude . . .' she added.

'. . . With great pleasure and sincere gratitude, we announce the death of Kees Johannes Maria Cornelissen.'

Then we both had to laugh like mad. Screech with laughter. We couldn't stop. My sides hurt. 'Stop it, stop it!' I pleaded with my sister, although I didn't know what it was I wanted her to stop.

My mother was still downstairs. She had made coffee for the police officers. She said you could distinctly hear us laughing from the living room. She was ashamed of us. 'It's nerves,' she apologised as she put the coffee cups down, her hands trembling.

It seems as if some people are more dead than others. My father, for example, is a good deal more dead than President Kennedy. If I had to name the ten most dead people I could think of, he'd come near the top of the list. The man has completely disappeared from view. Literally as well as figuratively. There isn't a single house with his photo on the wall. The anniversary of his death goes by unnoticed year after year. I don't suppose anyone misses him.

Apparently it's pretty lousy to have a dead father. I don't see why. The premature death of my father hasn't had much influence on my life. The atmosphere at home got a lot more pleasant, that's true. I moved up to the next class at school without any problem. I got my diploma. My mother's life didn't change much after my father died either. Her disintegrating marriage was finally over after twenty years. An entirely favourable outcome, even though she refuses to this day to take advantage of this stroke of good fortune.

Why my mother married my father back in 1957 is a mystery. Ditto reverso. The word 'mystery' is inadequate. The fact they ever got together is totally incomprehensible. It defies all logic. However you try to explain it – and I have tried – there's only one possible conclusion. That there was no reason at all. No economic, biological, sociological or any other kind of reason. If there were ever two people on this planet who ought to have avoided each other at all costs, it was them. I watched the double blind trial from the front row. When I think about my parents, I see two people standing screaming at each other.

My sister insists it wasn't always like that. When Birgit was small, it seems that my parents did occasionally go and lie next to each other on the bed. To talk. On Sundays, after drinks. They kept their clothes on. In her eyes it was the height of intimacy. She still hasn't completely freed herself from that misconception.

I never saw my father and mother being intimate with each other. It seems children find it embarrassing to see their parents kissing, but I'm sure I'd have found it fun to watch.

My parents hated each other. I grew up certain of that. I heard and saw so many arguments that I don't remember any of them. Oh, well, except that one with the chair. That was a real ripper.

I was ten. My mother had bought a white leather TV chair. One of those that swivel. It was gigantic. It was standing in the middle of the room when my father got home.

'What's that?' he growled.

My mother put her hand on her hip. 'A chair. For me.'

'What did that bloody thing cost?'

'You won't go hungry paying for it.'

My father walked around the chair. 'What an ugly thing! Really hideous. How could you buy it?'

'You don't need to sit on it. It's *my* chair.'

'Oh yeah? Who paid for it?'

Birgit and I were sitting by the fire reading Asterix and Obelix comic books. We heard my mother's voice get higher and shriller. My father kept goading. My mother kept rising to the bait. That was how it always went.

'. . . you won't let me have this chair? Aren't I allowed one thing for myself? Do you begrudge me even that?'

My father said something I didn't catch.

My mother ran to the kitchen. She came back with a large knife. It had a long, serrated blade.

Birgit and I stopped reading. I put my finger on the place I'd got to.

My mother went up to the chair. Screaming. She held the knife over the chair. 'Are you sure, Kees? Are you sure your wife isn't allowed a chair of her own?'

I can't remember what my father did. I was only watching my mother.

She hacked at the chair. She was hysterical. When my mother is hysterical her jaw goes completely stiff, and so do the tendons in her neck. She pressed her lower teeth into her upper lip. Holding her mouth like that she hacked at the chair.

Suddenly she stopped. She waved the knife under my father's nose. Her hair had come loose and was hanging in strands around her face. 'Stab me to death!' she shrieked. 'Just stab me to death! That's what you want, isn't it?' To make it easier for him, she was pressing the tip of the blade against her chest.

My father turned around and walked out of the room.

My mother lowered the knife.

Birgit went back to reading her book.

I stood up and inspected the chair. 'It's not too bad, Mum.'

We went shopping together every Saturday. On the way home from the A&P, my mother and I would talk about life.

'I don't understand why you stay with him.'

'I know, Lea, but what can I do?'

'Just get a divorce.'

'And then what?'

'Then at least we'd be rid of him.'

I don't know whether she took my advice to heart, or whether she realised for herself that it couldn't go on any longer. Whichever it was, I jumped for joy when my mother told me in the summer of 1979 that she was going to file for divorce.

The letdown came a few Saturdays later. We were walking back from the A&P. I was boisterously wheeling the shopping trolley along, sweeping it gracefully left and right, knowing for certain that no one else in the western suburbs of Amsterdam could do that so well as I could.

'Your father and I are going to give it one more try.'

'What?!'

'He's promised to improve. He begged me to give him one more chance.'

'And you fell for it?'

'That was a week ago and he's really been doing his best since then. Haven't you noticed?'

'Yeah, I've noticed him grovelling. But do you really think he'll keep it up? I don't believe a word of it.'

This time I was right. He couldn't keep it up. And after that my mother couldn't keep it up either. She finally filed a petition for divorce.

My father refused to cooperate. He didn't sign any of the forms. The marriage was dissolved all the same. My father would have to look for somewhere to live.

It didn't come to that. He died two weeks after the divorce.

I didn't go to the funeral. I said I didn't feel well. That was a lie. I felt right as rain, it was just that I didn't feel like going to a funeral. And certainly not to my father's. While my mother, my sister and my father's family paid him their last respects, I was eating macaroni.

I went to visit Yvonne and Peter, a couple with young children who lived a few doors away.

Peter made a big show out of every spoonful of macaroni the little ones had to eat. He was an actor and mad keen on slapstick. I thought he was very funny.

'You're a fine one,' Peter said, while he passed round the apple purée. 'Your father's being buried and you're here enjoying yourself.'

I wasn't in mourning for him. Not then, not a week later, and not after that either. I haven't grieved for him for a single day. The bastard was dead; time to party.

Sometimes you see pictures of people at the end of the war. They've been liberated, but they haven't really taken it in yet. They have dark shadows under their eyes and they're not laughing. My mother has had dark shadows under her eyes ever since my father died. I laugh. I laugh myself silly. I really do.

chapter fourteen

When I talk to you, you answer me in your own fashion, by making little throaty noises. That's great fun for all of us.

'Do you have any Biotex?' asked the home help.

I was lying in my own bed. I was wearing an old T-shirt of Harry's. My lower quarters were beaten to a pulp, my stomach was black and blue all over.

'In the cupboard under the sink, why?'

'Soon you're going to have a lovely bath to soak your bottom in Biotex.'

'Sorry?'

'It's good for your stitches. It's very cleansing. Then it won't get all infected.'

José went downstairs.

Bathe my bottom in Biotex. There was room for more humiliation yet, then. For the past forty-eight hours my life had been a sequence of humiliations. Half the medical world of Haarlem had seen my cunt. That's to say, half the medical world of Haarlem had been inside it up to their elbows.

The last morning in hospital I couldn't pee. My private parts were so sensitive I didn't dare to.

'You're not going home until you've urinated,' one of the nurses said. She gave me a jug of water. 'Pour this over yourself while you're doing it. You'll have to do that for the next few days in any case. Every time you pee, rinse well. Against infection.'

I hobbled back to the toilet and lowered myself over the seat. Sitting on it was not an option. The cold water splashed against my cunt, but no pee came. I pulled the flush and left the toilet.

The nurse was waiting for me in the corridor. 'Have you urinated?'

I leaned against the wall for support. 'I think so, yes,' I lied.

'You're lying.'

I went bright red.

'Drink lots of water and try again shortly. And I'll want to see it.'

She was serious. Twenty minutes later she came to fetch me. Arm in arm, we shuffled our way to the toilet.

'Just leave the door open.'

I pulled down my hospital knickers. Ridiculous elasticated things. The thick maternity sanitary towels without side panels didn't slip out of place, I had to admit. I was wearing three of them.

Jesus, I sure was bleeding!

'I'll get some clean sanitary towels for you,' the nurse said. 'Pee first.'

I shut my eyes, poured the water over my vagina and concentrated. I needed to go, but did I dare to?

'Go on, it won't hurt.'

Where have I heard that before?

The first drops started to come. It burned, although it wasn't
as bad as I'd expected. I let it stream out. I had to.

'That's the way.'

José came back into the room. 'I've got your bath ready.' She
helped me out of bed.

I needed the help. I walked bent over with pain. I wobbled
unsteadily to the bathroom like an old woman.

There was a shallow pool of water in the bath.

'You lower yourself into it and after a few minutes you get
out again. It's all over in no time,' said José breezily. She pulled
down my knickers. 'Hey, you're still bleeding quite a lot.'

'I know.'

She helped me out of Harry's T-shirt.

She helped me into the bath.

The Biotex stung my pussy.

'Alright?'

'Alright . . .'

'In a few days from now it'll be more painful. Then the cuts
will really be starting to heal.'

With that cheerful prospect in view I raised myself back out
of the bath.

'Do you want to go and sit downstairs for a while?'

'I can't sit. I want to lie down.'

José helped me into bed. 'Have you defecated since you gave
birth?'

'No.'

'I'll go and stew some prunes for you shortly. And cut you a slice of cake. You have to get those bowels moving.'

Shitting means pushing. Pushing means pain. Lea wouldn't be pushing for a while yet.

'Shall I go and get young Harry?'

'Why? He's sleeping, isn't he?'

'If you're going to breastfeed, we need to put him to the breast right now.'

'I'm not sure I am going to breastfeed.'

Harry came in at that moment. 'Of course you're going to breastfeed. That's what's best for the baby. Isn't it?'

José nodded.

A little later, Harry Junior lay next to me in bed. He still looked ghastly.

'What a sweet little thing, isn't he?' said José. It seemed to me that was a stock phrase for home helps. Page one of the textbook:

ALWAYS SAY THE BABY IS A SWEET LITTLE THING
EVEN IF IT'S A DWARF WITH WATER ON THE BRAIN
AND/OR A HARE LIP

What was the mother supposed to answer?

YES I'M HEAD OVER HEELS IN LOVE WITH HIM

I couldn't bring myself to say it.

'Lift up your T-shirt.' José had a wet flannel in her right hand.

Harry whistled in appreciation. 'That looks great, pet.'

That was better. Until now, Harry had been completely fixated on his offspring.

José wiped the cold flannel over my nipple. 'It's still a little retracted.' She pressed Harry Junior's face against my breast. 'Let's just see if he takes it.'

He took it. He sucked. He sucked my whole damned tit inside out. Suddenly it hurt like fury. As if my nipple was being stabbed full of needles.

'It may hurt a little. That's the milk coming through,' José explained.

'Get him off me.'

'It'll stop hurting in no time.'

'Get him off me!' I tried to pull Harry off my breast but I couldn't.

'He hasn't drunk enough yet,' said José.

'I don't care! Get him off!'

José put her little finger into the corner of Harry's mouth. He let go. I quickly pulled my T-shirt back down.

Junior started crying.

Harry was angry. 'What the hell are you doing, Lea? He's hungry.'

José picked Junior up and comforted him. 'Do you want to try again in a little while?' she asked in a friendly voice.

'No.'

'What do you mean "no", my child has to be fed.'

'Don't interfere, Harry.'

'Are you sure?' José asked.

Suddenly I was absolutely certain. Harry Junior would be put on the bottle. He'd done enough damage. Thanks to him I could forget about my sex life. Now he wanted to help destroy my tits too. I'd heard about women whose flesh had split right open, leaving a nipple hanging to the breast by a thread. I wasn't having any of that.

'I'll make up a bottle for him,' said José. 'What have you got?'

'Bottles, but no formula.'

'Doesn't matter, I've got a sample packet with me. Maybe you could go to the supermarket shortly and pick up a can of infant formula?' She looked inquiringly at Harry.

He nodded.

'Do you want to take Junior with you?' I asked José. 'Then I can get a bit of a rest.' I was worn out.

'Don't you want to give him his bottle?'

'Let Harry do it.'

Harry's face brightened immediately.

They left.

I was alone.

I closed my eyes. I wanted to sleep. I couldn't. I could hear José and Harry talking. I heard the phone ring. I heard the vacuum cleaner. I heard the washing machine. I could smell the flowers. Harry's colleagues at work had had an enormous bouquet delivered, José had put them next to my bed. A congratulatory telegram had arrived, from Harry's brother. The neighbours had put a big wooden stork in our garden. It was holding a nappy in its beak with a doll in it. Everyone seemed so happy with little Harry. There was no getting away from it.

> *Be happy, Lea, you have a healthy child*
> *Be happy, everything went well*

Be happy, your husband is crazy about him
Be happy, your in-laws are on cloud nine

There had to be some kind of logic to it. There must be a reason why everyone thought I should be happy. Woman gives birth to child – cunt ruined, child remains whole. Woman stripped of her womanhood, of her figure – the bonus, a child. A boy. Who can impregnate other women. So that they can also have children and lose their womanhood.

It's nature. Primeval laws. New life takes precedence over the old. The oak tree dies once it has borne fruit. *Nature*.

I was too young. Why did I have to give precedence to new life? This was my heyday. My prime.

I rolled over and thought about Queen Beatrix. According to my mother, members of the royal household routinely have Caesarean sections, because that presents the least risk to both mother and child.

Trix's cunt was still in one piece. But Claus was depressed. Something wasn't right there. Surely Trix wouldn't be so stupid as to choose natural childbirth. Would Trix, our Queen, have been introduced to the forceps? And would Claus have been watching? Good God, that man was so sensitive it would have been disastrous. Perhaps he'd performed a Van Gogh-style act. Had he cut off a bit of his prick afterwards out of a sense of powerlessness and misplaced solidarity . . .? It would explain an awful lot. It would explain everything, even their son's perpetual pursuit of leggy blondes.

Mary had an Immaculate Conception. She gave birth in a stable. Her son Jesus preached love. He ended up on the cross.

He preached Love and ended up on the Cross. The full impact of this had never struck me before. That was the message. That was His Message. Love makes you suffer. *No Love, no Suffering.* It was that simple. Jesus wanted his own generation to be the last. A generation that would neither love nor suffer. That would live in peace and die in peace. It would be a tremendous way to end. Live and die as He had said we should. End all Suffering, begin with yourself. No one had understood what he meant. Except for me. I understood. I had to reveal his message to the world. That was why it had happened. I had been chosen.

Suddenly I started sobbing uncontrollably. Maybe Junior could have been born perfectly normally. Those forceps might not have been necessary at all. Maybe I could only understand the message if I had suffered. So I had to suffer. The sacrifice was great – my cunt. *My cunt has been sacrificed for the sake of the Message* . . .

José came in with a bowl of fruit. 'Look, this will do you good.'

My hands shook as I took the bowl from her.

'Harry drank a whole bottle. The little lad was so hungry! Feeling a bit better?'

I looked at her. *Does José know about the Message?*

'Your husband gave him the bottle. It was such a touching sight. Such a big man with such a tiny little baby. Really lovely.'

She probably doesn't know about it.

'Shall I have a look at your stitches?'

I put the fruit on the bedside table.

José pulled off my knickers.

I parted my legs.

She looked closely. 'Looks good.'

I would be healed. That was it! Of course! Why hadn't I

realised it before! I'd had a natural childbirth and would heal naturally too. The healing would be swift. My womanhood would be fully restored. I would become a virgin like the Virgin Mary. Doctors would speak of a miracle. It would be my reward. I smiled. For the first time since Harry was born I felt happy. Everything would be all right. I was certain of it.

José pulled up my knickers. 'Your mother rang. She'll be along this afternoon.'

I looked down. *I mustn't give anything away*. 'That's nice.'

'And someone called Corine rang. Asked if you could call back.'

'Corine's my tennis partner.'

'You play tennis? That's nice. Where?'

'Here, in Aerdenhout.'

'I play badminton.'

'That's nice.'

'Thirteen years at the same club. It's very friendly. I met my husband there.'

I looked at my watch. 'What time's my mother coming?'

'Three o'clock. Shall I bring you the phone?'

'No. I want to rest for a bit.'

José left me alone. That was good. Her chatter was distracting. I had to think. The more I thought, the more I would understand. I felt agitated. It was all so exciting.

Suddenly I saw and understood so much more. The great totality, the Interconnectedness of Things. It was a revelation. A Revelation. A forceps delivery. I had been Delivered.

I picked up a piece of fruit and saw *Childbirth & After* lying on the bedside table.

I studied the cover closely.

> *Pregnancy*
> *Emotions*
> *Pain*

This was about me! I quickly read on.

> *Exercises*
> *Motherhood*
> *Surgery*
> *Home delivery*
> *Contractions*
> *Sex*

It all referred directly to me. I'd been through all of this.

> *Experiences*
> *Breastfeeding*
> *Work*

Work? Would I have to work? *Moi?*

Of course I would have to work. Not literally, but figuratively. I would have to go further in my spiritual quest, I would have to go deeper.

> *Thoroughly revised and expanded edition.*

That was a complicated one. It was probably a diversionary tactic. Otherwise ordinary readers would get suspicious. The book had been revised and expanded . . . but the message remained the same. That must be it.

Contact Publishing House

Oh God. A tremor ran through me. *Contact. They were trying to make contact.*

The book was written by eight women. Eight women. An octet. A witches' coven. The women had crazy names: Jetske Spanjer, Aafke Gorter, Hetty Hagens, Lilet Poortman . . . Pseudonyms. Why hadn't I seen that before? Those women didn't really exist. The names had been thought up to give the book credibility.

Lilet, I hear you!

What should I do now?

I turned the book over and got a shock.

On the back cover was a photograph. All eight women were laughing at me. *Have you finally got it?* they seemed to be saying. *Welcome, Lea!*

I looked at the women one by one. A few of them looked familiar. Suddenly I realised what it was. One of them looked just like Birgit. My sister. They'd put my sister in there between them. How incredibly thoughtful. They knew I'd see it. And that I'd understand.

My cheeks glowed. I was getting closer and closer to the heart of the matter. To the Supreme Truth. The mystery would be revealed. Did I have enough time? I looked at my watch. Twenty-two minutes past two.

Harry came into the room. 'How's it going in here?'

'Fine.'

'José says you're very tired. That you have to get plenty of rest.'

Okay José!

'Yes.' I hadn't had so much energy in ages, but Harry didn't need to know that.

'I've given Harry his bottle. He's sleeping now.'

'Great.'

Harry laid *De Telegraaf* on the bed. 'I'm sorry I got so angry just now. I do understand why you don't want to breastfeed. You've had a hard time. You have to recover first.'

José has had a good talk with him.

'I'm glad you understand.'

'I'll go to the printer's shortly.'

'Shall we leave the announcement cards for a while?'

'Why?'

Delay him. I have to use delaying tactics. Gain time. I need more time.

'I don't feel like having visitors yet. My stitches hurt so much, I can't even sit up.'

'Are you sure? We still have José now. Next week she won't be here any more.'

'That's what I want, all the same.'

'Okay, good.' Harry went away.

'Close the door, would you?'

He'd left the newspaper lying on the bed. Would I find my next instructions in it? Probably, but where? I gave it some thought. *Among the birth notices, where else?*

I found the right page. Not a single child had been born. People had only died or been married.

Suddenly I saw it. I got goose bumps.

> *See and hear this:*
> *the blind can see once more,*
> *cripples walk,*
> *lepers are cleansed,*
> *the deaf can hear,*
> *the dead are raised*
> *and the Good News is brought to the poor . . .*

My wishes! The wishes I'd made secretly as a child! I must be on the right track.

> *. . . On the evening of Monday 9th May 1998, towards midnight, the blind eyes of*

FATHER LEO BOS

> *saw a clear light and his deaf ears heard a soft voice calling to him. With this good news, this crippled man went peacefully to meet his Lord, in the knowledge that he had been purified and strengthened by the Extreme Unction and other sacraments . . .*

Leo Bos. *Leo and Lea*. He had seen the light. So had I. I hadn't heard a soft voice, but perhaps that would happen as well.

> *. . . Father Bos was born in Ilpendam on 3rd January 1900. He was ordained as a Priest in Vleteringen on 24th June 1929. From 1929 to 1964 he worked as a missionary in Sri Lanka . . .*

A man with a mission. Shit, you certainly had to read between the lines. Was his mission the same as mine?

*. . . From 1942 to 1945, however, he was interned by the Japanese
on Celebes, where he eased the suffering of many with his sense of
humour. From 1964 to 1981 he worked as Pastor at the home for
the elderly at Sankt Zierig (Germany). Thereafter he retired to
Ilpendam . . .*

Ease the suffering of many with your sense of humour. It had
potential, it definitely had potential. But how? Perhaps I ought
to become a stand-up comedian. Or a hospital clown.

*. . . In 1983 he moved into the nursing home 'De Einder' in
Amsterdam, where, in spite of his physical disabilities, he managed
to remain alert and very much himself . . .*

Remain yourself. A definite clue. No one must suspect anything. Remain yourself and work on your Mission.

*. . . He had a remarkable personality: sharp and witty, sensitive
but candid, displaying great determination in his work, his suffering and his prayer . . .*

Goddammit, this man was a saint! Did I have to measure up to
all this? Why me, why had I been chosen?

*. . . This man, a brother to us, reverend uncle or much loved col-
league, lived to the very end in true communion with Christ who
now, so we believe, has taken him unto himself in the House of God
the Father . . .*

I wiped away a tear with my little finger. Leo had gone to

the House of God the Father, into the lap of God, in other words. How fantastic for him! He'd arranged that very nicely . . .!

. . . His earthly body will be interred in the Northern Burial Ground in Amsterdam on 15th March after a requiem mass which will be held at twelve o'clock in the Chapel of the nursing home 'De Einder' in Amsterdam . . .

Ashes to ashes, dust to dust. They'd bury him in the ground.

Don't get all sad, Lea, the body is only an outward manifestation.

. . . From 2 pm onwards you can take your leave of Father Bos in person in the chapel, where his body will be lying in state.

> *On behalf of the family*
> *Mrs C. Tong*
> *Damstraat 14*
> *1377 AB Ilpendam . . .*

Mrs Tong! Not a very subtle hint. It was clear. I had just one chance to meet Leo. *Tomorrow he will be lying in state. I can get there to see him. He might be able to help me understand how to proceed. He is my predecessor. He doesn't have a wife or children. He has understood Jesus' message . . .*

There was a gentle knock at the door. José came in. 'Your mother's downstairs.'

I closed the newspaper. 'Isn't she coming up?'

'Little Harry is sitting on her lap. I've given her tea, and rusks with comfits*.'

'Where's Harry?'

'He went to the printer's.'

Feverishly, I assessed the situation. *Act normally. That's the most important thing. No one must notice anything. As far as the outside world is concerned, I am my mother's daughter and Harry's wife. Not the Woman with a Mission. I have to be a good daughter. And a good wife. What would a good daughter do?*

'Do you want a cup of tea too?' asked José.

That's it. Have some tea. With mothers you drink tea. 'Yes.'

'Do you want to have it downstairs or up here?'

'I'll come downstairs. Then I can see little Harry too for a while.' That last bit was a masterstroke.

José nodded, satisfied. 'Shall I help you down the stairs?'

'Yes please.'

My mother was sitting in the living room. She had laid Harry across her chest with his head on her shoulder. She was holding him tightly against her body and stroking his back.

I went and stood next to her. 'Hello Mum.'

'Hello Lea. Congratulations.'

'Thank you.'

'I always used to hold you like this. You could lie this way for hours.'

I smiled.

'Why does he keep making that odd whining noise?'

'He has a headache. From the forceps.'

'Terrible. The poor child has suffered so much.'

---

* Traditional Dutch treat to celebrate a birth.

'Yes, terrible.'

The Suffering won't last much longer. I am here to end the Suffering.

Harry came in with a box and a plastic bag. 'Here are the announcement cards. I've got a surprise for you.' He got a flat packet out of the bag. An inflatable rubber ring. 'José says it means you can sit down.'

'Oh, how sweet of you. Thanks.'

José inflated the ring straight away. It was white with jolly yellow suns all over it. The symbol of light, multiplied. Wonderful. I put my hands together and said a quick silent prayer of thanks.

Then I sat on the rubber ring and drank tea with my mother.

chapter fifteen

*For your last feed, at about midnight, you're allowed to get
into our bed with Daddy, you find that delightful. You lie
there looking at everything with big, wide open eyes.*

At night I had the house to myself. I sat on the floor in the lotus
position, with the rubber ring under my bottom. The silence
was blissful. I pressed my hands against my cheeks and let my
thoughts run free.

The only thing that stood in my way was little Harry. He
insisted on having a bottle at three in the morning. Giving him
twice as much at midnight didn't help. He just spewed it all back
up, so he was hungry again by three anyhow.

Harry could easily be the last of his generation. I wouldn't
need to do anything. No bottle, no Harry. It was that simple. I
would set an example. An example for others to follow.

I had so many plans. Harry was merely a link in the chain.
First I had to go and see Leo. I'd torn the death notice out of the
newspaper. The significance of it was unmistakable. On the

back of the cutting was a photo of a dark-haired ballerina on a folding chair. She was poking her tongue out at the audience. She looked like me. It was me. I too would do what no one expected. I would give the performance of my life.

In the morning I discovered two wet patches on my T-shirt. My breasts were leaking. They were warm and hard, as if there was a thick crust inside them. I took off my shirt. My nipples had white drops on them. Wasn't there something in the Bible about 'breasts like bunches of grapes'? If I pressed one of them, streams of milk poured out.

SAVE IT. IT WILL COME IN USEFUL.

I went downstairs and got a Tupperware bowl. I squeezed my breasts until there was a layer of milk in the bottom of the bowl. I took a tray of ice cubes out of the freezer, took out the blocks of ice and poured the milk in. It filled the space of four cubes. I put the tray in the freezer, right at the back.

Little Harry was crying. He was hungry. Again. I boiled some water, poured it into the bottle. One measure of feed per 30cc. Count the measures. I became confused so easily that I counted them out loud.

'One . . .

'. . . and one is two . . .

'. . . three . . .

'. . . and one is four.'

Put the top on. Shake. Cool the bottle under the tap.

I took Harry the bottle. 'Your son is hungry.'

He yawned. 'Why don't you do it?'

I opened the curtains. 'You're still here now. When are you going back to work, by the way?'

'I don't know. Hey, he's bawling his head off.'

'He's been doing that for the past ten minutes.'

'Then give him a bottle.' Harry sat up.

'It's your turn, I did it during the night.'

When José arrived, I told her about my breasts. They were very swollen and painful.

'They're too full, my dear.'

'Now what?'

'There's not much you can do. You could give little Harry a feed, but you don't want to. It'll have to clear up by itself. Have you got any sanitary towels or panty liners?'

'Yes.'

'I'll put a few of them in the freezer for you. When they're nice and cold, you can wrap them in plastic bags and put them inside your bra. That'll ease the pain.'

I went and lay down on the bed and thought about my mother.

For a long time my mother wore little bags of stones in her bra. Semi-precious stones. They have healing properties. Amethyst for this, tiger's eye for that. She used to put a small handful of stones in a little cloth bag, sew it shut and put it in her bra, underneath her breasts. She swore by their curative powers. Everyone should try stones. Myself included. I was given a piece of aquamarine to hang round my neck because I tended to get bronchitis.

When the stone age was past its peak, my mother got to know Doctor Vogel. On his advice she slept with potato peel and crushed cabbage leaves against her skin. During the day she drank pints of nettle tea. That did wonders for the bladder. To be on the safe side, she gargled three times a day with Molkosan, the foulest, most disgusting concoction I've ever tasted.

After my father died, my mother wandered about for ages in the counter-culture. She tried everything: tarot, I Ching, Reiki, astrology, numerology, hypnosis, reincarnation. The more unverifiable the theory, the more she was convinced she had found the meaning of life.

Since she thought she'd had a previous existence, she wanted to try hypnosis. However often she tried, it didn't work. Would I like to have a go? The Reiki instructor who rented a room in our house put me under within three minutes. At seventeen I had no difficulty dishing up two previous lives, one in Ireland, where I had been a peasant, and one in France; there I had been a clerk – and therefore a man – at the court of Louis the Something.

My mother took notes avidly. She thought it was wonderful, especially my description of my Irish husband on his deathbed.

'Didn't you find it terrible that he was dying?'

'No,' I said, truthfully. 'It didn't affect me at all. The man was old, used up.'

My mother was always searching for something she had once known. The purpose of her life had been revealed to her just once. It happened in the spring of 1972, when she was least pre-pared for it.

She was hanging out the washing.

'Suddenly I understood. It was very simple. I must tell Kees about it, I thought.' Kees was my father. 'I wanted to write it down, but by then I'd forgotten it already.'

I sniggered.

It's so simple, Mum. Once you know the answer it's almost comical. Life only makes sense if you put an end to it early enough. As long as you do that, anything is possible.

There was a bird on the windowsill.

Could it be Doctor Vogel, reincarnated as a house sparrow?

'Hi Doctor!' I waved, just to be on the safe side.

He didn't say anything. He didn't fly away either. What had the little creature come to tell me?

LEO!

Of course! I have to go and see Leo today. My friend. My shepherd. This is going to be a special day.

Harry came into the room. 'Everything okay in here?'

'Yes, fine.'

'I thought I heard you call.'

'I was watching television. A quiz. I got the answer before any of the contestants did.'

Harry looked at the TV. The screen was blank.

'I've just turned it off.'

Harry went and sat on the edge of the bed.

'Lea, would you mind if I went to work today? The lads called.'

Perfect. Just the way it has to be.

'Yes you go, my love.'

'You mean it? That would be great. I was afraid you'd be annoyed.'

'No, not at all. José's here. You can spend the whole day at the office.'

He grinned. 'I can treat everyone to rusks and comfits.'

*

Fifteen minutes later, Harry had gone.

I called José. 'Where's little Harry?'

'In bed.' She went over to the window, opened it and shook out her duster. 'I wanted to bath him but he's so fast asleep.'

'You can take the rest of the day off.'

'Really?' She shut the window.

'My mother will be here shortly. She wants to spend the day fussing over her grandson. You know how it is.'

'Are you sure I can go? Shall I do some shopping first?'

'No need. My mother's bringing lasagne.'

José fished her watch out from between her breasts. 'I must just take your temperature. What time is she coming?'

'In about an hour.'

'Then I'll quickly run you a Biotex bath too. Have you had a pooh yet?'

I shook my head.

'You have to do that, Lea. If you wait any longer it'll be worse than giving birth.'

The Biotex dip was painful. It burned like anything. I couldn't sit in it for longer than three seconds.

José kept pushing me back in. 'Come on, Lea, in for a moment longer. You can do it.'

Why did I have to suffer yet again? I'd suffered enough. Enough to be able to understand the Message. I wanted José to go away. She'd turned on the radio downstairs. I could understand every word they were singing.

> *I'd go down on my knees*
> *Kiss the ground that you walk on*
> *If I could just hold you again . . .*

It made me both happy and sad at the same time. I wanted to go down on my knees, but for whom? For Him, for little Harry, for big Harry, for Leo? I didn't know any more. José was disturbing my concentration. I wiped away a tear from my cheek.

'Oh love,' said José, 'are you crying? I was waiting for that. Maternity tears. They usually come on the third day.' She helped me out of the bath. 'Just let it all out, it's alright.'

I dried myself, put on a tracksuit and lay down on the bed.

'Shall I stay with you until your mother gets here?'

'No. There's no need. I feel better already. Could you turn the radio off?'

'Of course. See you tomorrow then, alright?'

'See you tomorrow.' I didn't get up.

José went downstairs.

The radio went silent. Right in the middle of an advertisement for sanitary towels. I felt my breasts. They still hurt.

The front door slammed shut.

It was quiet in the house. I sat up awkwardly. There was a lot to do.

I WILL GIVE YOU STRENGTH. GO ON.

I picked up the newspaper cutting. I had to leave for Amsterdam. I pulled on some trainers and went downstairs.

As I was looking for my car keys I heard crying. *Little Harry.*

Should he come with me? Was this a sign? I shut my eyes.

TAKE HIM WITH YOU. IT IS A JOURNEY HE HAS TO MAKE TOO.

I went back upstairs to the baby's room. There was Harry. He was wearing the Babygro with the blue rabbits on it.

LEO IS SURE TO LIKE THAT.

I got Harry out of the crib and carried him downstairs. The

Maxi-Cosi was in the hall. With trembling hands I laid him in it. Why did he keep on crying?

THE DUMMY.

I was so glad of the instructions. I could never have managed without them. I fetched the dummy. When I got downstairs the third time I was worn out. I leaned against the wall.

THE FATHER IS WAITING FOR YOU. ONLY TODAY.

I picked up the Maxi-Cosi and my rubber ring and walked to the car.

It seemed like centuries since I'd driven a car. The streets were so busy! Harry spat out the dummy and started to cry. He lashed out angrily with his fists in all directions. He probably had colic.

Twice I took a wrong turning. When I parked the car near the chapel, Harry was still crying. Maybe he was hungry. I didn't have a bottle with me. He'd have to stay in the car for a little while.

I turned the rear-view mirror towards me. How pale I looked! I ought to have spruced myself up a bit.

LEO LIKES IT WHEN YOU LAUGH.

I smiled. The first part of the assignment had almost been fulfilled; Leo and Lea would soon be together. The rest would follow of its own accord.

I gave Harry his dummy and locked the car. I walked into the chapel right after an old man in a raincoat. The man hung his coat in the cloakroom. I didn't have anything to hand in.

It was busy. Groups of people were waiting in the hallway. They talked in low voices. I walked past without acknowledging them.

There's Lea
To think she dares to come
Lea's here
Did you see Lea?

They were talking about me. All of them. I was causing confusion. They hadn't expected me to be there.

Someone tugged at my sleeve. 'You have to go to the back of the queue, madam.' Little piercing eyes behind big owlish spectacles. What business was it of hers?

'I have an appointment with Leo.'

'Are you next of kin?'

I walked on. Soft piano music was coming from Leo's room. I opened the door. There were two women in there. One blew her nose loudly, the other one was praying. I ignored them and went to the coffin. All around it there were large white lighted candles.

BLOW ONE OF THEM OUT.

I chuckled. Leo liked jokes. I blew out a candle.

'What on earth are you doing?' said the snivelling woman.

The praying woman looked up, annoyed.

'Leo's last wish,' I whispered. I looked into the half-open coffin. An old, grey-haired man was lying there, with a hollow face. He had a big nose.

An die Nase eines Mannes . . .

Leo winked at me.

The snivelling woman relit the candle I'd blown out.

'Who are you?' the other one asked.

Nobody, nobody, nobody knows
Rumplestiltskin is my name.

'You look so unhappy. Leo wouldn't have wanted that. Sex, drugs and rock 'n' roll, ladies.'

'She's drunk,' the sniveller whispered.

'I'll go and fetch someone,' said the other. She left the room.

My liaison with Leo would be a short one.

I pulled the grey cloth off the lid of the coffin and knocked three times on the wood. *If you still have anything to say to me, say it now.*

YOU HAVE UNDERSTOOD THE MESSAGE PERFECTLY. PUT AN END TO THE SUFFERING. BEGIN WITH YOUR-SELF. YOU KNOW WHAT YOU HAVE TO DO.

Thank you. Hasta la vista, baby. And have a good journey.

KISS!

Stupid. I should have thought of that. Leo mustn't go to his grave unkissed. I bent over and pressed my lips against his cold mouth.

TONGUES!

Give them an inch . . .

I tried to squeeze my tongue between his stiff lips. It wasn't all that easy.

'Stop that!' Sniveller reached me in two strides.

From outside the door I could hear a man's voice, deep and authoritative. 'Madam, would you come with me?'

Great, a gorilla in uniform.

'It's okay, I'm leaving.'

I stood up with some difficulty. My stitches pulled.

Three pairs of suspicious eyes followed my every move. These people were weird. It broke my heart to have to leave Leo with them. I blew a kiss in his direction.

'See what I mean?' said the second woman.

I turned my back on her and walked towards the gorilla – he didn't have hair on his chest, only a name badge. 'Move over, J.K.'

Jan Krabbendam was delighted with the order – he stepped aside immediately.

In the hallway, a group of people parted so I could get past. BLESSED ARE THOSE WHO KNOW NOTHING.

I left the chapel and walked to my parking place. A Surinamese couple was standing next to my car. I didn't know whether they were a couple, but I thought so. It didn't look like a coincidental formation to me. The woman peered through the window, concern on her face. Harry was lying there squealing like a stuck pig. I took my bunch of keys out of the pocket of my jogging pants.

'Is that child yours?' said the man, with barely concealed rage.

'*Your children do not belong to you*,' I answered, smiling.

'We've called the police. It's disgraceful.'

I opened the car door and sat behind the wheel. It stank like hell in the car. Harry had shat himself. I started the engine. The woman shouted something I couldn't understand. The man shook his head disapprovingly.

I drove out of the parking place. Harry cried incessantly. PUT AN END TO HIS SUFFERING.

When I got to the highway I couldn't decide what to do. Should I take a different route? I had to remain unpredictable. I mustn't let them find me.

I giggled. I'll go back the way I came. That's the last thing they'll be expecting.

*

Back home, I left the Maxi-Cosi on the floor in the hall. I went to the kitchen.

The breast milk was frozen. I put the cubes in a bottle and thawed them in the microwave.

His Last Supper.

I gave Harry the bottle while he was still in the little car seat. He drank greedily.

His face was red and puffy. I tried to see myself in him. Nothing about him seemed familiar. He looked like a baby. He was interchangeable. He was the beginning of the cycle. He would have to be the end of it too. Because of him, it had all gone wrong. I had to go back to the beginning. Time would be turned back. That was why time was now standing still. In this vacuum, everything could be put right. This evening, big Harry and I would go to bed, and when we woke up, the newspaper would fall onto the mat and it wouldn't be 1998 any more, it would be 1997.

The bottle was empty. Harry had drunk it all up.

HE COMES FROM WATER. HE MUST RETURN TO THE WATER.

I picked the baby up out of the Maxi-Cosi and took him upstairs with me. I ran a bath. I felt the water with my elbow to make sure it wasn't too hot, as José had taught me to do. 'If he gets restless, you can give him a bath. He loves that,' she had said.

I laid Harry on top of the chest of drawers and took off his clothes. He had a nappy full of greenish yellow shit, all the way up his back.

I carefully let him slide into the bath. I supported his head with my left hand. He looked at me inquisitively.

BAPTISE HIM.

With my right hand I poured water over his forehead. 'In the name of the Father, the Son and the Holy Ghost . . .'

Harry started to whimper.

LET HIM GO.

I pulled my hands away from him. Harry disappeared under the water. I turned around and walked out of the bathroom.

chapter sixteen

24th June 1966

I've been giving you brown beans with apple purée for lunch for about two weeks now. You won't eat it without sugar. It's good for you, so you have to eat it, that's why I add the sugar. You always find the first spoonful particularly disgusting. You pull such a comical face, it always makes me laugh.

I was startled by the crash. The pot of ferns lay in pieces around my feet. The marble pillar wobbled but remained upright.

Harry!

I'd forgotten all about him! He was still in the bath! How could I forget about him? They were right, I was a bad mother.

I raced back to the bathroom and pulled Harry out of the water. He didn't make a sound. I slapped him on the back and shook him. He coughed. Water came out of his mouth. He started to cry.

I heard someone coming up the stairs.

My husband. His jacket was hanging open. 'What's the matter?'

I looked at him anxiously. 'I don't know.'

'Did you give him a bath?'

'Yes.'

'Why don't you get a towel? He's crying. Don't just stand there.'

Harry got a hand towel from the rail and took Junior from me. 'Quiet now, little man.' He wrapped his son in the towel and held him close. 'Where's José?' he asked.

'I sent her home.'

'Why?'

'I wanted to be alone for a while.'

'You're in no fit state.' He sighed. 'You're so pig-headed. You could have waited for me to get back before giving him a bath.'

'I have to go and lie down for a while,' I said.

Harry followed me into the bedroom. He laid Junior next to me on the bed. 'Stay here with Mummy for a moment and I'll get you some clothes and a nappy.'

'Harry?'

'Yes?'

'I'm frightened.'

'Frightened? Of what?' He took off his coat.

'I don't feel too good.'

Harry laid his coat over the back of the chair. 'What do you mean?'

'I can't sleep.'

'Because of the stitches?'

'Yes. That too.'

'And?'

CAREFUL WHAT YOU SAY.

'I don't know.'

'Perhaps you should see the doctor. You haven't been yourself since the birth.'

'Don't you think it's weird? Everyone assumes I'm walking on air. They forget what I've been through.'

Harry came over to sit next to me on the bed and put his arms around me. 'I haven't forgotten. I was there, remember?'

I was no match for that amount of loving kindness. I started to cry.

Harry held me in his arms. 'Hey, girl . . .'

That did it. If anyone calls me 'girl' I'm off. I cried with long, howling sobs.

I dried my face on his shirt. I snuffled about in his armpits. Harry's smell was strongest there. 'It's been a long time,' I sighed.

Harry didn't answer. 'Oh, just look,' he said tenderly.

I glanced aside. Junior had fallen asleep wrapped in the towel. How could Harry find that little white skull interesting? More interesting than his own wife? And endearing? There was nothing endearing about it. It was a gnome. An intruder.

I stroked Harry's chest. My hand slid lower and lower. I kneaded his groin.

There was no reaction.

'Is little Harry having a nap too?'

'Lea.' His voice was full of incredulity.

'What is it now?'

'Our son's here.'

'He's sleeping.'

'You've just given birth.'

'But you haven't, have you?' I undid his belt.

Harry grabbed my hand.

'Let go.'

'I don't feel like it.'

'What did you say?'

'You heard me.'

His Lordship doesn't feel like it. Oh great. Another illusion shattered. I was always promised that men only wanted one thing and that they wanted it all the time. That they think about it every five seconds. That's why I became a heterosexual in the first place, for God's sake.

'Don't you find me attractive any more?' I immediately regretted it.

Of course he doesn't find me attractive any more. And I'm not, either. My stomach is a blubbery, white heap, there's no sign of my waist and my cunt is an abstract accumulation of scar tissue, held together with stitches. I'm wearing a tracksuit, my hair is greasy and stringy. I wouldn't get turned on by myself in a hundred thousand years, so why would Harry?

'I can't think about that right now.'

'Shall we take a shower together?'

Harry stood up. 'I'll get a nappy. He'll pee on the bed otherwise. Shall I call the doctor?'

'The doctor?'

'For you, we were just saying.'

'Oh yes. Fine.'

He disappeared and came back with a nappy and some pyjamas. He adroitly applied the disposable nappy to Junior's undersized buttocks.

The child went on sleeping, even while his pyjamas were being put on.

'Shall I lay him in the crib?'

'Yes, do.'

He picked Junior up carefully and carried him out of the room.

'Do you want something to drink?' he asked a little later. He'd stopped in the doorway.

'No. Come and lie in bed next to me for a while.'

He hesitated.

'Just for a moment,' I begged.

'Oh, alright then.'

He lay down on his back on the bed and crossed his arms behind his head.

I snuggled up against him. And I couldn't help it. My hand slid automatically down to the place where I was hoping to find an impressive erection.

He has reproduced himself. The work is finished.

I did what I could, but little Harry remained a mere shadow of his true potential.

'Are you going to make a doctor's appointment for yourself too?'

'Why?' Harry asked.

I squeezed it gently. 'It's not working.'

'Are you really incapable of thinking about anything else?'

'What should I be thinking about?'

'About our child. About the future.' He pushed me away and stood up. 'I'm going to put the announcement cards in the mail.'

He walked out of the room for the third time.

I was left behind.

He'd turned his back on me. This was all going wrong.

YOU HAVE TO GET BETTER.

You guys are right. I have to get better.

chapter seventeen

24th June 1966

You've had another injection, the 'four in one', against whooping cough, tetanus, polio and diphtheria. All very important.

I was sitting in the waiting room. I stared at the wall. It was busy. Most of those sitting there were old people and housewives. Two of the patients had been put there for my benefit. It was obvious, especially that Japanese woman with the paper mask over her mouth.

Next to me was a man with a baby in a carrier. He was carrying the baby on his stomach. No doubt the doctor wanted to know how I'd react to that. When she came to get me, I smiled at the man and his mite. I could see right through their little game.

In the surgery I folded my hands together in my lap. I avoided the doctor's eyes as much as possible.

'Mrs Meyer, your husband called to say he's worried about you.'

I nodded.

'You had a difficult labour, I hear?'

'Yes.'

'You haven't fully recovered yet?'

'No.'

'Have the stitches been taken out?'

I shook my head.

'Are they still causing you a lot of discomfort?'

'Yes.'

'I hear you're having trouble sleeping.'

'That's right.'

If she only knew. I don't sleep at all. I have to stay alert. I mustn't doze off. I can't, anyhow. My thoughts are too clear; my brain is too active. My mind is sharp. Sharp as a knife. Razor-sharp, incredibly sharp. Sharp-witted.

'Is that your main problem?'

'I think so.'

'Are you very tired?'

'Yes.'

'You lost a lot of blood during labour, perhaps we should have a look at your iron level.'

I nodded.

'My assistant will do that shortly.'

There was a moment's silence. I fiddled with the clasp of my bracelet.

'Your husband says you're very agitated. Restless. Is that right?'

I shrugged.

'Would you like me to give you a prescription for something to calm you down? Something to help you sleep?' She picked up a pen and a notepad. 'I can give you some sleeping pills, but we could start with something a bit milder.'

'I don't know. The milder stuff first, maybe?'

'That's what I was thinking. I'll give you a prescription for Passion Flower. They're homeopathic drops, they have a sedative effect.' She wrote out the prescription and gave it to me. 'Hopefully they'll help you to sleep better. If necessary you can always give me a call.'

'Good, thank you very much, doctor.'

The doctor took me to her assistant's room. 'Would you take a look at Mrs Meyer's Hb level?'

The assistant nodded. She had blond hair and fat tits. She was a Dolly Parton clone. She was on my side. Nothing surer.

The doctor left.

'This'll be done in no time, just take a seat,' said Dolly in a friendly manner.

IT'S GOING FINE. KEEP COOL.

She pricked my finger and took a drop of blood, which she smeared on a glass slide. 'You're not anaemic,' she told me shortly afterwards.

'What's the result?'

'Seven point eight.'

Towards the end of my pregnancy I'd had to take Machteld's iron tablets. They made me constipated and my shit went jet-black, but it did help.

'Seven point eight,' I repeated, satisfied. 'I can't complain then.'

'Have you just given birth?'

STAY ON YOUR GUARD.

'Yes.'

'What is it?'

'A boy.'

'Oh how lovely, a nipper. I've got two sons.'

I looked at her tits. *Yeah yeah, two sons. That figures.*

'Congratulations,' Dolly bleated.

'Thanks.'

'I'll inform the doctor it's normal.'

I stood up.

'Don't forget your prescription.'

'Oh yes. Thanks.'

I walked to the car. I was just about to put the key in the ignition when I had second thoughts. I'd walk. That was a good diversionary tactic. I got out and put the prescription in the pocket of my jacket. I kept my hand on it the whole way – no matter what happened, I mustn't lose the prescription, it was evidence.

The pharmacy was packed. I was shocked to see so many people. Behind the counter they were walking hastily to and fro. A telephone was ringing. A perm in a white coat picked up the receiver. She had a stack of paperwork in her hand. She looked around and lowered her voice as she spoke into the phone.

IT'S ABOUT YOU! THE DOCTOR IS WARNING HER. THEY'RE ONTO YOU.

Bloody hell, I'll have to hurry. The trap is closing.

I waited my turn impatiently. It was taking too long. Far too long.

'Can I help you, madam?' The question was asked by a neatly dressed young man with dark hair and glasses. He was wearing a grey university sweater with a blue trim.

The perm finished her phone call. She glanced in my

direction for a second, then went and sat at a computer. Wearing a tired expression she pressed a few keys.

YOUR DETAILS. SHE'S LOOKING FOR YOUR DETAILS.

It wasn't working. She shook her head and called a colleague over.

I smiled broadly. The system was jammed.

I confuse the system, wherever I go, computers run amok.

IT'S BEEN HAPPENING FOR YEARS. HAVEN'T YOU EVER NOTICED BEFORE? YOU CREATE INTERFERENCE.

'Madam?' said the lad with glasses.

I pushed my prescription towards him with shaking hands. 'I need these drops.'

'One moment.' He went to a cupboard and came back with a small packet. 'You don't need a prescription for this medication. It's not covered by the National Health Service. You'll have to pay for the drops. Seven ninety-five, please.'

'First the prescription,' I said.

'Pardon?'

'I want a copy of the prescription.'

'But you don't need one. The instructions are inside the packet. You'll find the exact dose in there.'

'I have to have a copy of the prescription.' I stressed every syllable.

'Madam, it's very busy. I don't have time to make copies.'

'No copy, no drops,' I said in a high-pitched voice.

The lad looked inquiringly at his colleague. It was the perm.

I started to get frightened. At any moment it could happen. I must play the game all the way to the finish now.

'I demand a copy! I have the right to a copy!' My voice cracked.

The glasses walked off.

Someone nudged me in the side with his elbow. 'If I were you I'd go ahead and take those drops straight away.'

I blushed from ear to ear. Ivo Niehe! 'Is it really you?'

A sphinx-like smile appeared on his lips. For a moment I thought he was going to kiss me.

'Madam!' the bespectacled lad was waving a sheet of A4 paper. 'Here you are, madam, your copy and your drops.'

I gave him ten guilders. 'Keep the change.'

It was cold outside but that didn't bother me. I returned to the car at a trot, the panels of my coat flapping behind me. I had to giggle. I'd made it! I'd led the whole lot of them up the garden path.

chapter eighteen

24th June 1966

*You're allowed minced vegetables now, I'll start you on
those once you've got over your jab. I wonder how you'll
react. I'll write again then. Until next time, little woman.*

José was doing the vacuuming when I got home. Sky Radio was
playing.

When she saw me she switched off the vacuum cleaner.
'Hello, Lea, how did it go at the doctor's?'

'Fine. I've got some drops.' I went to the sideboard and
pulled open a drawer. I had to hide the prescription.

*The Yellow Pages, that's a great place. They'll never look there.
Where shall I put the prescription? Under P for Passion Flower? No, too
obvious. Not L for Lea either. H would be absurdly transparent.*

'What's your last name, José?'

José had turned the vacuum cleaner on again. She didn't hear
me.

'José!' I pulled the plug out of the socket.

'Yes?'

'What's your surname?'

'Smit.'

I put the plug back in.

The S. They'll never think of that.

I stuck the copy of the prescription into the book next to *Scaffolding for rent* and imprinted the page on my memory.

The howl of the vacuum cleaner was getting on my nerves. José was on her knees next to the chaise longue.

I tapped her on the shoulder. 'I'm turning it off, okay?'

'Something the matter?'

'The doctor says I need peace and quiet. I'm going to lie down. I don't want to be disturbed. Can you do the vacuuming some other time?'

'Of course.'

I hung up my coat and got the Passion Flower out of my pocket.

'Your son's asleep,' José informed me without being asked. 'Your husband's given him a bottle. Then they had a bath together.' She smiled. 'They make such a lovely pair, those two.'

'Could you turn the radio down?'

I took the phone off the hook.

Peace and quiet. I had to get some peace and quiet. The doctor was right.

I went upstairs. Harry was in his study. I told him what had happened at the doctor's. In the bathroom I put ten drops of Passion Flower in a glass of water and drank it down with great gulps.

Passion Flower. Passion is my middle name.

I went and lay down on the bed. All I had to do now was to wait for a feeling of relaxation to come over me.

The doorbell rang.

THEY'RE COMING TO GET YOU!

I sprang up. Walked quickly to the landing. *Don't open it, José!* I wanted to shout, but no sound came from my throat.

José was almost at the door already. She opened it. On the doorstep was a man I didn't recognise.

That must be them. They've found me.

José spoke with the man. If only she didn't give me away. 'Thanks,' José said. She shut the door again. She looked up.

'Who was that?' I asked.

'You left your lights on. Where are the keys? I'll turn them off for you.'

I left my lights on. Yet another sign. I have seen the light. I must keep it burning. But how? I scratched my head. I didn't know any more.

'It's okay. I can see them,' said José.

I went back to the bedroom and carefully closed the door.

WE CAN HAVE MORE INTENSIVE CONTACT. BUT ONLY THROUGH THE RIGHT CHANNELS.

Channels? Sometimes I couldn't make head or tail of the instructions.

KEEP A BETTER LOOKOUT.

Keep a better lookout? I'm not doing anything else but, for God's sake. Why does it all have to be so cryptic? Couldn't you guys maybe just say what you mean for once?

I let my gaze wander through the bedroom. There was nothing unusual about it. The curtains were closed. The television was off.

The television!

UH-HUH, SMART OF YOU.

I grabbed the remote control from the bedside table and turned it on.

WELCOME TO 'THIS IS YOUR LIFE'. ZAP AND YOU SHALL FIND.

Unbelievable. They were sending messages through the television. Wherever I zapped, on every channel they were showing a programme that was made especially for me. Which was I supposed to choose? All the information was equally relevant.

Pippi Longstocking appeared.

Pippi!

And Annika.

Tommie.

Mr Nelson.

Lilla Gubben.

Nostalgia for childhood, logical to start there. Pippi, the girl with supernatural powers who has to look after herself.

PIPPI = LEA. LEA = PIPPI.

Do Annika and Tommie stand for José and Harry? No, it's about what happened long ago.

ANNIKA = BIRGIT. TOMMIE = THE BROTHER WE SHOULD HAVE HAD.

I followed developments on the screen, concentrating hard.

Annika and Tommie were visiting Pippi. They went up to the attic. Pippi said it was haunted up there. Annika nearly wet herself. When they got upstairs there wasn't a ghost to be seen. That was right, they were at the ghosts' annual meeting, Pippi remembered.

PIPPI ISN'T AFRAID OF ANYONE.

PIPPI LAUGHS AT GHOSTS, ANNIKA'S AFRAID OF THEM.

LEA LAUGHS AT THE PAST, BIRGIT'S AFRAID OF IT.

I must show her there's nothing to be afraid of. That's my task. I have to chase away the ghosts. Blow away the cobwebs. I'm the youngest, but the cleverest too. The funniest and the boldest. I must be all of those things. That's the way it's always been.

A soft tap at the door. Harry. 'Are you asleep?'

'No.'

He came in. 'Do the drops help?'

'Not really.'

Pippi waved at me from the screen.

> *Hey, Pippi Longstocking,*
> *falderie, faldidah, faldihopsasah!*

The music sounded so loud I could hardly hear what Harry was saying. I tried to turn off the TV. 'Could you switch the TV off, the remote isn't working.'

Astounded, Harry looked towards the wall. 'It's already off, isn't it?'

That was scary.

Harry can't see Pippi. But I can see her. I can still see her. Could you guys turn her off, please? I don't know how it works.

YOU CAN TURN HER OFF YOURSELF. TRY IT.

I looked away from the television.

'Are you sure you're alright?' Harry sounded worried.

Junior started to cry.

'I'll go,' said Harry.

Passion Flower.

I ran to the bathroom, got the bottle, unscrewed the top and let the drops fall directly onto my tongue.

A bitter taste purifies the heart.

I giggled. *'This won't do the trick, honey,'* I said to my reflection in the mirror. I could down three bottles of homeopathic tranquillizer and then still – then still the most I'd feel would be nausea. I looked at myself. With wide-open eyes I studied my face. Goosebumps crept up my arms. Something could happen at any moment. I knew what it would be, too. If I shut my eyes and then opened them again, I'd find myself looking at someone else.

WHO DO YOU WANT TO SEE? WHO DO YOU WANT TO MEET?

Nobody! Nobody, you hear! No devils, no spirits and LEAST OF ALL MY FATHER. I don't want that. Play your dirty tricks on someone else.

I shut my eyes tightly and felt my way out of the bathroom. In the bedroom I unplugged the TV from the wall socket. I looked up cautiously. The screen was blank.

I undressed, crawled into bed and pulled the sheets over my head.

Pippi is scared, are you satisfied now?

I stayed in my room for the rest of the day. Harry brought me up a plate of food. Steak with fried potatoes.

I took three mouthfuls and flushed the rest down the toilet.

YOU HAVE TO GO ON. THE MISSION HAS NOT YET BEEN ACCOMPLISHED.

When Harry got into bed beside me, I pretended to be asleep. I waited until I could hear regular breathing, then I slipped out of bed.

CORRECT THE GREATEST ERROR.

I went to Junior's room. He was asleep in his crib.

HE HAS TO GO. ONLY THEN CAN YOU MAKE A FRESH START.

He weighed almost nothing. He smelled of baby. I'd have to wash all his little clothes, otherwise everybody would be able to smell that he had existed. I held him against me. I had to be careful not to drop him. He would wake up then, and start crying.

SEE TO IT THAT HE BELONGS TO THE PAST.

The tasks got more and more complicated. Where do you find your past?

PIPPI.

In the attic! With the ghosts!

I walked up the stairs with some difficulty.

It was dark in the attic.

BE PATIENT. YOUR EYES HAVE TO ADJUST TO THE DARK.

My boxes were in a corner. The boxes I'd carried around with me all my life. There were school things in them, journals, swimming certificates. My poetry album. My father's collection of rocks.

I opened one of the boxes. If I moved a few files to one side, Junior would fit between them nicely.

The books were a bit hard, though.

I took off my nightshirt and laid it in the box. I wrapped Junior in the nightshirt. He went on sleeping. I put the lid on the box.

GO BACK TO BED.

I went downstairs.

First to the toilet. I had to have a shit for the first time since giving birth. I sat on the toilet nervously. I kept my eyes firmly shut and used as little pressure as possible. Slowly a turd slid out of my arse. It didn't hurt. I looked into the bowl. Smooth, light brown and thin.

SEE. THIS IS YOUR REWARD. EVERYTHING IS RETURNING TO NORMAL.

I crept happily into bed again.

I couldn't get to sleep, I was too cold and too tense.

The mission is practically accomplished. Now I can begin to live according to His word. I shall preach Love, just like Jesus. Just like Leo.

Smiling, I thought about my future. There were two possibilities. One, I would be recognised as the new Jesus and become world-famous. Two, I wouldn't be recognised as the new Jesus and . . . Sighing, I threw my legs over the edge of the bed. Just grab a T-shirt.

When I opened the wardrobe door, it happened.

A baby fell. I saw it.

He was lying on his back. He threw his arms out wide. He fell further and further into the depths. He was wearing a white woolly hat and a white Babygro.

WE'LL LET HIM DIE NOW.

I don't want to see it. I don't want to be a witness.

Make it stop!

I swung the wardrobe door shut with a loud bang.

Harry jolted awake. 'What's the matter?'

I stared absently at him.

'Why haven't you got anything on? What are you doing over there?'

The baby had gone.

Harry came over to me. He put his arm around me. 'Darling, you're stone-cold. Come on, get into bed. Did you have a bad dream?'

I nodded. That was it. *A bad dream*. The dream was over. Tomorrow everything would be alright again.

I lay down in the foetal position.

Harry pulled the covers over me.

I wanted to cry. I couldn't, so I pretended to. I made crying noises. 'Waa! Waaaa . . .!'

I put my thumb in my mouth. As a child I sucked my thumb for ages. So long that I had to wear a brace.

I sucked my thumb avidly.

Harry stroked my forehead. 'Shall I call the doctor, Lea?'

NO!

'No!' I took my thumb out of my mouth.

Harry hesitated. 'What's the matter with you, you're acting so strangely.'

'Nothing,' I said in a child's voice. 'There's nothing wrong at all. I'm going to sleepy-pies now. Are you going to sleepy-pies too?'

He shook his head, stood up and left the room.

KEEP IT UP, IT'S GOING WELL.

In the distance I heard swearing.

Two seconds later Harry stormed into the room. 'Where's Junior?'

'Who?' I asked.

'Our child, where is our child?'

It's going wrong. Harry wasn't supposed to look. He hasn't forgotten about Junior yet. That won't happen until tomorrow.

PLAY FOR TIME.

'Isn't he downstairs, in his baby bouncer?'

Harry didn't answer. He ran downstairs.

TAKE OVER JUNIOR'S ROLE.

I lay in the foetal position again and cried.

Downstairs I could hear doors being opened and slamming shut again. A little later I heard Harry's footsteps on the stairs.

'Waaaa! Waaaa . . .!'

My wailing didn't mollify him at all. He yanked the covers roughly off me. 'Shut up for God's sake! Where is Harry?'

'He's here, isn't he?' I giggled.

He shook me angrily. 'What have you done with my child? Where is he?' He let go.

I stroked my nose with my finger, the way Wicky the Viking does when he needs to think of a cunning plan: finger along the right side, the underside, the left side. 'Where would you put a baby, in the compost bin or in the ordinary trashbin?'

Harry went white. 'This isn't happening,' he whispered. He ran downstairs again.

He came back without a baby. I felt sorry for him. This had to be done, but still, he seemed so despairing. As if he really did mind that his child was gone.

'I'm asking you one last time, otherwise I'll call the police. Where is Junior?'

'I'm not allowed to say.'

'Who says you're not?'

I put my finger to my lips. 'It's a secret. A big secret. Come into bed with me, my love? Then we can have a good sleep.'

Harry buried his head in his hands and moaned.

A perfect drama. They've thought of all the crucial elements: the young father, the anger, the powerlessness, the sorrow . . .

I stroked the side of his leg comfortingly. 'Hush now, darling, it'll be alright.'

Harry gave a deep sigh.

'Are you coming to lie down? Then I'll sing you a lullaby.'

'Shut up!' Harry turned his head to one side.

I didn't want to hear it, but I did hear it. *A baby crying.*

Harry went out onto the landing.

Tense, he strained to hear where the noise was coming from.

'He's in the attic!' He stormed up the stairs.

He was back a moment later. He was holding Junior in his arms. Apparently the child was alive and kicking.

'He was in a box! Why? What's he ever done to you?'

INJURED INNOCENCE PERSONIFIED.

I raised my eyebrows as far as they would go. 'I don't know. I don't know how he got there. Honestly I don't.'

'He could have suffocated! He could have died!' Harry was talking more to himself than to me. He kissed the child. He mumbled, 'Daddy's going to give you a bottle, for the shock.' He tried to leave the room.

'No!' I got out of bed. 'Give him to me.' I grabbed Harry by the shoulder.

'Keep away from me!' Harry pulled himself away.

Harry held Junior tightly in one arm and pushed me backwards with the other. 'Lie down in bed! And stay there!' Holding the shrieking child close to his chest he ran downstairs.

I followed him down.

CONVINCE HIM.

'Listen, Harry. If we get rid of him today, everything will be alright again tomorrow.'

Harry didn't answer. He went into the living room.

I tried to pull the child out of his arms.

He took a swipe at me. His fist caught me right beside the ear.

I was shocked. *Pain*.

He hit me again.

He's never hit me before.

'Sit down!' Harry pointed to the sofa. 'And shut up!' He picked up the phone.

I couldn't follow what he was saying.

Harry hung up. 'He's coming.'

'Who?'

'The doctor.'

KEEP QUIET.

'Listen Lea, I'm going to put Junior to bed. You stay *here*. You keep away from him! Understood?'

I sniffed. My nose was running. I didn't have a handkerchief.

Harry looked at his watch. 'You go back to sleep for a bit, little man. You'll get your bottle shortly.'

I stayed put. Naked. Alone.

It was dark. Harry had only switched on the small lamp next to the phone.

They could be here at any moment.

GET OUT OF HERE.

I walked to the stairs. I went up.

Harry came out of the baby's room. He blocked the doorway.

'You were supposed to stay downstairs!'

'I want to go to bed.'

'You stay there.'

'I'm cold. I want to lie down.'

Harry looked at me without speaking.

'Can't I go to bed now please?'

'No. The doctor will be here shortly. I want you to stay downstairs.'

DO AS YOUR HUSBAND SAYS.

'Are you coming down too?' I asked quietly.

'Yes. I'll get your dressing gown.'

I went back downstairs. Why had Harry called the doctor? He hadn't hit me that hard, had he?

Shivering, I paced up and down the room.

Harry came down and gave me my dressing gown. He turned on the lights.

I went and lay down on the sofa. I closed my eyes.

Harry poured himself a glass of whisky. He didn't say anything.

The doorbell.

Harry emptied his glass in one gulp. He put it down on the dresser. 'Stay here!' he said.

THE FINAL COUNTDOWN.

Not so final for me, amigos.

I hared upstairs. I dived into bed, pulled the covers up over me and pretended to be asleep. They couldn't do anything to me. Not anything.

Voices. Downstairs.

'Le-a!' Harry was calling me. From the bottom of the stairs. 'She's gone up,' he said.

Thump thump thump.

'Here she is.' Harry.

They came into the bedroom. I peered out through my eyelashes and saw my doctor.

Doctor Boon's hair was tangled, he was wearing a skiing jacket and a pair of jeans. He put his medicine bag on the floor and knelt by the bed. 'Mrs Meyer, how are you?'

YOU HAVE THE RIGHT TO REMAIN SILENT.

I didn't answer.

'Your husband called me. He's very concerned.'

'Very concerned,' I said in a high-pitched voice, 'then it must be extremely serious mustn't it, if Harry is very concerned.'

'How are you feeling?'

'Fine!'

'You feel fine?'

'Yes.'

'No problems at all?

'No. Only my stitches. Do you want to take a look, maybe?'

'No, I only want to talk to you.'

'Now then, my child, so we'll talk. How nice.'

'You came to see us at the practice this morning, you saw my wife.'

'That's right.'

'You didn't feel too good then.'

'No, but I got some fan-tas-tic drops! A miraculous substance, it's a good thing you mention it, I'll go and get it right away.' I stood up.

Harry and the doctor looked at each other. They let me do as I pleased.

CONTROL YOURSELF. NOT TOO MANY STUNTS.

Whistling, I went to the bathroom. I didn't look in the mirror. I got the drops. I put ten of them into a glass of water and drank it. Whistling, I walked back.

Doctor Boon was sitting on the edge of my bed.

I went and sat next to him.

He looked at me seriously. 'Now tell me truthfully. How do you feel at this moment?'

'Very well. Certainly now that I've had my drops.'

'Very well. You feel very well. In your own reality, you mean.'

I laughed. 'Hear that, Harry? I feel very well in my own reality. Isn't that just fucking incredible!'

Harry said nothing.

'You know,' the doctor said, 'there are various sorts of reality.'

'Oh, really?' I asked, intrigued. 'How many have you got? Two, three, four? Maybe we could play happy families.'

He sighed. 'I mean that one can experience reality in various ways.'

I yawned.

It went quiet for a moment.

I looked at the radio alarm. 02.15. 'Jeez, is it that late? I think I'll go to sleep now.'

Doctor Boon turned to Harry. 'I can't get through to her. I'll call the Crisis Service.'

I put my little finger to my mouth, my thumb to my ear and said in a deep voice, 'Hello Crisis Service! Major Alert! Woman Goes to Sleep!'

Nobody laughed.

The doctor got his mobile out of his bag. He went out of the room, onto the landing.

'Have you seen my nightshirt?' I asked Harry.

'It's in the attic.'

I walked over to the attic stairs, gave the thumbs up to the telephoning doctor on the way past and went up.

chapter nineteen

25th June 1966

*Tomorrow we're going to Bakkum for a month, you can
enjoy the sea and the woodland air. So far you haven't
spent as much time outdoors as I'd have liked.*

My nightshirt was lying in the cardboard box. I took off my
dressing gown. I put on my nightshirt. It was lovely and quiet in
the attic. This was probably the safest place in the house. High
and dry. There was an old mattress leaning up against the wall.
I pulled it out and dragged it across the floor. At the back of the
attic was a walnut table. I pushed the mattress under the table
and lay down on it. It felt good, but I needed bedclothes. I
knew there must be an old shower curtain somewhere, the one
Harry had laid over the chaise longue when he was painting the
ceiling. I crawled out from under the table, found the curtain,
dragged it back and pulled it over me. It covered me but it
wasn't very warm. My dressing gown was still lying on the
floor. I got out of my shelter again. I got the dressing gown and
laid it over the curtain. Now I had a real little bed.

I shut my eyes tight.

THEY'LL BE HERE SOON. YOU MUST SLEEP. LIKE A LOG.

I breathed deeply in and out. I tried to relax my body bit by bit. First my toes, then the rest of my feet, my ankles, my shins . . .

I heard Dr Boon talking to Harry on the landing. 'How's the baby?'

'As far as I can see, he's fine.'

'Was she alone with him?'

'Yes. She put him in a cardboard box.'

'Shall I have a quick look at him, just to make sure?'

'Yes, do have a quick look.'

It was quiet for a moment.

Harry came upstairs. 'Lea, where are you?'

I didn't move.

He spotted me all the same. 'What are you doing there?'

'I'm trying to sleep. It's impossible with you and the doctor around.'

'Another doctor will be here shortly.'

'Another one? Go on then. Throw the cat another canary.'

'Shut up with your stupid jokes.'

'Why?'

'You really don't get it? This is a very serious situation. You've put our child in danger. God knows what could have happened.'

'You're telling me. God knew what could have happened. And what did God do? God sent Harry. Harry, of all people. And as if that wasn't enough, he sent Madame Passion Flower and Great King Drops, renowned for their treatment of mathematical genius in its terminal stages. And now, now Our Lord is sending the Crisis Service. God spare me.'

Goddamn.

God

Damn

Me.

Would He damn me? Why? I'd done everything right!

Harry rubbed his eyes. 'I'm going downstairs.'

He left me alone.

I couldn't hear anything any more, only the hum of the central heating boiler. I bit my nails. Something was missing. My happiness was incomplete. 'Harry!'

Silence.

'Haaarrry!'

Silence.

'Haaaaarrryyy!'

He rushed up the stairs. 'What's the matter?'

'Have you got a cigarette for me?'

'*What?*'

'I need a cigarette.'

'You don't smoke.'

'I've just started.'

'Get out from under that table first.'

'Where's Dr Boon?'

'Downstairs.'

The doorbell rang.

'That'll be the Crisis Service.' Harry went to the top of the stairs.

'Will they have cigarettes?'

'Shut up about cigarettes. Are you coming down with me or do you want them to find you up here?'

'Are they coming for me then?'

'Yes, they're coming for you.'

'Hm. It'll be quite a climb for the Crisis Service.'

Harry went down the stairs.

A little later he was back, bringing in his wake a man wearing a jacket with yellow stripes. The man was bald and looked suspiciously like Bozo the clown, but without the make-up. He had fat pouches under his eyes. His glasses were hanging by a cord, dangling against his chest.

THIS IS A TEST. THIS ISN'T A REAL DOCTOR.

'She's under there,' said Harry in an apologetic tone.

'Let's go and take a look,' said the pseudo-doc. He walked over to my shelter and crouched down.

I put my hand out, 'The Crisis Service, I presume?'

If he was impressed by the incisiveness of my late-night wit, then he didn't show it. A cool hand shook mine. 'Indeed, madam, I'm Dieter van Vlot and you are—'

'Not.'

'Pardon?'

'You're Dieter van Vlot and I'm not.'

He raised his eyebrows. 'You don't want to tell me your name?'

'Yes I do. Must I?'

'If you like.'

'I'm Lea Meyer.'

'You've just given birth?'

'Yes.'

'A girl or a boy?'

'A girl.'

'I understood that you had a son.'

'Then why do you ask?'

He opened his mouth and then shut it again.

It was quiet for a moment.

Bozo cleared his throat. 'How old is your son?'

'A few days.' Suddenly I felt frightened, I looked at Harry. 'Where's Junior?'

'He's in bed.'

'Has he had his feed tonight?'

'Yes, I've just done it.'

'Thank goodness. I was afraid I'd forgotten. You have to think of so many things when you have a baby, Dieter, you've no idea.'

'Why are you up here in the attic, Mrs Meyer?'

'Because I'm tired.'

'Wouldn't it be better to go to bed, then?'

'The doctor was keeping me awake. He's downstairs. He never stops talking. Have you met him?'

'Yes.'

'Nice young man, don't you think? I've had a lot of smear tests, as you can imagine. Harry! Where are your manners? Have you got Dieter a drink yet?'

'I don't want anything, thank you.' He cleared his throat. 'Why did you put your son in a cardboard box?'

'Have you got a cigarette for me?'

'I'd like you to answer my question first.'

'I talk better if I smoke.'

Dieter pulled a packet of Cabellero out of the inside pocket of his jacket.

Thank God — filter.

I took a cigarette out of the packet.

Dieter gave me a light.

I didn't inhale, because I couldn't. Instead, I blew great clouds of smoke towards both the men.

Harry coughed and flapped his hands.

Dieter didn't flinch. 'You were going to tell me why you put your son in a cardboard box.'

'I didn't do that.'

'Your husband says you did.'

'And you simply believed him?'

'Why would he lie?'

'Because he wants to put me in a bad light.' I looked angrily at Harry. 'Admit it. Ever since Junior's been here, you've wanted to get rid of me.'

'What on earth makes you think that?'

'It's Junior this and Junior that. I don't exist any more. I've served my purpose. You've used me and now you're finished with me.'

'Where did you get that ridiculous idea?'

'Do you know what they did to me, Dieter?

He shook his head.

'They cut my cunt open. With a great big pair of scissors. They just kept on cutting. Snip-snip-snip, there goes Lea's little cunt, snip-snip-snip. And then they put a pair of forceps in there to pull the child out. Enormous spoons, the biggest you've ever seen. And what did Harry do? Absolutely nothing! Harry was happy. Oh my goodness, how happy he was! He couldn't ring his mother quickly enough. And what did he say? "*Everything went fine, Mum, come on over and see.*" I took an angry drag on my cigarette. I blew the smoke in Harry's direction. 'And do you know what his mother looked at? At the child. Everyone looked at the child. Harry looked at the child, his father looked at the child, my mother looked at the child, José looked at the child. Oh my goodness, what a darling little child it was . . .!' I threw the dressing gown and the curtain aside. 'Shall I show you something, Dieter?' I laid the burning cigarette on the floor, lifted up my nightshirt and pulled down my knickers. There was a sanitary towel in them, because I was still bleeding. I spread my legs. 'See this? See this cunt? Destroyed. Completely ruined. Finito.'

Dieter looked away. 'Mrs Meyer, please cover yourself.' He picked up the cigarette and gave it to my husband. Harry stubbed it out on the floor.

'You're not looking. Not afraid of it are you? Haven't you ever seen a ruined cunt before?'

'I'm not a gynaecologist.'

'Oh, no, Dieter is a member of the Crisis Service, that's true. *Mayday*, *mayday*, there's a serious cunt crisis going on in the Meyer household!' I spread my legs even wider. 'See those stitches, Dieter? Have you counted them? There are eight of them. Dr Kallenbach put them in one by one. Such a wonderful doctor, that Kallenbach! He extracted my mother-in-law's fibroids. I think they probably served them for Christmas dinner, in a béarnaise sauce. Absolutely delicious. I won't hear a word against Dr Kallenbach.'

'Lea, pull your knickers up,' said Harry. He came over to me and tried to pull them up himself.

I kicked his hands away. 'Keep away from me! Everyone ought to see what's happened to my cunt. Go and get that other joker from downstairs so he can have a look too.'

'Mrs Meyer—' Dieter began.

'His wife gave me drops, you know. Excellent drops! Passion Flower! Perhaps you should put some in my asshole, they haven't done much for me so far. But I have the evidence! It's in the Yellow Pages, under S for *Scaffolding for hire*, that's where the prescription is. Harry, go and get Dieter my prescription! Dieter is from the Crisis Service. Dieter has to see the prescription!' I couldn't stop screaming by this point. It felt marvellous.

Dieter conferred with Harry. They looked serious.

'Mrs Meyer, I'm considering having you admitted.'

'First we'll take a look at the prescription for my drops.'

'Mrs Meyer, can you hear what I'm saying?'

'Loud and clear, Dieter. Reception's fine. Can you hear me too?'

'I can hear you, Mrs Meyer.'

I brought my face close to his. 'But do you understand me?'

'I think I understand you, yes.'

Dieter had pale blue eyes. He wore hard contact lenses. DON'T TRUST HIM. DON'T TRUST ANYONE.

'I suggest you go to the hospital. To calm down.'

I scratched my nose. Then I picked up an imaginary pen and wrote on the floor. It was a while before I was ready. 'Do you know what it says here, Dieter?'

'No.'

'Read it along with me. It says,

Dear Dieter,
There are two kinds of ideas. Good ideas and bad ideas. I regret to inform you that your idea is of the latter kind.
Yours sincerely and with best wishes,

Lea Meyer

See?'

'Does that mean that you do not agree to be admitted?'

'You're a very clever little man, van Vlottenstein, you may certainly pass on the message to your employers at your next performance assessment meeting, that I said that.'

'I agree with Mr van Vlot,' said Harry suddenly. 'It seems to me it would be best for you to go to the hospital.'

I ignored him. I pulled the shower curtain and the dressing gown back over me. 'Any further business, Dieter?'

'Mrs Meyer, I'd rather you came voluntarily.'

'No further business? Then the meeting is closed. I'll expect the minutes in my in-tray by tomorrow.' I addressed the last bit to Harry.

Dieter took Harry aside. He made a long speech.

All Harry did was nod. *The jerk.*

Dieter brought out an antique Motorola. The house really was riddled with telephoning doctors.

While Dieter tapped out the number, Boon's tangled mass of curls appeared in the stairwell.

'Doctor Boon!' I shouted.

He said something to Harry as if he hadn't heard me.

'Doctor Boon! Yoo-hoo!'

Dieter put his hand over his free ear and walked past me.

'Hey, Boon, are you deaf?!'

He came over to the shelter.

'How is my little man?'

'Who do you mean?'

'Harry Junior, of course. How is my little lad?'

'Fine.'

'Great. Wonderful.'

Boon put his hands in his pockets and took them out again. He looked around.

Dieter was still on the phone.

'Has my husband offered you a drink?'

'Er, yes.'

'Good. Would you go and get Junior, then?'

Boon was taken aback. 'I can't. He . . . er . . . he's asleep.'

'Doesn't matter, he always sleeps very soundly.'

'But it's still better if he stays in bed now.'

'Harry!'

'Yes?'

'Would you go and get Junior, darling?'

Harry looked at Dr Boon.

Dr Boon shook his head.

'We'll leave him to sleep, Lea.'

No one wanted to fetch my baby. It wasn't fair. 'Juu-nee-orr!' I called. 'My little whippersnapper, come to Mummy! Mummy's in the attic, Daddy too. Come on!'

It was silent for a moment.

'Ah, look, here he comes . . .' I pointed towards the stairwell.

Dr Boon and Harry looked around simultaneously.

'Got you!' I roared with laughter. 'Bunch of suckers. That child's three days old. He can't even roll over.'

Dieter had finished his call. He turned to face both men. Since I couldn't follow the conversation, I wrote a few more letters on the floor. They were very nice letters; shame I was the only one who could read them.

I was in the middle of a sentence when Dieter suddenly came and stood right in front of me. I didn't look up.

'Lea, an ambulance will be here soon. I want to give you a sedative.'

'Shh! I'm writing.'

He crouched down.

My pen stopped in mid air.

Dieter had a white pill in his hand and a glass of water. Where he'd got that from so quickly was a mystery. 'Would you take this?'

They want to give me pills, I wrote, *what do you think, Leo, should I take them?*

It would be at least a week before I got an answer. Today's mail delivered tomorrow? Fat chance.

'We feel it would be best if you took this pill right away.'

'Have you got another cigarette?'

Harry came and stood next to me. 'Take that pill, Lea. It'll do you good.'

'Bugger off, hypocritical shitbag! Since when have you cared what's good for me?'

Harry wanted to say something, but Dieter signalled to him to be quiet.

The doorbell rang again.

'Well well, that was quick.' Dieter sounded surprised.

Harry went down to answer the door. He came back with my mother. She still had her coat on. She glanced nervously up and down. Dieter and Dr Boon shook hands with her.

'Hey, Mum, what are you doing here? Did you get my letter?'

She walked cautiously towards me. 'Harry called me. How are you?'

'Excellent. These guys are just making a ridiculous amount of fuss about nothing. I'm not allowed to see Junior. I have to take pills. All crap, of course. Can *you* go and get Junior?'

'He's fast asleep, Lea, I've just been to look.'

'Oh. What a pity.'

'Do you have a fever?' She knelt down and felt my forehead. 'No, I don't think so.'

Harry came over and stood next to her. 'The doctor says Lea should take a pill, to calm her down a bit.'

My mother nodded understandingly. 'I'd take it if I were you, Lea.'

'Who else did you go and ring, you twit, is this yet another thing you couldn't manage by yourself?'

'Why don't you just take the pill?' said my mother.

'Dieter!' I shrieked.

He abruptly broke off his conversation with Dr Boon and came and stood next to me.

'Everyone in this room is of the opinion that I should take your pill.'

Dieter was still holding the glass of water.

'Come here with that thing.'

Bozo looked pleased. 'Very sensible, Lea.' He gave me the pill.

I laid the long, white tablet on the upturned palm of my hand and studied it in detail.

All those present watched, holding their breath.

I held the pill between my thumb and forefinger and turned it this way and that, close to my face.

'I've heard all sorts of good things about you,' I told the pill, 'but my grandfather always said that seeing is believing . . .'

'She never knew her grandfather,' my mother whispered.

'. . . if you're really so special, then you must be able to fly.'

When I got to the last word I swung my arm back. I threw

the pill as hard as I could away from me. It flew over the heads of the assembled throng and disappeared into the stairwell. I heard a couple of light taps and then it was quiet. 'Applause for the magic flying pill!' I was the only one who clapped.

Harry turned to Dieter, annoyed. 'Where's that ambulance got to?'

'They're on their way.'

Dr Boon went downstairs. 'I've found it!' I heard him call out.

'Dr Boon has just become a father,' I told my mother.

'Really?'

'Of twins.' I went on writing my airmail. There wasn't anything else to do.

Dieter spoke to Harry in a hushed voice.

Dr Boon came back. My mother congratulated him on his twins. His face clouded. 'My wife can't have children. She became pregnant after IVF treatment. With twins. But we lost them after a few weeks.'

The doorbell.

Harry went down.

He came back with a man and a woman, both wearing dark blue uniforms. Dieter shook hands with them.

After a short conversation, the woman came over to me. She had long dark hair, a straight ponytail and friendly brown eyes. She knelt down next to the mattress. 'Mrs Meyer, will you come with us?'

'Who are you?'

'Sorry, I'll introduce myself. My name is Sandra.'

'Have you seen my baby?' I whispered.

'No, I haven't seen him.'

'They say he's downstairs sleeping, but I don't believe them. I think he's dead.' I started to sob.

Sandra laid her hand on my shoulder. 'There's nothing the matter with your baby, nothing at all.'

I looked at her through my tears. 'How do *you* know? You haven't even seen him. Everyone here is lying. They're all trying to bamboozle me the whole time. No one takes me seriously, no one. And neither do you.'

She stroked my arm 'I take you seriously, honestly I do.'

'Have you heard about my cunt yet?'

'No—'

'That doctor destroyed it. It's giving me hell. But no one wants to look at it!' I started screaming again. 'All these doctors here know how to do is make phone calls! Phone, phone and phone again! And talk. Oh, they're *so* busy talking! No one bothers to look at the patient. I'm lying here RACKED WITH PAIN!!! I threw my dressing gown and the shower curtain aside and pulled up my nightshirt.

'Oh God, here we go again.' Harry.

I tugged at my knickers.

Sandra tried to stop me. She laid her hand firmly on top of mine. 'Don't do that, Lea, I can't do anything for you here. We're going to the hospital. That's a good place to get better.'

'You think so?'

'Absolutely.'

I sighed. She sounded so sure of herself, this Sandra. She smelled nice too. Of Nivea. But still. Something wasn't right. Something wasn't right somewhere. 'And Junior? What will happen to my baby?'

'Junior is in good hands. You don't need to worry about that.'

'A baby belongs with its mother. Where's my baby? I haven't seen him for ages. He's dead. My little man is dead!' I howled with great screeching sobs. 'My baby, my little Harry, I want my baby!'

Sandra looked aside, uncertainly.

Her colleague came towards us. He went down on his haunches. 'What's the problem?' The man had a spotty face and a droopy moustache.

'This is my colleague, his name is Ger,' Sandra said quickly.

I grabbed his arm with both hands. 'Will you go and get my baby, Ger? They say he's alive. But even if he's dead. I have to say goodbye to him, don't I?'

'Please try to control yourself first. You're screaming the whole neighbourhood down.' A strong Amsterdam accent. That's not something you often hear in Aerdenhout.

'I will, I promise. I promise I'll be quiet as a mouse.' I cleared my throat. 'If I'm quiet for two minutes, can I see my baby?'

Ger nodded.

I took a deep breath and firmly shut my mouth. When necessary, I have iron self-control.

I counted the seconds silently. Ger talked to Sandra. In the background I could hear the buzz of conversation from all the others. It was crowded in the attic. If a fire broke out, I could always resort to mime. Not a word would pass my lips.

. . . hundred and eighteen, hundred and nineteen, hundred and twenty. My two minutes were up. Radiant, I said, 'See, I can do it! Now go and get my baby, Ger, please?'

'Just a minute, I'll ask the doctor.' He went up to Dieter.

Van Vlot threw a glance in my direction and shook his head.

'I'm sorry,' said Ger, 'the doctor says no.'

I started to cry. It wasn't fair. 'It isn't fair. You promised.'

Sandra stroked my arm. 'I know. He can't do anything about it. It's not up to us.'

I pushed her hand away. 'A mother has a right to her baby! Who's depriving me of my rights? Who? I want my little Harry . . . Junior, can you hear me? It's me, your mummy! I love you, darling, I MISS YOU!' I screamed as loudly as I could. If I went on doing that, they'd bring Junior to me after all. They'd have to.

Harry took Dieter by the arm. 'Couldn't she just see him briefly? Only for a moment, then perhaps she'll calm down.'

Dieter was implacable.

I continued my lament. 'No one knows what I've been through. No one! Children come into the world in one piece, mothers are throwaway packaging! I'm ruined, my child is whole, and now I have to go away! What have I done wrong? Why do I have to go away?!' Although I was screaming louder and louder, I could feel the audience's attention slipping away. So much was happening around me, it was hard to follow it all.

Ger disappeared.

Sandra stopped trying to stroke me.

Ger came back. He laid a stretcher on the floor.

Sandra suddenly had a hypodermic needle in her hand. 'Can you hold her?' she said.

Ger and Dieter knelt down next to the mattress.

If they think I give up easily, they've got another think coming. I'm extremely strong, especially if someone threatens to inject me against my will.

I kicked out as hard as I could and thrashed about with my arms. I fought like a lion, but there were too many of them.

Ger and Dieter held me tight. They rolled me onto my stomach and pressed me against the mattress. Sandra lifted up my nightshirt and pulled my knickers down.

I felt sorry for my mother. Sorry that she had to witness the forced sedation of her youngest daughter . . .

The needle went into my buttock.

When Sandra had finished, Ger and Dieter turned me onto my back and laid me on the stretcher. Straps were buckled.

The attic revolved around me. Fragments of conversation got through to me. Ger said something to Sandra about steep staircases. They wanted to take me away.

I must resist them.

The straps weren't as tight as I'd thought. I wormed and twisted. No one noticed.

Suddenly I got loose. I rolled to one side, off the stretcher. I was free – Lea Houdini had done the impossible.

'Oh no, now look . . .' My mother was the first to discover my escape.

Harry swore.

My freedom was short-lived. Strong male hands grabbed me, laid me back and tied me up, very tightly this time.

I could no longer move. I couldn't scream either.

My eyelids became heavy.

chapter twenty

*You're starting to recover now. It all started the second
week of our stay in Bakkum. You got a tummy bug, such a
bad one that I didn't dare sleep at night. Everything you
ate, which wasn't much, came straight back up again.*

I'm sitting on Daddy's shoulders. He's singing to me. *Ride-ride-
ride-in-the-waggon-and-if-you-can't-ride-I'll-carry-you*. Daddy is
galloping across the room. *A-lump-in-the-road-a-bump-in-the-
road-a-ditch-in-the-road!* He suddenly bends his knees. I want to
laugh. He always makes me laugh. No sound comes out of my
throat. I can't. A bit nauseous. No so fast, Daddy! Don't wobble
like that. I'm going to fall. Cold wind. Cold on my face. Why
am I lying on my back? *Quiet now, Lea. I'm with you.* I know that
voice. I want to answer. *Grandmother, what a big nose you have!* My
throat is dry. Swallow first. Little wheels, I'm lying on little
wheels. The wheels are turning. I'm gliding along. From indoors
out. From outdoors in. Straight on. A long corridor. My hair,
someone's stroking my hair. Push me faster, quick, quick. This
is an emergency. My cunt. I'm bleeding to death. They have to

take a scalpel to my cunt. They have to take a scalpel to my cunt urgently. It was a botched job, Kallenbach. Such a young woman. Deformed. Marked for life. Kallenbach grins. Big yellow teeth. We'll do it at night. No one needs to know. I shiver . . .

Someone is pulling at me. I have to get up. I blink against the light. Fluorescent lighting. Weak legs. Hands under my armpits. A pitted face, very close. Droopy moustache growls. *That way*. A small office. A desk. Two chairs in front of it. A woman. Behind the desk. A respectable-looking woman. THE MEDICAL DISCIPLINARY BOARD! So they *have* been told . . .! Kallenbach won't get off scot-free after all.

Someone pushes me into a chair. I sit there. In front of the desk. My chin is on my chest. My head is too heavy.

I gaze off to one side. What's going to happen now? There's Harry. My husband. He's talking to the woman. She's writing something. Now she looks at me. What a nice laugh she has . . .

'What's your little boy's name?'

'Maurice,' I say.

I wink at Harry. I'll never betray our child, in spite of what he's done to me.

Someone coughs. A young man with spiky hair comes and stands next to the desk. He's wearing a sweatshirt. On his sweatshirt it says BULLDOG in big letters.

The woman nods at the young man.

The young man nods back. He nods at Harry too.

Harry nods back.

I get dizzy.

'I'll take you to your room.'

Now Harry nods at me. 'You go on, I'll be along soon.'

I want to nod too. Seems I've landed in the middle of a nodding convention. By the time I finally get my head to move, it's too late. Harry's no longer looking.

The young man pulls me upright.

Who could he be? Can't be a doctor. A nurse perhaps? But he's not wearing a uniform. He's wearing a sweatshirt with BULLDOG written on it.

A corridor. It's difficult to keep up with him. He doesn't offer me his arm.

Doors everywhere. Green doors. With numbers on them.

Suddenly the young man stops.

'Here it is.'

chapter twenty-one

The doctor came to the campsite and gave you some medicine, it didn't seem to help very much and you just went on and on crying. You had such an awful stomach-ache. One morning you cried so much I couldn't stand it any more. I took you to the doctor. He gave you a suppository. Slowly but surely you started to get better.

Room 214 was sober, neat. There was a bed against the right-hand wall with a dark blue bedspread. Against the left-hand wall was a table with two chairs. The crimson curtains were drawn.

'Here's the sink and a cupboard for your clothes.'

'Where's my husband?' I saw a bit of fluff on the carpet and prodded Bulldog. 'Pick it up for me, would you?'

He didn't react. 'Your husband still has a few things to sort out yet. He'll be here shortly to say goodbye. You should get straight into bed.'

Suddenly I saw that I had my nightshirt on. Maybe it would be a good idea to go to sleep. An operation like that is no walkover. You have to be fit and rested for it.

The young man left me alone.

I got into bed.

It was very quiet. No one came.

I got out of bed and left the room.

I looked along the corridor. I no longer knew where the little office was. I took a guess and turned left. I went around a corner and found myself face to face with a Surinamese man. He was washing the floor with a floorcloth on a long handle. He was wearing a white uniform.

YOU MUST GO TO BED WITH HIM. YOU MUST SLEEP WITH THE ENEMY.

A shiver ran down my spine. Could it be true? Would I have to go to bed with this cleaner? I'd never fucked a negro.

The man grinned at me. I saw a few glinting gold teeth.

I held my breath.

But he didn't make any kind of move in my direction. Instead, he went on mopping the floor.

'Do you know where my husband is?'

He wrung out the cloth over the bucket in a leisurely manner. He leaned on the handle and pointed the way to the office.

I went in.

Harry was still sitting there talking to the woman. 'You back?' he asked. He didn't sound angry, he sounded kind.

Without saying anything I went and sat next to him.

The woman and Harry went on talking. When they'd finished, the Bulldog guy came in again. I walked back to my room with him and Harry.

'Just get into bed,' said Harry. 'I'll see you tomorrow.'

He went away. The young man also.

I tried to sleep but I couldn't. Perhaps Harry was still in the office. I knew how to get there now.

The cleaner had gone. I saw no one at all in the corridor. Harry wasn't in the office. Where could he be? The woman from the disciplinary board had gone too.

The Bulldog guy was there though. He had a steaming mug of tea in front of him. He sighed when he saw me. 'You're supposed to stay in your room, Mrs Meyer.'

He took me there for the third time.

Somehow or other, I just couldn't stay in bed. Wandering along the corridors, I ended up back at the office.

Bulldog was still sitting there doing nothing.

'I can't sleep,' I said.

'Do you want some warm milk?' He stood up.

'No, I want a goodnight kiss.'

He shook his head.

I walked up to him and raised my face towards his.

'I won't be able to sleep otherwise. A little girl should never go to bed unkissed. That's what my grandfather always said.'

Spike still refused.

'Come on, what kind of a pansy are you?' I pulled him towards me by his sweatshirt and pressed my lips to his. Instead of responding to my kiss, he pushed me away.

I've never known that to happen before. Is he really a poof then?

Bulldog grabbed me roughly by the arm and pulled me along after him.

At the end of the corridor was a door. He pushed me through it and let go of my arm. I opened my mouth to say something. *Too late*. The door slammed shut behind me.

I was alone.

*

The space inside was small, a good bit smaller than my own room. The walls were bare, the floor was made of concrete. The window looked out on a courtyard. There was no curtain. In one corner, under the window, was a mattress. On the wall next to the door was a white push-button. That must be a bell. The door had no handle. I pushed against the door. It was shut. That idiot had imprisoned me. This was all a mistake, I had to put it right immediately. Through the little window in the door, I could see a small hallway. There was nothing in it except a single chair.

Limbo. The gateway to hell. You've arrived in hell, Lea.

I pushed the bell.

A woman appeared in the hallway. It wasn't the woman from the disciplinary board. I didn't recognise this woman. She looked through the little window.

'Let me out of here!'

She shook her head and disappeared.

I rang the bell again.

No one came.

I rang it very frequently and for long periods.

No one reacted.

TRY TO ESCAPE.

Of course. I had to break out, that was my only chance.

I went to the window. I'd smash it and run away. There was nothing in the room to smash the window with, so I'd have to do it with my bare hands. I would cut myself, blood would flow. But that didn't matter. The important thing was that I'd be saved.

I took a deep breath, made a fist and hit the window hard.

It didn't break.

I shut my eyes and threw another punch.

Again nothing happened, except that my hand hurt.

I took a good look at the window. It was plastic.

Goddammit, they've thought of everything.

Okay, don't panic. There must be a way to get out of here. First try ringing the bell again.

I pushed the button for several minutes at a time and waited.

The hallway remained empty.

I turned around and inspected the cell from top to bottom. There was no air vent, no drain, nothing. The window was fixed in place with thick bolts. I'd never be able to get those out, not in a hundred years.

On the floor there were three plastic cups of water and three cardboard containers with rims at the top, like upturned hats.

Three cups.

The holy number.

The holy trinity.

The symbolism was obvious. I had to do something with these things, but what?

CLEANSE YOURSELF.

I picked up a cup and poured the water over my head. My hair got wet, my nightshirt too. Other than that, nothing happened.

Annoyed, I kicked the two remaining cups over.

I peed in one of the cardboard hats.

There wasn't any toilet paper. My sanitary towel was heavy with blood. I didn't have a clean one with me.

I pulled up my underpants and looked out of the window.

There was a tree in the courtyard. Its branches waved softly to and fro. Were they waving at me? I pressed my nose to the window and waved back. Tears came to my eyes. How I'd love to be out there with it . . . I'd take all my clothes off and hug it tight. I'd tickle it under its branches and cover its trunk with kisses. We'd be together for always. We'd drink rainwater and let the wind caress us.

THE WATER'S GONE. YOU'LL DIE VERY RAPIDLY WITHOUT ANYTHING TO DRINK. YOU'LL DIE IN HERE ALONE. NO ONE WILL COME TO GET YOU OUT.

And what about Harry? Where's Harry?

HE'S NEXT TO YOU, IN THE OTHER CELL. CAN YOU SEE HIM? HE'S WEARING HIS WHITE SHIRT. HE'S IN THE CORNER OF THE CELL, WITH HIS HEAD IN HIS HANDS. THEY'VE IMPRISONED HIM, JUST LIKE YOU.

My heart pounded in my throat. I shut my eyes tightly and saw flashing, bright pink neon letters.

DON'T PANIC!

I immediately opened my eyes again. I didn't want it to happen. I didn't want to see any more signs.

YOU'RE RIGHT. THIS IS THE PERFECT MOMENT TO PANIC. YOU'RE HOPELESSLY LOST. UNLESS—

Unless what?

THERE'S JUST ONE THING YOU CAN DO.

What?

DO WHAT YOUR FEELINGS TELL YOU TO DO.

I went and stood in the centre of the cell.

THAT'S THE WAY.

What next?

YOUR BODY CAN'T LEAVE THE ROOM, BUT YOU CAN LEAVE YOUR BODY.

What do you mean?

TRY TO MAKE CONTACT. TRY TO MAKE CONTACT WITH THE HIGHER REALMS. YOU CAN DO IT. YOU HAVE THE GIFT.

I'm frightened.

DO IT!

How?

SAY WHAT YOU WANT OUT LOUD.

'I want to get out of here.'

LOUDER!

'I want to get out of here!'

EVEN LOUDER!

'I want to get out of here, I want to get out, I WANT TO GET OUT, I WANT OUT!' I screamed louder and louder. I bent over, grasped my ankles, stood up straight again and stretched out my hands towards the ceiling. 'I want to get out of here, I want to get out, I want to get out, I WANT OUT, I WANT OUT!' I screamed until I was hoarse.

No one lifted me up.

I didn't leave my body.

I stayed precisely where I was.

I stopped screaming and breathed deeply in and out a few times. Actually, I was quite relieved. If I'd succeeded in getting out, where would I have ended up? Would I ever have been able to find the way back to my own body? Maybe it didn't work because I wasn't completely convinced I wanted it to. Maybe it was time to face reality. I'd die in this room, alone, without ever seeing or speaking to anyone. The tree would be the last thing I ever laid eyes on.

I'd keep my eyes trained on it. It would comfort me. It wasn't much, but it was better than nothing.

I went and lay down on the mattress. It felt cosy, as if it was warmed by electricity. I looked around, but I couldn't see a cable or a socket.

I pulled the blanket up over me.

I suddenly realised how tired I was.

chapter twenty-two

When we got back from Amsterdam, you'd lost so much ground that we made every effort to build you up again. Boiled porridge pressed through a sieve, that went down nicely and you got a bit of colour back.

'Lea? Are you asleep?'

Someone was shaking my shoulder.

'Lea, can you hear me? It's me.'

'Mum?'

She pulled back the duvet. 'Open your eyes. It's ten thirty.' My mother's face was close to mine. The corners of her mouth hung down. If I looked at her upside down, she'd be laughing and she'd have very small top front teeth.

I giggled.

'What is it, what are you thinking?'

'Mm? Oh, nothing.' I sat up.

'I've bought you some underwear. Clean knickers. Birgit chose them.'

'Birgit. Clean knickers from Birgit. Great.'

'Not from Birgit, the knickers are from me. They're in your cupboard. The flowers are from Birgit.' There were two pots of crocuses standing on the table. 'I borrowed some saucers from the kitchen. Just so you know. You'll have to water them every day. You won't forget, will you?'

'Water every day. Saucers from the kitchen.'

My mother looked at me quizzically. 'Have you eaten yet?'

'Since when?'

'Since you got here, of course.'

'I don't know.'

'You must eat, Lea.'

'Yes, Mum.'

'Birgit sends best wishes. Oh yes, she asked if you'd keep the bulbs.'

'What?'

'When the crocuses have finished flowering, will you keep the bulbs for Birgit? She wants to plant them in her garden.'

I couldn't keep my eyes open. I lay down again. I was tired. So tired. I pulled the duvet up over me and turned to face the wall.

My mother pushed down on the bed as she got to her feet. 'I'll be off then. Your knickers are in the cupboard.'

It was light in the room. Someone had opened the curtains. Next to the crocuses was a tray of food. I got out of bed. There was a white piece of paper on the tray.

Breakfast – 214 – L. Meyer.

On the plate were two pieces of brown bread with two slices of cheese wrapped in see-through plastic. Next to the plate was a dark brown bowl. I took off the lid. There was a firm, white substance in it, with a smell I couldn't quite place.

BLANCMANGE.

Ah, an appeal to my childhood. Blancmange for Lea, very clever; they were obviously thinking, she's sure to eat that. A good thing I didn't fall for it. I quickly put the lid back on the bowl.

I picked up one of the slices of bread and held it up to the light. As far as I could see it was an ordinary piece of wholemeal bread. I pulled off a bit of the crust and put it in my mouth. I chewed it carefully. It tasted like bread. To be precise, like bread crust. They'd put together a damn good imitation. I went to the wash basin and spat it out. I rinsed out my mouth until it was completely clean, so that there wasn't a crumb left.

I left the cheese well alone.

Finally there was the banana. A banana is a banana is a banana. Surely they couldn't have faked that? When I'd peeled it I still couldn't find anything suspicious. Naked, yellow and curved, it lay on the table. I laid the floppy skin on top of it.

YOU MAY PARTAKE OF IT. IT IS NOT FORBIDDEN FRUIT.

No, it's too risky, for all I know they may have injected it with something.

There was a soft tap at the door.

'Just a minute!'

I put the banana back in its skin. I laid the cheese on top of the banana. Then I pushed the tray away from me.

'Come in.'

'Good morning, Mrs Meyer.' A woman came into the room. She shook my hand and sat down next to me.

I knew her from somewhere.

She looked impeccable in her light blue suit. Her blond hair was tied in a bun and she was wearing nail varnish.

I looked at my own nails. The salmon pink varnish was chipped all over the place.

'How are you feeling now?' She put her open notebook on the table and got out a pen.

I suddenly remembered. This morning. She was standing in the hallway when they let me out of the cell.

She looked at me inquiringly.

I mumbled something.

She played with her pen for a second or two, but she didn't write anything down. 'Your husband rang. He'll be here shortly.'

'Harry rang? Really? When's he coming?'

'At half past eleven.'

'Can I go home then?'

'I'm sorry. You can't leave yet.' She got something out of her pocket. 'I've just spoken to Dr Posthumous and—'

'Who's he?'

'He's the head of department, you saw him this morning.'

'I saw so many people this morning.'

'Dr Posthumous has a beard.'

'Oh, *him*.' I brushed some crumbs off the table.

'Dr Posthumous thinks it would be sensible to start on some medication.' She showed me a small plastic packet with a white pill in it. She pressed the pill out of the packet. 'I'd very much like you to take this.'

'Okay, fine.' I took the pill from her and put it on the table. 'What a nice suit you have on, there aren't many women who can wear that sort of colour. Donna Karan?'

'Er, no, it's from C&A.'

'No need to be ashamed of that, it's beautiful. I've got a special DKNY wardrobe at home, I'm completely crazy about her. Harry sometimes says he'll go bankrupt—'

'You are supposed to take your medication now, Mrs Meyer.' She pointed to the wash basin. 'Would you like a glass of water?'

'No thanks, no need.'

I knew what I had to do, I'd seen it often enough on TV. I put the pill in my mouth and held it under my tongue. Then I pretended to swallow it.

She looked satisfied. She picked up her notebook and pen from the table and stood up. 'I'll leave you now, then. Unless you have any questions?'

I shook my head.

'If you want anything, you can always go and ask the nurses in the office. You know where it is?'

I nodded. I most certainly did.

She shook my hand. 'See you, then.'

When she'd gone, I waited for twenty seconds. Then I took the pill out of my mouth. I washed it down the plughole. The empty packet was still on the table. There was a sticker on it.

PIMOZIDE 2 MG

It didn't mean anything to me. But I'd find out, I'd investigate it down to the last possible detail. I put the packet away in my clothes cupboard. If that woman came back, I'd tell her I didn't know where it was. No doubt she'd get a rocket from Posthumous for being stupid enough to leave it lying around.

I walked round and round the room. There was nothing to

do. I had to wait. Wait until Harry arrived. Wait for the doctor. Wait until the mayor said I could go home. My whole bloody life was on hold.

I heard the singsong voice of Harry's secretary. *I'll put you through, one moment . . . He's in a meeting, could you hold the line?* It was a bad connection.

I'd often told Harry they ought to play music. Something with piano, say, by that Wibi Soeriwhatyermiflip. Or André Rieu with his palm-court orchestra, that would be a tremendous asset to the real estate sector. If it worked, clients would hang up if they got put through too quickly.

Just before eleven thirty there was a knock at the door. Harry. With an A&P carrier bag in either hand.

'What happened to you?'

'What do you mean?'

'You look dreadful.' I giggled. 'You look like a tramp. That jacket! Are the dry cleaners on holiday?' I stroked his chin. 'And when did you last have a shave, Mr Meyer?'

He pushed my hand away.

'It's a good thing you're here, darling. I was just thinking. Have you found a piece of music yet?'

He put the bags down on the bed.

'For the office, I mean, while you're waiting. That Rieu seems a good idea to me.'

Harry looked at me, mystified.

'Never mind. What have you brought?' I opened the bags.

'Trousers, jumpers, knickers and bras,' Harry enumerated. 'José helped me. She says to get well soon.'

He hadn't brought any sanitary towels, I noticed.

'I've got something else for you too,' said Harry. He took a rolled-up newspaper out of his inside pocket. I grabbed it out of his hands.

VIOLA HOLT ADMITTED. DETOX OR FOURTH FACE LIFT?
BEATRIX PREFERS IT DOGGY FASHION.
HENNIE HUISMAN, 'I WAS A FORCEPS DELIVERY. THAT'S WHY.'

Vrij Nederland[*].

I clapped my hand over my mouth. 'Jesus, Harry, see that? How do they know all those things? It's about us. We like to do it doggy fashion, they're right about the forceps and I've been forcibly admitted, in *Vrij Nederland*. Good God.'

'Have they actually given you any medication yet?'

'Shh!' I put my index finger to my lips. Then I led Harry to a corner of the room.

'Wait here. Don't say anything.'

'I wish I'd only brought *Libelle*,' Harry mumbled.

I got the empty packet out of the cupboard and put it under my nightshirt. I crept up to him on tiptoe. I stood very close to him.

'See this?' I got the packet out from under my nightshirt.

'Why are you whispering?'

'They wanted to give me this. Pimozide. Strange name for a pill, don't you think?'

This is the packet, Lea, where are the contents?'

---

[*] National weekly newspaper.

'There was a little gypsy girl, sitting on a stone. Crying, crying, crying all alone.'

'Lea, I asked you a question!'

I pointed to the wash basin. 'Don't tell Posthumous. I've thrown the baby out with the bathwater.'

'Look at me! Did you take the pill?'

I shook my head. 'Of course not. I don't trust them. You can't trust anyone here. Do you know what they did to me last night?'

'I heard about it, yes.'

'Will you take me with you, Harry, before they do it again? I want to go home. Please can I go home?'

Harry looked at the floor. 'I'm sorry. You'll have to stay here for a few more days.'

'Can't you arrange something for me? Please?'

He shook his head. 'Go and sit on the bed.'

I did as he said.

Harry crouched down in front of me. The last time he did that was when he asked me to marry him. 'Lea, I want you to listen to me carefully.' Harry took both my hands in his. 'You have to get better. That's only possible if you stay here. Here they know how to treat you. Everyone has your own interests at heart, they really do. For God's sake take your medication. You'll be home all the sooner, with me and Junior.'

'You really think so?'

'I don't think so, I know so. There's no other way. Believe me.'

My earlobe itched. 'So you think I should take that Pimozide?'

'Absolutely.' He came and sat next to me. 'Have they told you about the tribunal yet?'

'No. They don't tell you anything in here. They give you pills, they bring you bunches of bananas and then they leave you to your fate. You've no idea, Harry, what it's like in here.'

'Calmly now. You can't leave right away because you've been compulsorily detained. Soon there'll be an official hearing to decide whether or not you have to stay.'

'A hearing, where?'

'Here in the hospital.'

'Really? Will the magistrate come here, for me?'

'For you, yes. You'll have a lawyer, and there'll be a public prosecutor too.'

I rummaged in the bags. 'Jesus, Harry, a tribunal, I'll have to wear something appropriate.' I pulled a few bits of clothing out of the bags. 'This won't do, won't do at all. When is the hearing?'

'I don't know exactly, I think tomorrow or the next day. It has to be within a few days.'

I took a deep breath. 'Okay. Listen. You're going home soon. You know my Donna Karan wardrobe?'

'I know it, yes,' sighed Harry.

'You stand in front of the wardrobe. You open it. On the second or third hanger from the right there's a short, grey jacket. That's perfect for an occasion like this. Should I wear a blouse under it or a casual T-shirt?'

'You're asking me?'

I drummed my fingers on the bedside table. 'Make it a T-shirt. But I'll wear my Cartier choker with it, you know where it is don't you, in my jewellery drawer?'

'Do you think you should? What if someone in here nicks it?'

'If necessary you can take it back with you after the hearing, but it's absolutely essential, otherwise the whole thing's too shabby. You'll find the T-shirt on the shelf above the clothes rail, it's white with short sleeves. Then I'll need that long, slinky grey skirt with the split, I think it's hanging next to the jacket.'

Harry got a notebook and a pen out of his inside pocket and made notes.

'Women in New York think nothing of wearing training shoes with that kind of outfit, did you know that?'

Harry didn't say anything.

I considered it for a moment. 'No. They wouldn't recognise that as a fashion statement here, they'd think, that woman's round the bend.'

'Just your black court shoes, then?' asked Harry.

'The silver-grey ones from Miu Miu, darling, they're still in their box.'

As soon as Harry had gone, I went to the office to ask for another pill. I was given one and I took it straight away. Now I wouldn't be able to have second thoughts.

On the way back I met a thin young woman. She was leaning against the doorframe of her room. She had two ponytails tied with jolly ribbons, and she was wearing a brightly coloured jumper and leggings with legwarmers. 'Hi,' she said. She was holding a bag of marshmallows. 'Would you like one?'

I took a marshmallow. I looked inquisitively over her shoulder. 'Is this your room?'

'Yes, do you want to see it?'

She took me in with her.

There was a poster of a half-naked Mariah Carey on the wall.

She'd obviously never had a baby. And if she wanted to remain two-dimensional then she shouldn't, not on any account.

There were decorative cushions on the bed, and a bedcover with a horse's head on it.

'Have you been here long?' I asked.

'Yes, a while.'

'What's your name?'

'Cynthia. And yours?'

'Lea.'

'Nice name.'

'Thanks. You have a nice name too.'

'Want another marshmallow?'

'No, I've had enough.'

Cynthia put two marshmallows in her mouth. She chewed. She blinked a few times.

'Shall we lie down on the bed for a moment?' I don't really know why I asked that.

We lay down facing each other. Cynthia consumed one marshmallow after another. She wound strands of hair around her finger. She had large blue eyes with long eyelashes and flushed cheeks.

'How old are you?' I asked.

'Twenty-three.'

She looked younger, much younger. She looked like a child.

Hesitantly, I stuck out my index finger. Her face was sure to be very soft.

'Let me just see what time it is,' mumbled Cynthia. She turned towards her bedside table. 'Yes! I'm allowed one.' She jumped up and produced a packet of cigarettes from her right legwarmer. 'You want a cigarette too?'

'I don't smoke.'

She put the cigarette in her mouth and went out into the corridor.

'Hey, Martin!' she shouted at a man who came out of the office. 'Have you got a light?'

'Is it time already?'

'Yes!'

I got off the bed too. There was a piece of paper stuck to the inside of Cynthia's door. It was covered with writing in purple felt pen.

'What's that?'

'That's my timetable.'

Cynthia was allowed two cigarettes per hour, sweets three times a day and two phone calls.

'Did they come up with all those rules?' I asked indignantly.

'Oh no, I did it myself. Want a cigarette?'

'I don't smoke.'

'Another piece of liquorice, then?'

I shook my head.

Cynthia fidgeted, shifting her weight from one foot to the other. 'Would you like to cycle for a bit?'

'Are you allowed out then?'

'On the exercise bikes, I mean.'

'Okay.'

'Come on then.' She pulled me after her.

'So, Mrs Meyer, have you met our will-o'-the-wisp?' The woman in the suit was also walking along the corridor.

Cynthia bowed deeply when she saw her.

The suit smiled.

'Good, they're both free.' With her cigarette still in her

mouth, Cynthia jumped onto an exercise bike. She started to pedal like mad. I tried to get up onto the machine, but there wasn't much play in my stitches.

'Come on, where have you got to?'

'Hold on, I've just given birth, you know.'

Cynthia stopped pedalling immediately. 'Have you got a baby?'

'Yes.' I suddenly realised that Harry hadn't said anything about Junior. And that I hadn't asked about him either.

'A boy or a girl?'

'A boy.'

She scrunched up her shoulders and clapped her hands ecstatically.

'How lovely! Now that's really cool. A baby. Where is he?'

'At home, with my husband.'

'Is he the father?'

'Yes, he's the father.'

'So you have a husband and a baby.'

'I have a husband and baby,' I said slowly.

'Then you're a lucky devil, Lea.'

chapter twenty-three

We got a television a little while ago and you sit watching it so precociously. You sit in the living room in your crib with a cushion behind your back. If anyone obstructs your view, you push them away.

On the day of the tribunal I woke up with stiff jaws. My teeth were pressed so tightly together that I could only produce monotone grunts.

When Harry came to visit, I thrust a note into his hand.

I'm not allowed to speak!

'What do you mean, what's wrong?'

'Husst hissen.'

'Who says you're not allowed to speak, then?'

I pointed upwards.

'Nonsense, Lea, it's just that there's something wrong with your jaw. Open your mouth for a moment.'

I tried to. Saliva dribbled down my chin.

'I'll go and fetch someone.'

Harry came back with Dr Posthumous. The doctor hurried into my room. He shook my hand and barely looked at me. Harry must have interrupted him while he was doing something extremely important. 'Your husband says you have a problem with your jaw.'

I nodded.

Posthumous came and stood in front of me. He was a good two heads taller than me. 'Say something.'

'Aaah,' I said, shakily.

He lifted my lower jaw and shook it. 'Again.'

'Aaah.'

He gave a little slap to the sides of my chin, left and right.

'Aaah.' My voice sounded just as strange as before.

'No doubt about it,' said Posthumous. He turned around and walked out of the room.

Harry went after him.

'What an arrogant sod he is,' he mumbled when he got back. 'You've got lockjaw, Lea. It's a side effect of the medication. They've given you something for it. Hold out your hand.' Harry laid a pill on it. 'Swallow it right away. From now on you'll have to take this along with the Pimozide.'

I put the pill in my mouth and swallowed it.

'Let me see.'

I parted my teeth as wide as possible.

'Tongue up.' Harry peered into my mouth. 'You really have swallowed it. Very good! It'll work pretty rapidly, they told me.'

I nodded absently. The hearing was about to begin and I still had to put on my Donna Karan outfit. Fortunately, Harry had brought everything I needed – the only thing he'd forgotten was a pair of tights.

A little later my heels clicked down the corridor. Harry walked next to me in silence.

The door to the smoking room was closed. The woman in the suit and the head nurse were sitting with their backs to the window. Opposite them sat a small, bald man and two women. They had briefcases with them. The bald one must be the magistrate. He had a pile of papers on his lap.

I took a deep breath and went in.

Everyone stood up.

I shook hands with the magistrate.

'Paul Kramer, good morning, you're Mrs Meyer's lawyer?'

'I wam Wrs Weyem.'

Kramer was confused for a moment, but recovered himself quickly. 'You are Mrs Meyer, of course. Pleased to meet you, and you are . . .?'

'Her husband, Harry Meyer.'

'Paul Kramer, pleased to meet you.'

I shook hands with everyone in the room.

Harry did likewise.

The head nurse showed Harry and me to our seats. Everyone sat down. No one said anything.

After a while the door opened.

Agaath den Hartog came in. I'd met her the day before. My lawyer was a corpulent middle-aged woman. She had short grey hair and a pair of large-rimmed glasses. 'You look a bit like my mother,' I'd told her.

She smiled at me, introduced herself to everyone and sat on the empty chair to my left.

The magistrate opened the hearing.

'Mrs Helena Helma Maria Meyer-Cornelissen was placed in psychiatric detention three days ago on the authority of the mayor. We are gathered here to decide whether or not the period of detention should be extended. Is that clear?'

Kramer's eyes were focused on me.

I nodded.

'Before I come to a decision, I want to hear from all those involved, that is to say from Mrs Meyer, her husband, the doctor in charge of treatment and the public prosecutor.'

I looked to my right, absolutely astounded. Harry would speak too, he hadn't mentioned that at all. Did he know about that all along?

'This is the public prosecutor, Mrs Hemmes, and this is the clerk, Mrs van Tol. I would like to ask Mrs Meyer to speak first. What do you think about the possibility of being detained for a further period?'

I wiped my chin. Sometimes I couldn't tell I was dribbling. 'I'we uhh . . .' *Why did I have to sound like a halfwit today of all days?* I looked up to catch Harry's eye. He was staring straight ahead.

I felt someone pat my thigh. 'My name is Agaath den Hartog,' said a clear voice. 'Mrs Meyer has asked me to speak on her behalf.'

I'd done no such thing. I'd felt a bit insulted at our first meeting, as I'd been expecting a wily advocate of the calibre of Bram Moszkowicz. *This is no Tupperware party, Mrs den Hartog. Come along if you like, but keep your mouth shut, I'll do the talking. Maybe you'll learn something,* I'd said. I didn't have lockjaw then.

'Mrs Meyer is of the opinion that her detention should come to an end as soon as possible. The fact that detention was resorted to in the first place has deeply shocked her. As you know, Mrs Meyer has recently given birth. Her son was delivered with forceps, an intrusive and painful procedure which Mrs Meyer found very traumatic.'

I sat there avidly nodding in agreement. For the first time in my life, I was glad that someone had refused to take me seriously. This lawyer of mine was superb. A wolf in sheep's clothing, that's what she was.

'Mrs Meyer recognises that she was in a confused state for some days after the birth. She is currently being treated by Dr Mulder. She is taking medication which is working well. Mrs Meyer would like to go home, to her husband and child, because she believes that she can recover most quickly and thoroughly in her own familiar environment.' Agaath den Hartog paused for a moment. 'If her doctor believes that Mrs Meyer is still not well enough to go home, then Mrs Meyer is willing to remain in hospital on a voluntary basis until her treatment has been completed. Mrs Meyer assumes that this will take no more than one or two weeks, whereas if her detention is prolonged she will have to remain here for at least three weeks.

I looked around triumphantly at all the various faces. *Try telling me that's not a watertight argument, guys.*

'Your view is clear,' said magistrate Kramer. 'I would now like to hear from Dr Mulder, the doctor in charge of treatment.'

The suit stood up. 'Mrs Meyer was brought to this department three days ago. She was admitted at night and spent some time in isolation. I saw her for the first time the following morning and have been treating her ever since then . . .'

I yawned. Did she really have to bother the magistrate with all these irrelevant details?

'. . . at first Mrs Meyer did not cooperate with her treatment. When Dr Posthumous, the head of psychiatry, took her out of the isolation room, she refused to speak to him. A course of medication was started that morning, but Mrs Meyer made the unilateral decision not to take it, without informing us . . .'

How does she know that? Harry! Harry must have told her! He's the only one who knew. Why did he go and tell her that?

'. . . since then, Mr Meyer has persuaded his wife to take her medication, and as far as we know she has been doing so . . .'

As far as we know. What kind of goddamn crap is this! I prodded my lawyer.

She spoke up immediately. 'I can assure you, your honour, that Mrs Meyer has been consistently taking her medication. As you may perhaps have noticed, she has difficulty speaking at the moment, a recognised side effect of Pimozide, a drug that has been prescribed to her. Dr Mulder will be able to confirm this.'

A brilliant move! I could have kissed my lawyer.

Dr Mulder cleared her throat. 'As I said, it does indeed appear that Mrs Meyer is now taking her medication, but she has not been doing so for long enough to enable us to draw any con-clusions regarding her longer-term progress. Given that we cannot adequately estimate how Mrs Meyer's recovery will pro-ceed, it seems to us advisable to keep her in detention for the time being, to be on the safe side.'

The off-the-peg slut was going to drop me in it. What a bitch. Surely it was obvious to the magistrate that her argument was full of holes. If she really wanted to be on the safe side, she'd have to place her-self under lock and key.

I sighed and laid my hand on Harry's knee. I hoped he'd come well prepared.

Harry had a serious look on his face.

I smiled at him.

He didn't smile back.

'I'm now going to ask Mrs Meyer's husband to speak,' the magistrate said.

Harry straightened his tie. 'Ladies and gentlemen. First of all I want to use this opportunity to thank the hospital, by which I mean Dr Mulder and all the nurses, for taking such good care of my wife up to now . . .'

Dr Mulder and the head nurse gave him friendly nods.

'. . . there are things my wife is not able to express at this stage, but I am sure that she shares my feelings in this matter. Without all of you, we could not have managed, not at all . . .'

The magistrate nodded too this time.

I sniffed.

Soon he'll get on his hands and knees and start crawling around kissing everyone's feet.

'. . . I know Lea would prefer to go home. And I understand why. I think all those present understand. Unfortunately, that's not sufficient. We have to do what's best for Lea. I have her best interests at heart, we all do. Lea finds that difficult to believe sometimes, but it is true . . .'

I stiffened. What on earth was Harry playing at?

'. . . I think it would be best for Lea to stay where she is. She has told her lawyer that she would be willing to continue her treatment in the hospital on a voluntary basis, but to be honest – and I hope you will forgive me, Lea – I can't guarantee that she would actually do that. Knowing my wife, she'll pack her bags as soon as she gets the chance . . .'

I was dumbfounded. Harry didn't trust me any more! He wanted me to stay in hospital, far away from him and Junior. Far away from my child.

The public prosecutor looked at the magistrate, eyebrows raised. The magistrate nodded at her.

At this signal, the prosecutor started speaking. 'May I ask you a question, Mr Meyer?'

'Of course, your honour.'

'If I understand you correctly, you are saying that you are afraid your wife will come home as soon as her detention is lifted.'

'That's right.'

'Why are you afraid of that?'

'However much I would like to, I can't keep an eye on her twenty-four hours a day. The baby demands a lot of attention, there's the shopping to do, I have to show my face at work from time to time . . . and then there are the nights . . .'

'Let's be clear about this; do you think that she is still a danger to herself or to those around her?'

'Very possibly.'

'Do you have any reason to suppose that to be the case?'

'Perhaps.'

'What do you mean?'

'It's in the family, you know. Her father committed suicide.'

What?! My face jerked around towards him.

Harry acted as if he hadn't seen me.

'Was her father also admitted to hospital?' asked the prosecutor.

I shook my head slowly.

'Not as far as I know,' said Harry. 'It seems he was a manic-depressive, but he never sought treatment.'

I turned my face away. I folded my arms tightly in front of me and stared at my lap. I breathed heavily and laboriously in and out. I felt the tension in my jaws recede. The pill was working. I could say something now, but I didn't. I mustn't react. Any reaction would be the wrong one.

My lawyer cleared her throat. 'I think we're getting off the subject, your honour. We are here today to discuss the case of Lea Meyer. Her father's personal history is not relevant. Mr Meyer is making all kinds of connections based purely on hearsay.'

Harry's cheeks went bright red. 'I'm simply saying that I don't want it on my conscience if something goes wrong. I'm concerned for Lea's safety. And that of my son. She's already put him in a cardboard box. God knows what else she's planning to do.'

You don't have to listen to this. You don't have to.

I started to get up to walk out.

Agaath den Hertog grabbed my hand. 'Stay here a moment, Lea,' she whispered urgently. 'Please. We're nearly finished.'

'I understand your concern, Mr Meyer,' said magistrate Kramer, 'and I will take what you have said into account when I make my final judgement. I would however like to point out to you that a further period of detention will only relieve you in the short term. Before long you will arrive at the point at which you and your wife will have to pick up the threads again, along with your son. That's only possible on the basis of trust. Perhaps you can use the coming period to work on that together.'

If Harry goes on like this, all he'll have to work on will be divorce proceedings.

'Mrs Hemmes, you have the last word.'

'I'll keep it short.' The public prosecutor stood up. 'Mrs Meyer has been detained as a result of a situation which got seriously out of hand, in which among other things she was extremely negligent in her treatment of her newborn son. After her compulsory admission, it was some time before Mrs Meyer had sufficient insight to accept that she was in need of treatment and medication. Given the serious nature of these events, the Prosecutor's Office is of the same opinion as the doctor now handling this case, that the detention of this patient should be extended.'

Three against one. Thanks to my husband. Harry the traitor, Harry the turncoat has signed my death warrant.

The public prosecutor sat down again.

'I will read you my decision.' All eyes were turned to Kramer. He picked up a piece of paper from his lap. 'Having heard submissions from the subject of this hearing, from her lawyer, the doctor in charge of treatment, her husband and the public prosecutor, and taking into account the fact that according to these submissions there exists a strong likelihood that as the result of a psychiatric disorder the patient represents a serious danger to herself, to others, or to public order, the further detention of the patient is deemed necessary in order to guard against such a danger. According to article twenty-one, section one, of the law governing special admissions to psychiatric institutions, I hereby empower this hospital to detain for a further period Helena Helma Maria Cornelissen, born in . . .'

chapter twenty-four

I've neglected you terribly. In this book I mean, not other-
wise. You're growing well and you've become very much
part of the family. You always take things as they come.
When you were a year old you still didn't have a single
tooth in your head. The first one didn't come through until
you were fourteen months old.

'Lea, listen to me.'

I kicked off my shoes. Harry had followed me out of the
smoking room, even though I'd spat in his face when the magistrate announced his verdict. A marvellous, full gob of phlegm,
right between the eyes.

'I know you're angry, but just look at it from my point of
view. Have you got a handkerchief?'

I threw my skirt down at his feet.

Harry picked it up and hung it over the chair.

'You wanted a handkerchief, didn't you? Here!' I picked up
the skirt and tore it in two from the split. 'Oh wow, what am I
doing now? I must be mad! It's a good thing my husband's had
me locked away. Women who destroy clothes represent a serious threat to public order.'

'Do you know how much that skirt cost?'

'Ha! Now I recognise you again!' I took off the jacket and dropped it. Then I took off my knickers.

'If you go on like this, I'll fetch one of the nurses.'

I squatted down and pissed on the jacket.

Harry reached me in two strides. He pulled me up roughly.

'Did I pee on the floor? Oh, I'm sorry darling, I learned to do that in solitary. They didn't have a toilet in there, you know, I had to pee on the floor then too.' I wiped my cunt with the jacket and pulled my knickers back on. 'Don't you think you should arrange that with your hospital friend, get Dr Mulder to put me in solitary for a few more nights. To "be on the safe side"?'

'It's better this way, believe me.'

'Better? I'll be locked up for the next three weeks. In an institution, surrounded by idiots. And I don't mean the patients, I mean the staff. I've never seen so many schlemiels in one place. Know what they gave me yesterday? The department information folder.' I scrabbled about on the table and found the stencilled leaflet. 'Would you like to know what my daily schedule looks like?'

Harry made a defensive gesture.

'Oh, yes sir! You think you know what's best for Lea? I'll tell you, like it or not. From half past seven until a quarter past eight, I have *the chance to eat breakfast*. From a quarter past eight until a quarter past nine *opportunity to take a walk*. Do you know where I'm allowed to walk? Within this department. The rest of the hospital is out of bounds. From the furthest corner of the common room to the door is exactly seventy-six paces. I know that, because my schizophrenic friend Enzo has counted them.

He does nothing else all day but walk to and fro. His wife has got herself another man, he's not allowed to see his child. Our Enzo gets a lot of pleasure out of his walking time, as you can imagine.'

'Just sit down, Lea.'

'I haven't finished yet. From nine until half past eleven *therapy*. I don't have therapy, so instead I'm allowed to walk! From eleven thirty until twelve everybody has *the opportunity to take a walk,* from twelve to twelve thirty a hot meal and from one to one thirty *opportunity to take a walk.*' I waved the folder. 'You don't believe me? Just look here, from half past four until half past five, *opportunity to take a walk,* then a snack and from eight till eight thirty, *opportunity to take a walk (except on Mondays).* On Tuesdays and on Thursday afternoons you can have visitors between half past one and a quarter past two. If you don't have any visitors, then that's an extra *walking opportunity*! Yippediedoodah! From nine o'clock onwards there's *the opportunity to go to bed*! If you're not mad already, you'll go mad here.'

'They've cured your lockjaw, I see.' Harry loosened his tie and sat on the bed. 'You're better off here than at home, believe me.'

'How? Why? What have I done for God's sake that I don't get the opportunity to go to bed in my own bedroom?'

'Have you forgotten everything that's happened?'

I pulled on some tracksuit trousers and slippers. 'Give me that mobile for a moment.'

'What for?'

'I want to call my mother.'

'Your mother isn't home. She's looking after Junior. Why do you want to call her?'

'Perhaps I can stay with her.'

'Don't bother.'

'Why not?'

'You're in psychiatric detention, you're not allowed out. And even if you were, she's the last person who'd want to take you in.'

I raised my eyebrows.

'Do you really still not understand? You're mother's terrified of you. She held a family conference yesterday with your sister and one of your aunts. They decided unanimously that you should be locked up for as long as possible. Your mother and Birgit came round yesterday evening. They insisted you should be put away for at least a year. In the meantime, my mother is happy to look after Junior.'

I rubbed my eyes. *He's lying.*

'For God's sake go and sit down, you look as if you could collapse at any minute. Do you actually eat something now and then?'

Mechanically, I fetched myself a chair.

Harry ran his hand through his hair. 'At first I wanted to argue that they shouldn't hold you against your will any longer, too. Your mother persuaded me not to do that. She kept going on about your father, she said she didn't want to go through that nightmare again.'

'Oh. So she's the one who's suffering. I'm locked up, but she's suffering.'

'It's not easy for her, Lea, she's worked in the psychiatric field, it's terrible for her to see you like this.'

'That was half a century ago. And she couldn't stand it even then. She can't stand anything! Whether it's blood, the smell of sweat or a stiff dick, my mother starts to retch. She can't cope with the physical side of existence . . .!'

'Yes yes, I know. And you weren't cuddled enough as a child. The same goes for all of us, Lea, that's the way things were in those days.'

'Jesus Christ! You should go and get yourself some evening classes in psychology!'

'I've done what seemed best for everyone.'

'For everyone, right. Except for me. I'll tell you one thing, Mr Harry Meyer, the trick you pulled on me in that hearing, I'll never forgive you for it. God, how I wish I'd never told you anything about my past . . .!'

chapter twenty-five

You could talk fairly well after your own fashion, words I could recognise and understand very clearly. At fifteen months you took your first tottering steps. There was no holding you then. You could walk, so you would walk.

'Aha.'

I'd told Beau van Kooten that my father was dead.

'Suicide,' I added quickly.

'So,' said Beau.

Was I imagining it, or did his eyes light up for a moment? That would make a welcome change. Whenever I tell anyone about my father's death, a recurrent pattern emerges.

We're driving in Corine's Alfa Romeo Cabrio along the Zeeweg to Bloemendaal. It's a beautiful summer's day.

Corine asks me what my father does. Corine is my tennis partner.

I answer with my eyes closed. 'He's dead, but he was a bookkeeper.'

She obviously finds the first fact more interesting than

the second. She turns the radio down. 'Dead? Oh. For long?'

'About twenty years.'

'That long, eh? What did he die of?'

The conversation will now take an unexpected turn. For Corine, at least. For me what follows is utterly predictable.

'He committed suicide.'

I still enjoy dropping that bombshell. Most people have fathers who died of perfectly ordinary strokes, or of cancer. They ought to try the suicide version some time. Success guaranteed.

'When I was thirteen.'

I add that bit for extra effect.

Silence.

Corine is in acute shock for about three seconds. She slows down. She shoots me a panicky look. She licks her lips.

I can see her thinking, *Jesus Christ, her father committed suicide! I sure do hope she doesn't start blubbing . . .* No doubt she's sorry she asked, poor dear. Time for the reassuring smile. I pull my face into the correct shape and lay my hand on her bare thigh. 'I know, Corine, it sounds grim but it's really not that bad. I'm not unhappy about it. My father was a nasty, dominating man. He terrorised my family for years. His death was really a liberation, you know? Look out!' The Zeeweg bends sharply left at this point.

'Do you have any brothers or sisters?' asked Beau.

'I've got one older sister.'

'What's her name?'

'Birgit.'

'Birgit.' Beau repeated the name slowly, to imprint it on his memory.

'Actually two older sisters. After Birgit my parents had another daughter. Agnes. She died of a heart abnormality two hours after she was born.'

'So you're the youngest.'

'Yes.'

'What kind of relationship did you have with your father?'

I looked out of the window. 'Do you want the long answer or the short answer?'

'Whichever you prefer.'

'Right now I'd prefer a cup of coffee, Mr van Kooten.' I laughed mischievously. 'First things first, right?'

Van Kooten didn't seem to have understood the joke completely, but he got up all the same.

He watched me while I drank my coffee. I took my time. Van Kooten was generally quiet and thoughtful, this was the first time I'd noticed anything about him that I could describe as slight agitation.

'What were we talking about?' I said after about three minutes. I felt like winding my shrink up.

'Your relationship with your father.' Van Kooten's eyebrows performed a little dance.

I scratched my head. 'Oh yes. It's a long time ago now, you know. I'd rather talk about my relationship with Harry.'

'Harry?' Beau leaned back in his chair.

'My husband. There's a lot of tension between us.'

'Really?' He didn't make much of an effort to look interested.

'First of all there's the sex, of course.'

Van Kooten straightened up.

'Do you know that since Junior was born we haven't screwed each other once?'

Beau nodded. 'That's not uncommon. Most women have less need of sexual intercourse after a powerful emotional experience like the birth of a child.'

'That's not what I mean. I want it, but I can't get it. My private parts have been a disaster area since the birth. It's horribly sore. But the worst thing is that Harry doesn't mind at all. You know what he says? *Just a little cuddle is great too.*' I stuck my finger down my throat. 'What do you advise?'

'Have you seen a gynaecologist?'

'Of course. He said I'd have to be patient. That I had to give it time to heal. That's easy for him to say. Sometimes I really feel I'm about to burst, you know what I mean? Harry doesn't even want to do the little trick.'

'The little trick?'

'Fingering,' I giggled, 'he doesn't even want to give me the finger.'

'Right, okay.'

'Don't you think that's weird?'

'It's impossible to comprehend,' Beau concurred. 'How do you cope with it?'

'If I'm really honest, I'm not coping with it. Every man I see makes me think immediately of sex.'

'Do they really?'

'Yes. Including you. What I'd like most of all is for you throw me onto my back, pull off all my clothes and give me a thorough seeing-to.'

'Really?'

'I've heard that your tongue can work miracles, Mr van Kooten.'

He looked away. 'Oh come on now, that's a gross exaggeration.'

'Loretta never stops talking about it.'

'Loretta? Oh yes, of course. Our Loretta. A difficult case.'

'You have healed old wounds, Mr van Kooten.'

'That's what they say.'

I went over to him and knelt in front of his chair. 'Heal me too. I'll do anything you say. Heal me, please.'

Van Kooten stroked my hair. 'I don't know, Lea, I don't know if you're ready for that.'

I unbuttoned my blouse and granted him a full view of my black lacy bra. 'I've never been more ready, Beau-ie,' I said huskily.

He sprang to his feet. He pulled me over to the sofa and manoeuvred me onto my back. His hands lifted my skirt. 'Little temptress, you're driving me crazy,' he moaned, when he discovered I wasn't wearing any knickers.

'Sorry darling, I'll never do it again.'

With trembling fingers he ripped my tights in two.

'Help yourself, my love,' I whispered.

His head went down between my legs.

I opened my eyes.

'No Lea, I don't find that strange at all,' said Beau, 'childbirth is a traumatic experience for men too. A baby comes out of the most intimate part of a woman's body. That's a shocking sight. It may be a while before Harry can think of you as a sexual being again.'

'So you think I should be patient too?'

'There's no other way.'

Sighing, I turned the empty cup round and round in my fingers. Patience was never my strong point.

'You said just now that there was a lot of tension between you and Harry. Do other things play a role in that too? Other than sex?'

I cleared my throat. 'Well actually, I'm still pissed off with him.'

'Why?'

'He betrayed me. I spent three weeks in hospital because of him. He told the hearing that my father committed suicide. Said my father was a manic-depressive and that it obviously runs in the family. That destroyed any chance I had of getting out of there.'

'I see.'

'That was a foul trick to play on me. Wasn't it?'

'That depends.' Van Kooten stood up to get a cigarette. 'Why do you think your husband felt compelled to tell them?'

'My mother talked him into it.'

'Your mother?'

'She was convinced I'd never get better. Lea behind bars, hand the baby over to her and Bob's your uncle, that was the idea.'

Van Kooten blew out a cloud of smoke. 'What do you think?'

'Ah, I can't blame her. She had to cope with that whole business with my father, no wonder she was scared to death when I was admitted.'

'If I say "mother", what's the first word that comes to mind?'

I thought about it for a moment. 'Gratitude.'

Van Kooten simply looked at me.

'Now you want me to explain?'

He nodded.

'Why do you want to know all this stuff?'

'So I can help you to get better.'

'I am better, aren't I?'

'I hear a lot of distrust in your voice.'

I had to laugh. 'You hear all sorts of things in my voice, Mr van Kooten.'

He turned the palms of his hands towards me. 'Listen, Lea. You have to trust me, otherwise we'll never get anywhere. See yourself as a tree.'

'Sorry?'

'You're a tree, but we don't know yet what kind of tree. Do you have a strong, thick trunk or are you a bendy little tree? Maybe your bark is hard and impenetrable, but are you soft inside or not? – I can't tell from the outside. Your roots are in your childhood. That's where we have to start.'

'I can assure you I'm soft inside, Mr van Kooten.' I winked at him.

He didn't notice, he was glancing at his watch.

'I know, Lea. You are very vulnerable. I want to give you something to do for next time. Have a good think about your past. About your relationship with your mother. About your role in the family. About how you felt when your father died.'

'Could you write that down for me?'

'You won't forget.'

'Are you sure there's any point, Mr van Kooten? I mean, I'm living now. I have to go on. With Harry and with Junior.'

Van Kooten stood up and put his hand on my shoulder. The

warmth of his fingers burned right through my see-through blouse. His strong but tender grip gave me fierce stomach cramps. 'Think about it and then come back to me, Lea,' he said softly.

I'd always come back to him. If only so I could feel those hands touching my body. I'd love to talk about my childhood for the rest of my life. For Beau. With Beau.

My Beau.

chapter twenty-six

Once you were eighteen months old, I had to get out; I felt claustrophobic in the flat, I absolutely had to prove to myself that I could do something other than stay at home all day looking after the children and so on.

It was walk time. I walked a little way with Enzo.

'It looks as if I'll have to stay here for the time being.'

'Oh good,' he grinned.

'You go at quite a pace.'

'Always.'

'Don't you ever sit still for a while?'

'I do try, but I can't, unless I'm sleeping or eating. It's a side effect of the medication.' Enzo had a big book under his arm.

'What's that?'

'DSM, fourth edition.'

I'd no idea what he meant.

'Haven't you heard of it? DSM is my Bible. It's all in here.' Enzo tapped himself on the temple with his forefinger. 'Everything that goes on in your little head is in here.'

He showed me the cover.

DIAGNOSTIC AND STATISTICAL MANUAL
OF MENTAL DISORDERS
FOURTH EDITION

'Why are you here, actually?' asked Enzo.

'I thought I was the new Jesus,' I answered. I felt a blush spread over my cheeks.

He laughed. 'That's nothing. We all think that in here. A very common delusion.'

When Enzo put it like that it sounded a lot less worrying.

'Do you know what I sometimes think?' said Enzo. 'That Jesus had a disorder too. Maybe there had been a Jesus before him, the real one, let's say. What if our Jesus, the year-zero one, had the delusion, just like us, that he was Jesus, but he – unlike us – managed to convince people it was true, so that the deranged Jesus went down in the history books as the real Jesus.'

'Wow, Enzo, did you think that up all by yourself?'

He nodded radiantly.

'How brilliant! Impossible to verify now, but still. It is possible. It's very possible. And perhaps there wasn't only one Jesus before the official Jesus, maybe there was a whole succession of Jesuses.'

'Exactly!' cried Enzo. 'Just like there are now.'

'Only they're no longer recognised.'

'No, they end up in another Bible.' He held up his DSM again for a second.

We walked around the corner.

'Ah, her Ladyship is at it again,' Enzo observed.

A woman was standing in the corridor stark naked. Her medium-length, grey hair wreathed her face. The only thing she was wearing was a gold watch. 'Do either of you know what time it is?' Her Ladyship had a very posh accent.

'Will you deal with this?' asked Enzo. He carried on walking.

'Do you perhaps have the time?' her Ladyship asked again.

I'd never seen a woman of that age without any clothes on before. It wasn't anywhere near as bad as I'd have thought. Her waist, hips and breasts were well proportioned. Only her skin betrayed her age. She wasn't smooth anywhere any more, there were long, thin marks running all over her body.

'You have a very fine figure, madam.'

She pointed at her watch. 'It's slow. Or fast. Could you take a look?'

This happened all the time with her Ladyship, I soon discovered. She was perpetually convinced that there was something wrong with her sense of time. There was too, but it wasn't the fault of her watch.

'Let me see. No, that's right. It's a quarter to two.'

'One thirty already?'

I took her arm. 'Shall I take you back to your room, then you can get dressed. Where is your room?'

'That way.'

Her Ladyship's room was further on, beyond the office.

We were outside number 194 when she suddenly pulled her arm out from mine and started walking close to the wall away from the doors.

'What are you doing now?'

With large, fearful eyes she nodded towards the room. A

woman of about fifty was sitting in the doorway. She was wearing a dark blue jumper, a pale pink pleated skirt covered in
stains and a pair of slippers.

'Hello.' I gave her a friendly nod.

'Watch out!' her Ladyship shouted. It was too late.

The woman flew at me and grabbed me by the throat. She
clawed her nails into my flesh and dragged them downwards.

I screamed and tried to get free, but she had the strength of
a lunatic.

'Mrs Schreuder, don't!' A nurse ran up to us. He pulled the
woman off me.

I had four red scratches down my neck, they went all the way
down to my chest. Blood was seeping out of two of them.

'Didn't anyone warn you?' asked the nurse.

I shook my head.

He gave me a paper tissue. 'You'd better stay out of her way.'
He led Mrs Schreuder back to her chair.

'Is it time for dinner yet?' Her Ladyship looked at her watch.

'No. I'll take you to your room.'

When her Ladyship had been safely delivered, I had to go back
past room 194. There was no alternative route. The nurse was
nowhere to be seen. Mrs Schreuder was sitting on her chair talking to herself. I pressed my back against the wall and walked past
very carefully. As soon as she saw me, she stood up. I stiffened.
She strode briskly up to me.

'Mrs Schreuder, what were you trying to do?'

Enzo appeared from nowhere. He put his arm around her.
'Just you come and sit down quietly.' He accompanied her back
to the chair.

She lowered herself onto it without protest.

'She really had a good go at you,' said Enzo as we walked on.

'What a terrible person. They ought to lock her away.' I pressed the tissue against my neck.

'She's not so terrible. It's just that she can't regulate her own strength. That's her way of making contact.'

'Oh yeah? She went for my throat out of pure goodwill.'

'In a certain sense, yes. She doesn't mean any harm by it, she really doesn't.'

'How come she doesn't try it with you?'

'She knows me. And anyhow, I know how to handle her. Sometimes I let her pinch my hands. She can do it as hard as she likes, only she's not allowed to scratch. She enjoys it tremendously.'

Across from the exercise bikes there was a telephone attached to the wall.

<u>Telephone calls</u>
Only short calls may be made from this wing, by means of the payphone.
   No calls may be made at night. For longer calls, use may be made of the public phones in the hospital entrance hall.

'Have you got a couple of quarters for me?'

Enzo pulled a handful of change out of his pocket.

'Thanks, you'll get it back tomorrow.'

'I know where to find you.' He winked and went on walking.

I rang home and heard my own voice.

'This is the answering machine of Harry and Lea Meyer. We

are not in. Or we don't want to answer the phone. Give your name and number after the beep. Nine times out of ten we'll ring back.'

I hung up and dialled Harry's mobile number.

'This is the voicemail service of Harry Meyer. Please leave your message after the tone. Thank you.'

I rang Harry's work number.

'Hello Mrs Meyer.' Kristel stammered a little. She never normally did that.

'Can I speak to Harry for a moment?'

'Harry, I mean Mr Meyer, isn't here.'

'Do you know where he is?'

'I'll just look in his diary. Oh yes, I can see already. He's in Amsterdam.'

'With a client?'

'Er . . . no . . . he's, er . . . you really don't know where he is?'

'I wouldn't ask if I did. What's wrong, Kristel? Has he hired the Yab Yum sex club again?'

'No, no, of course not. He's at your mother's.'

'Well my dear, I can call him there then, right?' I couldn't understand why Kristel was being so unhelpful. I rang my mother's number.

'Mrs Cornelissen speaking.'

'Hi Mum, it's me.'

'Hello Lea.'

'How are you?'

'Fine. And you?' she asked warily.

'Okay. Is Harry there with you?'

'How did you know that?'

'An astral message got through to me. Could I have a word with Harry?'

'One moment.'

Just before she put her hand over the receiver, I heard a familiar noise.

'Harry speaking.'

'Hi, it's me. I was wondering if you were coming over today.'

'I wasn't intending to.'

'Oh.'

'What do you expect? First you curse the hell out of me and now you want me to come over.'

'Is Junior there with you?'

'Yes.'

'I thought I could hear him. What are you doing at my mother's, anyway?'

'She's offered to look after Junior.'

'Oh?'

'I can't stay away from work any longer, Lea. He often cries at night, it's impossible.'

'Does he stay there overnight, then?'

'He's staying with your mother for the time being, yes.'

'Couldn't you have given things a bit more time?'

'I didn't have any choice.'

'No, imagine if you had a choice. You wouldn't know what to do.'

'Here's your coffee, dear,' said my mother, a little too loudly.

'I'm going to hang up now, Lea.'

'Not so fast. How's it going with the family's plan to have me locked up for a year?'

'I'll talk them out of it.'

'So they really mean it?'

'Shall we talk about this some other time?'

'Lea!'

My sister yanked the phone out of Harry's hand.

'Hey, Lea. Long time no speak.'

'Hi, Birgit.'

'What's this I hear, are you going through a bit of a dip, is it a deep dip, darling?'

'Well, I—'

'. . . you planned that very nicely. I organised an Easter brunch. Everyone was going to come, I hired extra crockery. That's all up the spout now . . .'

'I really am terribly sorry, Birgit—'

'. . . and an Easter tablecloth. I bought that, too. Really beautiful. It's got the same pattern as the top of my net curtains. No one notices that kind of detail, but I do. I love that sort of thing. Now Steef and I will have to brunch on our own. That's nice too. We'll have the whole lot to ourselves.'

'Don't you have to work today?'

'They've introduced a shorter working week. And I wanted to see my nephew. Mum's bought him such a sweet little romper suit. Bright red with a pointy hood. Really fabulous. He looks just like a pixie. Do you remember the book of fairy tales we used to have?'

'Maybe.'

'Surely you remember. The fairy-tale book! Think, Lea. On the right-hand page of the fourth story there was a pixie. One of those really funny little men with fat red cheeks. He was sitting on a tree stump. And he was wearing a little red jacket with a pointy hat. Junior looks the spitting image of him, I promise you.'

'Nice.'

'How do the bulbs look?'

'Sorry?'

'My crocuses! You have unwrapped them, haven't you, since . . .?'

The crocuses were reading half past six. They were on top of the radiator.

'. . . they're beautiful, aren't they? I chose white deliberately, they're simply the prettiest. Much prettier than yellow or purple. Those are such hard colours. White looks best in my border, too. When they've finished flowering, you have to cut them off at the base, Lea . . .'

'Will do.' I wouldn't. I was intending to tip them straight into the garbage bin very soon.

'. . . my garden looks great. You must come over and look some time. There's always something flowering, all year long. You'll never guess what Junior's just had to eat . . .'

Cynthia was walking towards me. She had a lollipop in her mouth.

'. . . home-made apple purée! I still had some in the freezer from last year. We had such a wonderful harvest, remember . . .?'

'Harry's been eating apple purée?'

Cynthia went and sat on the exercise bicycle. She waved at me.

'And how! Mum did add a bit of extra sugar, otherwise he wouldn't have eaten it.'

'But he shouldn't be given sugar at all, should he?'

'Oh, a few teaspoons, what's wrong with that? You should have seen him tucking in. The child thought it was delicious . . .'

'I'm going to hang up on you, Birgit.'

'Okay. Seeya, Lee.'

'You want a lolly too?' asked Cynthia.

'No, thanks.' I stroked the saddle of the other exercise bike.

Cynthia looked at me. 'She did it to me too.'

'What's that?' I was still thinking about Birgit.

She pointed at my neck. 'Mrs Schreuder. I had scratches like that too. My mother was horrified when she came to visit.'

'I haven't got any visitors today.'

'Isn't your husband coming?'

'No.'

'He's probably busy with the baby.'

Cynthia jumped off her bicycle. 'Just going to smoke a cigarette. You want one?'

I shook my head. I still had three quarters. I could try to ring Corine. No, no point, she'd be on the tennis court, of course. Corine is my tennis partner.

During visiting hours I watched 'The Bold' in the common room. After that I played five sets of table tennis with a male fellow patient. I don't know what his name was. I won three of the five sets.

At around ten, when visiting hours were long over, the nurse came round with a trolley full of drinks. It seems he did that every evening. I didn't know, because I was always in my room by then. You had a choice of various soft drinks, fruit juices and green or red squash.

The nurse pushed the trolley up to the table, where a handful of patients was sitting. Mr Zevenhoven was there too. He had dementia and couldn't talk any more. He ought to have been in a nursing home, but there wasn't a place for him. Mr Zevenhoven wouldn't hurt a fly. His clothes stank horribly, he had dark rings around his crotch, but he smiled all day long.

'Here you go, here's your drink, Mr Zevenhoven,' said the nurse. She'd poured him a glass of green squash.

I took a can of Pepsi. *Maximum taste, no sugar.* Good stuff if you're counting the calories. Cola Light tastes of postage stamps.

'How do you know he wants the green one?' I asked the nurse.

'I don't.'

'Haven't you ever asked him?'

'He never says anything, does he?' She gave me an empty glass for my Pepsi.

'Mr Zevenhoven!'

The old guy gave me a friendly look.

'There are two kinds of squash. Red and green.' I pointed to the jugs. 'Which one would you like?'

With a trembling hand he pointed to the red one.

'Well, you shall have the red one then.' I poured him a large glassful. 'You don't have to drink that green muck, you know.'

Mr Zevenhoven slurped his drink with satisfaction. At least a quarter of the contents got spilled on his jumper, but what did that matter? It really couldn't have mattered less.

After the drinks came the medicine trolley. The nurse gave everyone their little cup of pills. There was Temazepam in mine, my nightcap.

Medication
Any prescribed medication will be given to patients by the
nursing staff at predetermined times of day.

'Can I have an extra sleeping pill?' asked Nora, a heavily built,
sombre woman with whom I didn't have much contact.

Nora was allowed an extra pill. 'Good luck tomorrow,' the
nurse said to her as she wheeled the trolley away.

'What's happening tomorrow?' I asked.

Nora sighed. 'I get my electro-shock treatment.'

I immediately had visions of Nora lying on her back on a
table with great jolts of electricity going through her, wearing a
strange cap on her head with all sorts of wires coming out of it.
'I didn't know they still did that.'

'They put me under first, so I don't know it's happening.'

'And does it help?'

'It might help. I hope so. I'm feeling very depressed. As far as
I'm concerned I don't want to go on. I'd like to end it all right
away. All I do now is eat and sleep. I'm hungry, too. I'd like to
eat all day.'

'You always get a separate serving, right?'

I'd noticed that at the table. Nora fervently complained that
no one could live on the quantities she got. Next to her, Lidwien
the anorexia patient sat poking disgustedly at her hot meal. She
spent more time pushing the food around her plate than eating
it, daydreaming about the glorious period when she'd consumed
no more than one small pot of baby food per day.

Meals
As regards mealtimes, you are requested to start and finish

at the same time as others. This gives you and the other
patients the opportunity to eat calmly and quietly.

'They've put me on a diet. That's why I get measured portions.
But it's so little. Nowhere near enough for me. Every evening I
see that stick insect sitting at the table, not wanting to eat anything but getting nice big portions all the same. Give her food to
me, I always think. It's not fair.'

The kitchen in this department is <u>not</u> intended for the use
of patients in the preparation of their own meals.

'That was the last time, guys, tomorrow I'm going home.' Theo
banged his glass down on the table. I'd heard from Enzo that
Theo was a teacher at a technical school, but that he hadn't
been able to work for ages because of overwhelming panic
attacks. I reckoned Theo must be in his mid forties. He always
wore grey sweaters, with the collar of a check shirt sticking
out over the top.

'Nice for you,' I said, because no one else had said anything.

'I'm truly dreading it. They say I'm ready to leave, but I'm
not at all sure I am. I hope I can cope.'

'Of course you can cope, why wouldn't you be able to cope?'

'What am I supposed to do at home? There's no one there.
I've been back a few times for trial periods. I didn't speak to a
soul all those weekends. I was crawling up the walls with
misery.'

'Couldn't you invite someone round?'

'Such as? Who'd want to come and see me? I've only had one
visit in this hospital. A colleague came round. He talked about

school the whole time. About the boys, about the new
timetable. That man knew perfectly well I'd never be coming
back. But he went on about it all the same. After thirty-eight
minutes he ran out of things to say. Then he left.'

You may not sit in the main hall of the hospital with
visitors.
Each visitor is allowed <u>one cup of coffee.</u> During visits, no
unnecessary noise is permitted in the form of music, television etc.

'It was still nice of him to come.'
Theo shrugged his shoulders.
'Aren't you at all happy to be going home?'
'Let me guess. You want to go, but you're not allowed to.'
When I nodded, Theo started to laugh. 'Anyone who doesn't
want to go home has to go. Anyone who doesn't want any pills
has to take them. Anyone who wants more pills gets fewer.
Anyone who wants to stay in bed has to go and use the fret saw.
I've made six stupid wooden bears already. They're sitting in my
room in a row, neatly painted and varnished. Would you like
one? Otherwise I'm stuck with them. It's an upside-down world
in here, my dear. None of it makes any bloody sense at all.'

If you have any problems or complaints, discuss them as far
as possible with the member of staff responsible, for example with the head nurse or the chief psychiatrist.

Two days later Lidwien buttonholed me at breakfast. 'Have you
heard? Cynthia's leaving.'

I was shocked.

'She's being transferred. She's packing right now.'

I gobbled down the rest of my toast.

Lidwien pulled a face.

I went to Cynthia's room. The door was open. Cynthia was standing on the bed in bare feet pulling Mariah Carey off the wall.

Suddenly I had an idea. I ran to the exit. I'd recently been allowed to leave the wing if I wanted to. *The door is open for Mike, Hamid, Lea, Lidwien and Nora*, the nurse had said during the group meeting.

I went to the little shop in the hall near the main exit and bought a bag of wine gums for Cynthia. And a shiny balloon filled with laughing gas. It was heart-shaped with roses on it. They had some with rabbits on too. I'd have to buy one tomorrow for Junior.

I ran back to the wing. Two ambulance men were walking along the corridor with a stretcher. I had to take big strides to catch up with them. 'Have you come for Cynthia?' I asked, panting.

'How do you mean?' He looked suspicious.

'A young woman. She's being transferred today. Have you come to get her?'

'Why do you want to know?'

'Could you wait a moment? I just want to give her something. To say goodbye . . .'

The man smiled. He had a droopy moustache and a pock-marked face. 'Go on, quickly then. We'll take our time.'

Cynthia was sitting on her bed smoking. There were a few plastic bags at her feet. There was no one else with her.

'Hi Lea,' she said flatly.

'You're leaving, eh?'

'Yes.'

'These are for you.' I gave her the bag of sweets and the balloon.

'Thank you.' She stood up, went over to the wash basin and held her cigarette under the tap.

I walked over and stood behind her and gave her a hug.

Cynthia turned around and leaned towards me. 'Will you give the baby a kiss from me?' she whispered in my ear.

I nodded.

What a shame Cynthia's never seen Junior.

The ambulance man stuck his head around the door.

Cynthia got her bags. She held the balloon and the wine gums in her right hand.

'Do you want to get on the stretcher?' asked the man.

She shook her head.

She walked to the exit along with the men.

I watched her go. Tears came to my eyes. I missed her already. And I missed Harry. I missed my men.

chapter twenty-seven

I started working in the evenings, demonstrating and selling Tupperware. You didn't mind much, you were usually asleep by then and Daddy was always home, so the two of you were never alone.

'Beau thinks I should examine my past.'

Harry cut into his steak. Our Filipino girl was upstairs with Junior.

'Which bit of your past does he have in mind exactly? Your years with Eddie-give-'em-all-you've-got, your bimbo phase or the meagre few hours you spent at various schools?'

'Do you have to be so coarse, Harry?'

He took a mouthful of beer.

'Mr van Kooten means my childhood, naturally.'

'Oh yes. Nice and easy. Soon you'll be able to say it's all Mummy and Daddy's fault. Are there any chips left?'

I looked into the bag and shook my head.

'Why don't you ever get enough?'

'Don't gripe, Harry. Or get them yourself next time.'

Harry pushed his plate away.

'I don't understand why you want to bother your head about your past. Just be glad it's over.'

'Maybe I haven't come to terms with it properly.'

'What is there to "come to terms" with?' You always told me you were overjoyed when your father finished himself off.'

I sighed. 'I was, yes. But Beau understands these things. And he says that I haven't properly come to terms . . .'

'You know what I'd do? I'd get a second opinion.'

'Jesus, Harry, you're so distrustful. That's just not done! Beau van Kooten is a highly respected psychiatrist.'

'As if he was completely infallible.'

'You've never met Beau. He's really special. He understands me. Almost without words.'

Harry stood up and threw his napkin down on the table. 'If you two understand each other so well, then don't bother me with all this crap. Go and have a nice rake about in the past with Beau.' He walked away.

My entrecôte was cold. I warmed it up in the microwave and went on eating by myself.

The next morning my mother came round. She wanted to go for a walk with Junior and me in the woods.

'Wrap him up well, there's a biting wind,' she said.

I pushed the Maxi-Taxi along the sandy paths. The wobbly pram didn't seem to have reckoned on a cross-country expedition. My mother kept worrying Junior would get bounced out. We continued our walk on the cycle path around the perimeter of the woods.

'How's it going with your head?' asked my mother.

'My head? Oh, that's okay now.'

'So you've sorted yourself out?'

I nodded.

My mother put her hands in her pockets. 'I know what it was, you know. You weren't getting enough vitamin B.'

I adroitly avoided a pile of horse dung.

'It's the sort of thing you get when that happens,' my mother went on. 'It was in the newspapers even twenty years ago. I remember telling your father, you ought to take vitamin B-complex capsules.'

'I've been taking multivitamins for years, Mum.'

'That's not enough. You have to have extra. Extra vitamin B. That's what I told your father, too. Not that he listened. He never listened to me.'

'They gave me all sorts of pills in the hospital, but no vitamin pills.'

Junior spat out his dummy.

My mother put it in again.

'Have you ever been back to Dad's grave?' I asked.

'Not me. Why should I?'

'Where is it again? Somewhere in the northern suburbs, right?'

My mother laughed scornfully. 'You could spend a long time looking. That grave was cleared ages ago.'

'Are you sure?'

She wasn't sure, but she thought so. Ten years ago she'd got a letter from the cemetery. Asking her whether she wanted to have the grave maintained. Pay up or ship out, that's what it came down to. No way she'd pay up, the widow had no desire to do that. 'I rang them straight away to say that I wouldn't do it, that they'd have to approach your father's brothers and sisters.'

'Don't you think you should have asked Birgit and me?'

'What do you mean?'

'He was our father. You could at least have asked us.'

'Why would I do that? That grave doesn't mean anything to you. You didn't even go to the funeral . . .'

'Did Dad's family take charge of the grave?'

'I've no idea. You'll have to ask them.'

We arrived at the pancake farm.

'Shall we have a cup of coffee here?'

'Yes, let's,' said my mother. 'I need a loo, badly.'

In the restaurant she kept her coat on. She was cold and complained about pains in her legs. 'I can't walk these long distances any more.'

'You were the one who wanted to come to the woods.'

'Yes, but I can't do it any more. I see that now, again, that I just can't do it any more.'

'Would you like a pancake?'

'No, just a glass of water. I have a bit of tummy trouble.'

I ordered a cup of coffee and a glass of water. 'Here's to your health, Mum.'

She took a sip of water. 'Do you know I hated you, Lea?'

I wondered whether I'd understood her correctly.

'You were acting so strangely. Before you were admitted and afterwards, when you were so determined to go home. I really hated you.'

chapter twenty-eight

*I did Tupperware parties for fourteen months, until I grad-
ually came to realise that sometimes you have to make a
decision in life; you can either enjoy your children while
you have them and be a part of their lives, or do two
things, neither of them with complete conviction.*

'I think I know what kind of tree I am, Mr van Kooten.'

He came away from the window to sit down opposite me.

'Really?'

Beau had those sweet little wrinkles near his eyes. And messy
eyebrows. If I were to follow my instincts, I'd carefully take his
glasses off his nose and stroke his eyebrows with the tips of my
fingers.

'It took me a long time to work it out, but now I know. I'm
a Christmas tree.'

He put his hands together and pressed his pursed lips against
the sides of his index fingers. Those lips were very distracting. I
didn't dare say anything about them.

'Why are you a Christmas tree, Lea?'

'I like to feel all glittery.'

'Do you mean that literally or figuratively?'

'Both. That's the thing. That's how I know for sure that I'm a Christmas tree. Look, I love gold.' I rattled my armbands. 'I like everything that glitters. And I love it when men chat me up.'

'Do you?'

'Of course. All women find that delightful, don't they? When men chase after you?'

'Why do you enjoy that?'

'I just do. It's nice to be the object of desire. To know you're driving men crazy.'

'That's not called a Christmas tree, that's called a cockteaser.'

'Whoa, wait a minute. Don't jump to conclusions. I give as good as I get, Mr van Kooten.'

'I see . . .'

'And there's another big difference between me and other trees.'

'Which is?'

'Can't you guess? Deciduous trees lose their leaves. I don't. I keep my needles on. In other words, my true self always remains hidden.'

'Very interesting,' said Van Kooten. He went over to his desk and got a notebook and pen out of the drawer.

'Shouldn't you put it in the computer?'

He glanced at the iMac and sighed. 'I'd like to, but it's not working. It got jammed up yesterday. There's nothing I can do to get a response out of it.'

'How dreadful, Mr van Kooten.'

'That's putting it mildly.'

'You have made back-ups, I assume. You must always do that, you know.'

'No,' he said tersely. The full extent of the disaster seemed to sink in anew. He ran his hands through his hair, sat down and put the notebook on his knee.

'Where were we? Oh yes, you were a conifer.' He started to write.

'A Christmas tree,' I corrected him.

'Okay, that'll do too. Have you felt like a Christmas tree all your life?'

'I think so, yes,' I said, after thinking about it for a moment.

'You didn't start out as a beech, for instance? And only start to wear that cloak of needles later on?'

'A "cloak of needles", what a wonderful way to put it.'

'Thank you.'

'I don't know, I've no idea. I never think about that kind of thing. It's just that you said I should.'

'How old were you when your father killed himself?'

'Thirteen.'

'How old was your sister?'

'Sixteen.'

'How did you feel at the time?'

I looked at my nails. Loes had got them back into tiptop condition. 'Happy.'

'Happy?'

What's the difference between a shrink and an echoing well?
An echoing well is free.

'Overjoyed.'

Birgit and I screeched with laughter when we heard about it.

The day after my father was found, we fried chips early

in the morning and ate them in front of the television with
big glasses of Coke and lashings of mayonnaise. We left the
TV on all day, we played very loud music. In the afternoon,
Birgit and I drank a whole bottle of Cointreau with our
neighbour Dickie. I found a cigar in my father's desk drawer
and smoked the whole thing, while the three of us played
hearts. Birgit and Dickie got pissed as newts and I got sick
as a dog.

'Weren't you distressed?'

'No. Good riddance. That's what I thought. And that's what
I still think. That man was unbearable, Mr van Kooten.'

'What did he do to you?'

'He . . .' My voice faltered slightly. 'It's not so much what he
did to me personally . . . It's the influence he had on the family.'

'That's too much of a generalisation for me.'

'You really ought to ask my mother. She knows a lot more
about it than I do. She's told me everything I know about it. She
told me how nasty he was and about all the dreadful things he
did.'

'Oh, so your information is second-hand?'

'Surely my mother wouldn't lie about it.'

Van Kooten didn't reply. He wrote something down. 'What's
your earliest memory of your father?'

I thought for a moment. 'When I was little, I always ran to
the door when I heard him coming home from work. He used to
stand in the hallway with his dripping rain cape on. "Pick me up,
pick me up!" I used to shout. "Let me get home first, Lea" my
father always said. "But you are home," I used to say . . .'

Van Kooten smiled. 'And what did your father do then?'

'He took off his cape and his coat, picked me up and carried me all around the room.' I could smell my father's wet cape. I could feel the cold from his cheeks, as I pressed my own against them.

'He doesn't sound like such a terrible man, Lea.'

I swallowed hard and stared into my lap. 'Not then, no.'

'What else do you remember about that time?'

'On Sunday afternoons my father sometimes took Birgit and me to the Vliegerbos. We used to catch sticklebacks there, and water fleas.'

For catching fleas my father has an ingenious invention of his own. He's taken the strings off a tennis racket. He gets a pair of my mother's tights, cuts off the legs at the thighs and ties the stumps together. He fixes the waistband to the empty racket.

'My father kept the sticklebacks in an aquarium. The water fleas were live food. If there were any left over, he froze them. My aunt once put one of the ice blocks in her wine. That was funny.'

'So you kept sticklebacks as pets?'

'Yes. And black-fringed water beetles.'

The black-fringed water beetle is a shiny, whopping big jet-black beetle. According to my father, the black-fringed water beetle is on the verge of extinction. Unlike the yellow-fringed water beetle, which he always tosses out of his net with a dismissive gesture.

In our two-bedroom flat in Amsterdam West, we can

follow the life cycle of the black-fringed water beetle from
beginning to end. It all starts in the living room, where the
nests that father has fished out of the ditch float in big glass
pots. They're white and about the same size as chestnuts.
The nest is under water, but there's a sort of little chimney
sticking out of it – made of a leaf curled up to form a
pipe – so that oxygen can get in. At a certain point the nest
splits open and dozens of little larvae tumble out. Small,
brown larvae, which can grow to be fat larvae the size of
your little finger. They have sharp jaws, with which they
really can bite. My father sometimes lets them dangle from
his finger to show us how strong they are. He's proud of
them. The larvae are put on the balcony in wide pots of wet
earth. They crawl into the dirt to turn into beetles.

It always takes too long for my father. He picks away at
the soil to check they're alright in there. A habit that's often
sealed the fate of a larva in the process of metamorphosis.
He does it with their nests too. He snips them open with a
pair of nail scissors if in his view nature is taking too long
about it. The idea is that enormous swarms of black-fringed
water beetles will take off from our balcony.

Van Kooten made a note. 'Your father loved nature,' he
observed without looking up.

'Oh yes. Very much so.'

'Why did he decide to protect the water beetle of all things?'

'No idea. He had a thing about water, for a start. He was
always good at fishing. He taught me to fish.'

'You know how to fish?' Van Kooten looked up.

'Of course,' I grinned. 'It's just that I never do it any more.'

chapter twenty-nine

20th October 1968

So I chose the first option and stayed home in the evenings like before. During the day I'd had a lot of preparatory work to do, after all, and you'd stand there in your playpen longing for a kind word, a cuddle or something, and I couldn't afford the time for any of that.

'There are the buds, see? And there! The honeysuckle's sending out shoots already too . . .! Beautiful, eh?'

Birgit was showing me around her garden.

'This corner's going to be completely different. Steef's going to dig it over this afternoon when he gets home from work. I want to try a combination of cow parsley, ground ivy and poppies. It's going to look fantastic . . .' She crouched down and pulled out some small green plants. '. . . as long as you keep up with them, weeds aren't a problem, did you know that? You just have to check through all the beds every day. A little bit of attention . . .' The cat rubbed itself against her legs, its tail sticking up straight as an arrow. '. . . I'll feed you in just a minute, Maximillian . . .' Birgit mumbled. She wiped her nose on the sleeve of her jumper.

Has she forgotten I'm here?

'Mum says you were asking about Dad's grave.' She went on rootling about in the soil.

'My psychiatrist was talking about it.'

'Do you talk to him about Dad?'

'Yes.'

'Has he said anything about it yet?'

'What do you mean?'

'Has your psychiatrist told you why Dad did it?' She was tying a broken stem to a cane.

'No.'

'What do you think?' asked Birgit.

'I think he was psychotic. Maybe he thought he was Jesus too. Thought he could walk on water or something.'

'Do you get very hungry if you're psychotic?'

I frowned. 'I don't think so. I hardly ate anything, I was chewing things over the whole time. In my mind, I mean.'

Birgit shook her head. 'Then it definitely wasn't that. The evening before he went away, we had chicken soup. He had four helpings. I remember thinking, Jesus man, isn't that enough . . .!'

My mother's chicken soup as his last supper. I don't remember that at all. In fact I don't remember a single thing about the evening before he disappeared.

'Then what did he do?'

'Don't you remember?' asked Birgit, surprised. 'We looked at some slides. I'd just got back from my holiday with Annet.' Annet was Birgit's bosom friend. 'Annet had taken slides of me. I was incredibly brown, I looked pretty good. Dad thought the slides were great. When mother and you had gone to bed, he wanted to see them again . . .'

A sun-tanned, laughing Birgit was the last image he ever laid eyes on.

I felt a cramp somewhere near my heart. I didn't really want to hear any more. But Beau had told me I had to.

'. . . that holiday was the first time I'd fallen properly in love. With Günther, a German. He came round not long after . . .' She stared ahead, smiling. '. . . all I wanted to do that evening was sit in my room dreaming about Günther. Dad kept coming and disturbing me. One time to see the slides again. And later he came in all ingratiating and sat on my bed to talk about my holiday. I didn't feel like doing that at all. I made it fairly clear that he wasn't welcome.'

He didn't come to see me. I'm sure of that.

'I had to get up for a pee at two in the morning. I saw the light on in the living room. He always stayed up late. I usually said goodnight to him again. Not this time. I did put my head round the door. He was playing electric piano with the headphones on.' Birgit stopped talking.

A plane flew over.

Our father disappears the next day. There's no note. The first thing my mother does is to look down over the edge of the balcony. Kees doesn't turn up for work that Monday. Nothing is heard from him for days. Günther turns up unexpectedly at the door, with two other German guys. My mother lets them stay. If father comes back now he'll be angry, I think to myself.

Kees didn't come back. A week after he disappeared, a walker saw something floating in the Sloterplas.

chapter thirty

So all that changed. We played, larked about, washed the
windows together and so life went on. You were always very
sociable; you were perfectly content to play by yourself, but
you preferred it if I joined in.

'Baby book' is putting it a bit strongly. A grey ring-back folder with
six sheets of paper in it. Birgit has a folder too, but hers is much
thicker. Mine looks nice and full because there are four cardboard
dividers in it and one page with the Multo Guarantee on it.

Multo, everything you need in one folder!
Multo expands your possibilities!
Multo Alphabets. Multo Subject Dividers, Multo Stencils.
Multo Subject Dividers are designed to fit folders of the
21.5 × 16.5 cm format and are made of strong card in five
different colours, with ready-punched holes.

'Hi Mum, it's me.'
'Hello Lea.'

'Hey Mum, I found my old baby book in the attic. I read a piece about Dad. About how I was allowed to lie next to him in the double bed every evening.' I took a deep breath. 'Did Dad like that, having me lying next to him?'

'I never noticed. I put you there, he never asked me to.'

I ought to have known. My mother would rather play a round of Russian roulette than say anything nice about my father.

'Why are you asking me about this, Lea?'

'My psychiatrist wants to know what kind of family I come from. He says you and Dad must have been in love at some time. Otherwise you wouldn't have got married and had three children.'

My mother sniffed. 'Your psychiatrist never met your father.' She told the story of their honeymoon in Paris.

The just-marrieds saunter arm in arm along the street. My mother is hoping for a few words of endearment. Instead, my father says, 'Great, now I'm married. At least they'll see me as a responsible citizen now.' 'What do you mean?' asks my mother uncertainly. 'Have you been in jail, then?' 'No, but if you're not married, people are quick to assume there's something wrong with you.'

Only a few weeks after the wedding, they decided to go out for a Chinese meal.

They've arranged to meet at the door, but my mother can't see her husband there. She waits ten minutes, a quarter of an hour, twenty minutes and then decides to take a look inside.

My father is sitting alone at a table. The fried rice was very good. He pushes an empty plate away from him, finishes the last of his beer and burps. 'I've finished, where did you get to? Let's go home,' he snaps at her.

Their first Christmas ended in confrontation too.

My mother buys a chicken for ten guilders, thereby more or less using up my father's entire week's salary. Uncle Jan, my father's brother, comes to visit unexpectedly. My mother opens the sherry that my father won at the anglers' club. He comes home, flies into a rage, throws his brother out of the house and takes a swig from the bottle. My mother takes the chicken out of the oven, wraps it in newspaper and heads off out of the door. That evening at the dinner table you could cut the atmosphere with a knife.

'Yes, that's what your father was like,' my mother concluded. 'That's how he always was. I thought you knew that.'

I hung up. *Im Westen nichts neues.* I could tell stories from my mother's chamber of horrors even in my sleep.

chapter thirty-one

10th December 1968

The St Nicholas' Eve party was a highlight of the season for you, especially when you found a surprise in your shoe in the morning. In the evening, when we all gave each other presents, that was the most exciting of all. You didn't understand what was going on, but all the parcels were opened with a great sense of anticipation and everything delighted you.

'Does that machine of yours make tea too?'

'It certainly does.'

'I've brought some liquorice tea with me. I like it sometimes as a change. In my opinion you drink too much coffee.' I produced two teabags from my handbag.

'Very thoughtful, thank you,' said Van Kooten.

After a few minutes he put two steaming mugs of tea on the table and sat down. 'How have you been doing the past week?'

'Good, very good. I made an apple tart yesterday. My Filipino girl had never tasted anything like it! I wanted to bring you a piece, but I was afraid you'd think it was strange if I did.'

Van Kooten patted my knee for a second. 'Come on, Lea, you know better than that.'

Blushing, I took a sip of tea.

'Have you been thinking about your father?'

I gave Beau a full account of all the conversations I'd had with my mother and with Birgit. He listened and nodded, but he didn't write much of it down.

'So whether or not the grave is still there is something I have yet to find out. He wasn't psychotic the evening before his death, because Birgit says he had four bowls of chicken soup.' I hoped Beau would be proud of me. His deputy sheriff had brought a whole series of new facts to light.

'It's good to hear you've been working on it, Lea, but there's something missing.'

'What's that?' I could barely conceal my disappointment.

'Ultimately, this is about him and you. How do *you* feel about him?'

'I didn't have all that close a relationship with him, Mr van Kooten.'

When I was born my father was terribly disappointed. My mother presented this information to me every year on my birthday.

'Your father very much wanted a son. He'd told everyone, "You'll see, the third one will be a boy." The day before you were born I thought, let's have fried rice this evening, then perhaps the child will be born. It was 12th January when I made that fried rice and you were due on 15th January. We went to sleep and a couple of hours later I could feel that it was about to happen. I woke your father and told him to ring the doctor. "The baby's on its way," I said.

"'It can't be," said your father, "it's not due yet." He didn't want to get out of bed, so I had to get up myself to call the doctor. Your sister slept through it, she didn't hear a thing. The labour went well. I remember I had to move my bowels at one point. The doctor thought it was the urge to push, but I said, "No, I only have to squeeze." He didn't believe me, I wasn't allowed out of bed and that's why the pooh came out while he was watching. I felt awful about it. Then you came out. The first thing I said was, "What an ugly child!" The maternity nurse was shocked. I told her, "I ought to know, I've had three and this is the ugliest." You looked very weird. You didn't have any eyebrows and there was hair growing out of your earlobes. You had a horrible squint. Your father wondered whether you were normal. It came right after a while. Your father thought it was such a pity you weren't a boy. If you were you'd have been called Kees, like him. He didn't ring anyone to tell them you'd been born, it was such a letdown for him.'

'Did your father ever tell you how disappointed he was?' asked Beau.

I shook my head.

'So it may well be that he quickly got used to the fact that he'd had a daughter again.'

'Yes, of course, a week later he was walking on air. Goodness, how crazy he was about me! Strange that I never saw any sign of it.'

'Did he hit you?' Van Kooten tilted his head to one side.

'No.'

'Did he denigrate you?'

'No.'

'Did he abuse you?'

I laughed. 'That'd be money for old rope, eh Beau? Lea Meyer's incest story, brought to light in a mere four sessions.'

Van Kooten wasn't the first whose thoughts had wandered in that well-trodden direction.

Jean-Claude, one of Birgit's hundreds of exes – a manic-depressive nutter who looked the spitting image of our dad – claimed that my father had had it off with Birgit. He spread the rumour far and wide after Birgit split up with him. One time I bumped into him in town and he started foaming at the mouth as soon as he saw me. 'Just ask your sister what went on between her and your father. Just you ask her, then you'll understand why that cunt is so frigid.' I shrugged my shoulders and kept on walking. Incest, of course. Why not that on top of everything else? Just to make sure, I checked out the story with the supposed victim.

'Bullshit,' said Birgit on the phone.

'And that stuff about you being frigid?'

'That's true. But it was Jean-Claude who made me that way. As it happens, I've got a pencil in my pussy right now.'

'Sorry?'

'My sex therapist told me to do it. If it goes okay, I can put a candle in there tomorrow. Do you know what I'm afraid of?'

'That the cucumber won't find you attractive?'

'No. That I'll have a heart attack. And the ambulance men will find me with a candle in my cunt.'

'Don't worry, you can cross the incest scenario off your list,' I said to Beau.

He lit a cigarette.

'The things you mentioned just now, my father did them alright, only not with me.'

'Oh?'

'He denigrated my mother, he denigrated my sister. Sometimes he gave Birgit a slap, although he also praised her to high heaven with great regularity. She was simply a genius. Just like him.'

'And you were always out of range?'

'Yes. Lucky, wasn't I?'

'That remains to be seen. How did he go about denigrating people?'

'Birgit went to grammar school. When she chose to do languages instead of sciences my father was furious. His best-laid plans were wrecked. Birgit was supposed to win the Nobel Prize.'

'And after that?'

'After that Birgit was a worthless good-for-nothing. He tore a strip off her every single day. He told her she'd end up selling sausages at Hema.'

Posthumously, my father was proved right. Birgit never finished her grammar-school studies. She spent the last two years of school permanently stoned. She actually did work

at the local branch of Hema for a while. In the tart department. Once she'd put on ten kilos in weight, she switched
tills to work at C&A.

'What did your father think of you?'

'No idea.'

Beau took a drag on his cigarette and blew the smoke towards
the ceiling. 'You weren't interesting enough to be hit. You
weren't important enough to be denigrated.'

'If you go on like that I'll start to think it was a pity I escaped.'

Van Kooten nodded slowly. I got the idea that he understood
more about it than I did.

My father asked me a personal question just once in my life.
I was eleven. It was a Thursday evening and I was lying in
bed.

'How are you doing in school?' he asked.

I was totally stunned by his sudden interest, and the fact
that he was sitting on the edge of my bed. 'Okay,' I
answered. 'Not all that well, but not too badly either.
Average, I guess.'

Wrong! Wrong! Wrong! I realised that even while I was
saying it.

My father nodded as if that was what he'd suspected all
along, got up and went away.

End of conversation.

Van Kooten nodded as if that was what he'd suspected all along.
'Let's go back for a moment to the days after he left. You didn't
go to the funeral?'

'No.'

'You were cheerful.'

'Yes.'

'You didn't cry'

'Once, but that was because of my mother.'

When they dredged my father up, he'd been in the water for a week. Not a pretty sight, although it could have been worse. Imagine if he'd decided to hang himself. Then one of us would have found him, dangling at the end of a rope, with an ashen-grey face, protruding eyes and his tongue sticking out of his mouth . . .

The police told my mother that she mustn't on any account go to see my father's body. My father's brother Jan was going to go and identify him, but he backed out when he got there. No one who knew him ever saw him again.

My mother was given an unmarked plastic bag with my father's belongings in it. I was there when she opened it. We were standing in the kitchen. She started taking his things out, her face white as a sheet. First his wallet, which he always carried in his hip pocket, so that it had taken on the shape of his right buttock. Then his watch. When she pulled that out of the bag, she started screaming. 'I remember buying this for him! It was a birthday present. He said it was too expensive. Another thing Sir thought was too expensive! The row we had about it!' She waved the watch in the air. 'I told him, give it back to me then! But oh no, he wouldn't do that. First kick up a stink, and then wear the thing after all. Now he *has* given it back to me. It's broken, but he doesn't care about that . . .!' She burst into tears. I couldn't stand it. Screaming was okay. Screaming was normal. But crying . . . I put my arm around her.

'Come on Mum, quietly now.' Sobbing, she rootled about in the bag. She found his trainers and pulled them out. The leather was all cracked. My mother turned the bag upside down and shook it. It was empty. 'The front door key isn't here. He must have had that with him,' she said.

My father had not merely pulled the door shut after him. He had also turned the key in the night lock. He was punctilious in that sense. He left his family safe.

'I hear a lot of grief in your voice,' said my shrink.

I'd gone over to the window. There was a swing in my shrink's garden. I'd often looked out, but I'd never noticed the swing before. I didn't know whether or not Van Kooten had children. Perhaps he had grandchildren.

'I love it when you are silent, then it's just as if you are not here . . .'

I shut my eyes. '. . . *and hear me from afar, and my voice doesn't touch you . . .'*

'You know it,' said Beau in disbelief.

I went and stood next to him with my hands on my hips. 'Pinching poetry from Neruda to impress your patients. Shame on you, Mr van Kooten, what kind of sharp practice is that?'

A schoolboy grin appeared on his face. 'Sometimes it helps.'

I lowered myself into my chair.

'*Allow me to speak to you in your silence too*,' said Beau, 'I think I know how I can help you . . .'

Bang! With a crash the window, the one I'd just walked away from, was smashed to smithereens.

'Jesus Christ what's that?'

Shards of glass fell out of the window frame. The floor was carpeted with fragments. A cold wind blew in through the hole. Half a paving stone was lying next to the radiator.

Van Kooten stood up and led me to the door. 'Stay here!'

Outside, someone was screaming.

A face appeared at the window, white as a ghost. The woman was wearing a pink bathing cap with tufts of wet hair sticking out of it. She grasped the window seat firmly and tried to climb in through the broken glass. Her arms began to bleed but she didn't seem to notice.

Van Kooten strode over to the window. He gave the woman's shoulders a shove.

I started to feel sorry for her. The woman wobbled and fell back into the garden.

'Go away! I'm calling the police!' shouted Beau.

It was quiet for a second, then the woman started shouting insults again.

Van Kooten looked around. There was nothing he could use to barricade the window. So he simply closed the curtain.

The woman went on screaming.

My shrink picked up the phone. With his left hand he opened a drawer. He rummaged around nervously in the drawer. 'What's the number again?'

'One-one-two.'

He threw me a grateful look.

After he'd made the call, he walked over to me.

'You alright?'

'I'll be fine.' I stood there, my legs trembling.

He put an arm around me. 'I'm terribly sorry, Lea.'

'Who is that woman?'

'An ex-patient of mine. Lost cause.'

The curtain ballooned inwards. We both turned round simultaneously to look at the window.

I pressed myself involuntarily closer to my shrink.

'You just go, Lea, I'll deal with this from here.' He opened the door.

'Are you sure?' I could have stood leaning against his chest like that for hours.

'I'll manage. The police will get here soon. I'll see you next week. You're on the right track. Immerse yourself in your feelings. The way you felt back then.' He gave a slight push to the small of my back.

As soon as I was out in the hallway, the door shut behind me.

chapter thirty-two

You were enchanted by the Christmas tree with all its decorations and fairy lights. The crib with all the little figures in it spent more time in you and your sister's room than next to the tree. That's fine, as long as you both have fun.

'Lea Meyer speaking.'

'Hello Lea, it's me.'

'Hello Mum.'

'Listen, I've been thinking. About you and that psychiatrist.'

'Yes?'

'I don't want you saying unpleasant things about my marriage.'

'What?!'

'I don't want you to blacken your father's name.'

I burst out laughing.

'The man's dead, Lea. He can't defend himself. I don't think it's fair.'

'Not fair? Who's the one who's always blackened his name? My whole life I've been forced to hear about all the things he did wrong!'

'I've been open with you, yes. But you wanted me to be. You always wanted to know everything and I've always told you everything. As honestly as I could . . .'

My mother was right. Honesty was something she valued very highly. If I asked a question, she'd give me an answer. That was why I'd always been aware of how unbearable my mother's existence must have been.

It started the day she was born. A month before she was due my grandmother's womb ruptured. Bleeding like an ox, they took my mother's mother to the hospital. Family tradition has it that she stood on her head in the ambulance. They drove straight past the nearest hospital, because it was protestant and my grandmother was a catholic, like my father's parents. So they chugged along for another ten minutes. Unborn life was sacred. If a choice had to be made between mother and child, the child would take precedence, that was a fact you couldn't argue with.

'For God's sake save my wife,' my grandfather begged. 'I've already got four children at home . . .'

The baby came into the world blue and lifeless. It was laid at the foot of the bed. The hospital staff did all they possibly could to save my grandmother. They succeeded.

Only much later did they notice that the baby was moving. A girl.

My grandmother took against the little girl from the very start. My mother described to us in graphic detail how our grandmother used to roll her up in a carpet and stamp on her. How she hit her, denigrated her, abused her. And how she resolved never to do that to her own brood. *Make me a good mother to my children. Make me a good mother to my children. Make me a good mother to my children.* My mother repeated this mantra to herself as she stepped up to the altar with my father.

Perhaps she ought to have resolved to become a good wife too. Perhaps that might have helped . . .

'Lea Meyer speaking.'

'Hi, Lea!'

'Hello Birgit.'

'Did you get my tape yet?'

'Tape? What tape?'

'I sent you a video. With clips on it. Me singing and Steef playing guitar. Steef's father filmed it. He bought a new camera specially. It looks really cool.'

'Nice.'

'Nice? This isn't a hobby, don't get the wrong idea, this is deadly serious. I'm going to keep working at it. Steef's going to make copies of the tape so we can send them to a bunch of record companies. And to Hennie Huisman. This'll definitely be my breakthrough. There's a load of really good songs on it. One of them's about Dad.'

'Oh. About Dad.'

'Yes, I thought maybe you'd like that one. I've figured it out, by the way.'

'What have you figured out?'

'Well, last week I had this discussion with Steef. I was wondering what I'd do if I had only a few hours to live. How you'd want to fill the time, so to speak. I know the answer now . . .'

I walked out into the hall. There was a fat envelope on the floor with Birgit's handwriting on it. 'Hey, I think I can see that tape of yours lying on the mat.'

'. . . I'd want to be in a concert hall with a symphony orchestra. A big orchestra with all the instruments. I'm singing, accompanied by the orchestra. That would be great. Them playing my music and me singing.'

'And then you'd want to die?'

'Yes. Why not? Once I'd done that, there'd be no point doing anything else. That would be such a kick. The ultimate kick. Oh, Lee, I can see Steef coming . . . He's nice and early. I'm going to cook dinner. I'll hang up now. You'll look at my video, won't you?'

The engaged tone.

Birgit had written SONGS FOR MY LITTLE SISTER LEA in red felt pen on the sleeve of the video, with little hearts all around the words. 'Skin-diving' was the second track. Under the song titles it said in blue felt pen '*And One Lullaby for my Little Nephew*'. There were little stars next to that one.

I stuck the tape in the video machine and ran it forward to the second clip. It started with a close-up of Steef's hand on the guitar. When the camera panned back, you could see that he was sitting cross-legged on the floor next to the open fireplace. I recognised the interior of Birgit's house. The fire was lit. Birgit was sitting in front of it. She was wearing a cowboy hat and a black leather jacket. Steef had jeans on, and a grey woollen sweater. Once the intro was over, the camera focused on my sister. She sang in a low, husky voice.

I'm just a teenage girl
not a woman yet
hear the slammin' door
don't get out of bed

Realising later
'tis my dad who went away
not just for a short time —
for an infinite stay

I'm just a teenage girl
not a woman yet
still he decided
to go under and get wet

Skin-diving's what he was thinking
his body and his brains
nothing to remember
the slamming door remains

No other memories
than a hot August day
his last exhalation
he's gone and stays away.

chapter thirty-three

12th March 1969

When you were almost three you got the measles, but they were gone again completely after a few days.

'Tell me, Lea, why did you bring forward our appointment?'

'I just had to talk to you. Partly because of last time. Did you manage to sort it out alright?'

The window had been boarded up with chipboard.

'Don't worry. That all worked out fine. I called the Crisis Service. They took the woman into their care.'

'Oh. The Crisis Service. Well, that's good then. It really was terrible, wasn't it?'

'Yes, very unpleasant.' Van Kooten went over to his espresso machine. 'Coffee?'

'Yes please. You're looking very smart today.'

'Thank you.'

My shrink was wearing a stylish black Italian suit. His shoes were freshly polished, the toes gleamed at me.

'Here's your coffee.' His glance met mine for a second. The sparkle had gone from his eyes. He looked tired, dejected even. It didn't suit him.

'The other reason I'm here is Birgit.'

'Your older sister, right?'

'Yes. She sent me a videotape. With songs she's written. One of them was about my father.'

Van Kooten put his cup down on the table. I had his full attention.

'I looked at the clip. And do you know what happened? I cried. Really, floods of tears. I must have cried for at least three minutes. All the time the song was playing.'

Van Kooten nodded with satisfaction. 'Good. Very good.'

'How can you say that? It wasn't good at all. It was god-awful.'

My shrink smiled. 'My dear Lea, let me explain.'

I went pale. He'd never called me dear before.

'I wanted to tell you last time, but I was interrupted.'

We both looked at the window.

'Before I go on, I want to ask you a question.' Van Kooten tried to make eye contact with me. Was he finally about to make an indecent suggestion? I crossed my fingers behind my back. 'Have you had any more fits of crying since you heard the song?'

'No.'

Beau looked disappointed for a moment. Then his face lit up again. 'Would you bring the video with you some time? Then we can watch it together.'

Guiltily, I stared at my feet.

'You've still got it, haven't you?'

I shrugged.

The last shot was of Birgit's open fireplace. The credits rolled across it.

Produced by Birgit Cornelissen
Performed by Birgit Cornelissen
Lyrics by Birgit Cornelissen
Music by Birgit Cornelissen
Styling by Birgit Cornelissen
Make-up by Birgit Cornelissen
Video by Wim de Wit
Video-editing by Wim de Wit
Guitar: Stefan de Wit
Copyright: Birgit Cornelissen

The closing shot had given me an idea.

Burned by Lea Cornelissen

'You burned the tape? How could you do that?' Van Kooten stood up and walked exasperatedly to and fro.

'I didn't ever want to watch it again, not ever! Can't you understand that?'

For a second, and totally unexpectedly, he placed the palm of his hand on the top of my head. 'Relax. It doesn't matter. We'll find a solution.' While I did a lightning calculation of when I'd last washed my hair, my shrink sat down again. 'I've been thinking about you a lot over the past few days.'

'Oh, really?'

Van Kooten heaved a deep sigh. 'I never usually share

personal feelings with my patients. I regard that as a rule, a code of my profession, which not only I but all my colleagues have a duty to respect.'

Come on, come on. Cut the crap, honey.

My shrink cleared his throat. 'I regard you as the exception that proves the rule . . .'

Yes. With a few nonchalant tugs at the lever I'd done it. The jackpot clattered noisily into the tray. *Beau thinks I'm special. I'm more than just an ordinary patient. He has personal feelings for me which he's now going to tell me about. I'll be a good sport. I'll pat him on the back and say, that's alright old man, this sort of thing can happen to the best of us. I forgive you. As long as you take me out for dinner tonight.*

'. . . my mother died the day before yesterday.'

My coffee went down the wrong way. 'Ah, Mr van Kooten,' I managed to say, 'how terrible. My condolences.' I had an uncontrollable fit of coughing.

Van Kooten offered me a Kleenex.

'Was she very old?'

Thank God I can talk normally again.

'Seventy-seven.' My shrink shut his eyes. A look of pain passed across his face. I had a lurking suspicion that he could see his mother before him. 'Marie-Antoinette was a special woman, a very special woman. A beautiful woman. Warm, a warm woman . . . no one can deny that. Unfortunately she was unable to enjoy the autumn of her life. Instead she had to fight. Fight against the many forms of cancer that tormented her.'

Beau was rehearsing his funeral speech. Holy smoke – that's why he had a black suit on! He was probably going to bury her today.

I stood up. 'Shall I go now, Mr van Kooten? You probably have other things to think about than my dead father.'

Van Kooten shook his head.

I hesitated. 'It doesn't matter, not at all. My own problems can wait. I'm so sorry to have come unexpectedly. If I'd known . . .'

'You couldn't have known, Lea. It's alright. Sit down. I'm a doctor first and foremost. If I can help a patient, then I will. My mother would have understood that and approved of it, I'm certain she would.'

'That's extremely decent of your mother, but she's only been dead for a day and a half and my father's been dead for twenty years. She's got more of a right to your er . . . your attention, so to speak.'

Van Kooten gave me a penetrating look. This was neither the time nor the place, but that man's looks made me go weak at the knees.

'That's a very remarkable thing to say, Lea . . .'

I'd actually managed to score a point. Exactly how I'd done it was still a mystery.

'. . . you've put your finger on the most sensitive aspect of the problem, probably without realising . . .'

Shit — he's onto me.

'. . . when your father died . . .'

'Committed suicide, yes.'

'. . . when he died, you didn't pay any particular attention . . .'

Suddenly I understood what he was getting at. 'Mr van Kooten, we're not going to start confusing apples with oranges here, are we? You said yourself just now that your mother was a warm person, and so forth. Perhaps she was even proud of you.'

'She certainly was.'

'My father wasn't proud of me. He was barely aware I existed. Why in God's name should I have "paid attention" when he died?'

Van Kooten stroked his chin with his hand. He hadn't shaved. He was usually Gilette-smooth. Was it normal for psychiatrists to let their stubble grow after a bereavement?

'Whether you like it or not, Lea, when a loved one dies you have to go through a grieving process.'

'Exactly – "a loved one". Your mother may have been among your loved ones but my father wasn't one of mine, I can assure you.'

'But he was once. You were attached to him at one time, there's no getting around it. The first man in your life . . .'

I suddenly had an urgent and inexplicable need to chew something. I searched through my handbag. I always had dental floss and a packet of Xylitol with me for Harry.

'. . . that's your problem in a nutshell,' Van Kooten went on. 'Your father put an end to his own life when you were thirteen. You didn't shed a single tear. That's an abnormal reaction . . .'

I squirmed to and fro in my chair. What an idiotic analysis! I'd never heard anything so ridiculous. 'Who are you to say what's normal and what isn't? My reaction was completely normal. Under the circumstances. And entirely logical too.'

'Don't get angry, Lea . . .'

'It was the end of the holidays, remember? I was going up from seventh grade to high school. I had to go to school that

Monday. I got piles of homework straight away. Do you think I could have gone to the teachers and said, "Sorry, I'm going through a grieving process"?'

'Didn't the school help you then?' asked Van Kooten, surprised.

'They didn't know about it. No one knew. The teachers didn't and neither did the other girls in my class. Do you think I was going to shout it from the rooftops? "How was your holiday?" "Very nice, our whole family went to Spain." "And yours?" "Very nice, my father drowned himself."'

'Do you feel guilty about the fact that you didn't go to the funeral?'

'No. Should I?'

'Certainly not,' said Beau quickly. 'You did what was best for you at the time. As you said, you had to get on with your life, with school, with your friends. As you saw it, you had no choice but to get back into your normal routine as quickly as you could.'

'It wasn't really a matter of choice, Mr van Kooten. I didn't feel anything. I felt nothing for that man at all. Alive or dead, it didn't make a blind bit of difference.'

Van Kooten slowly shook his head. 'But all the same, the grieving process is unavoidable. I even suspect that the fact you went off the rails after Harry Junior was born had something to do with it.'

I gasped for breath. 'Excuse me, but you really are starting to talk psychobabble now. I had a psychosis. One of those postpartum things. It happens to one in every so many women, they told me at the hospital. I was simply unlucky.'

'Nonsense. There's no such thing as a postpartum psychosis.

The question is, why did you turn your back on reality? Just think about it. You've told me that Harry's crazy about the little one. That ever since Junior was born he's wanted to live to be a hundred. Perhaps that was too much to bear. Perhaps your brain thought, "This isn't logical. Father Harry wants to live for ever, father Kees jumps in the Sloterplas. Something has gone wrong somewhere. Something in my life has gone very wrong." And that's when your mind started to wander.'

'Wait a minute, let's keep our feet on the ground here. Something went wrong alright. My forceps delivery, remember? That's the reason I went round the bend.'

Van Kooten made a dismissive gesture. 'That was just the trigger. The real cause lies deeper. Much deeper. There are plenty of women who go through a dreadful childbirth. They don't all end up in solitary confinement.'

I didn't know what to say to that.

My shrink didn't say anything more either.

He probably wants to give his words time to sink in.

I chewed fanatically on my Xylitol and stared at the chipboard.

Van Kooten remained silent.

'If I understand you correctly, you say I have yet to go through a grieving process. Because of my father's death.'

'Exactly,' my shrink answered happily.

'You make it sound as if it's up to me simply to get on with it.'

'Allow me to help you. This is the perfect time to bring your feelings to the surface. The birth of your child has exposed your nerves, so to speak.'

'Mm . . .'

'I know you're not exactly keen on the idea. Patients are

rarely filled with enthusiasm when I suggest they look the past full in the face. That's why I always tell them, think of me as a dentist. The dentist tells you it's high time for a root canal treatment. Roots, roots – know what I mean?'

I rolled my eyes.

'It's painful. I can't deny that. It's an unpleasant, painful procedure. But it does you an enormous amount of good. Who knows how much misery it may spare you.'

'Supposing I try it – and I say supposing. How do I go about it, how does one start such a process?'

Van Kooten nodded earnestly. 'To be honest, I think it will be very difficult in your case. You've repressed your grief for twenty years. Your feelings about your father are hidden away beneath a thick, deeply frozen layer of ice.'

'And you're going to melt it?' At last an idea that I liked the sound of. If it were to involve an open hearth, a bearskin rug and a bottle of bubbly, it would be heaven.

He smiled. 'We've already made a start. Why do you think I was so enthusiastic when you told me your sister's video made you cry? It's a real shame you threw that tape away.'

'I'm sure Birgit would give me another copy . . .'

'You think so? That would be excellent. Although I don't think it's going to be enough.' Van Kooten stood up and paced up and down his office. His black suit fitted him like a glove.

'Are you in mourning too now?' I asked, curious.

He stopped. 'Actually I am, yes. The process started when I was sitting next to my mother in the hospital. She was on a heavy dose of morphine. I held her hand. My brother was sitting on the other side of the bed. We knew she might leave us at any moment.'

'And your father?'

'He died five years ago.'

'A stroke?' I guessed.

'Traffic accident.'

'Gee . . .'

'My brother's a psychiatrist too. He's two years older than me. My mother passed away without regaining consciousness. We kissed her and then fell into each other's arms. It was a special moment. "I wish you a good grieving process," my brother said. He wished me the same when my father died.'

'And did it work?'

Van Kooten nodded. 'Yes. It was a very intense period, but I got through it and out the other side.'

'And now you're about to go through it again?'

'I hope so, yes.'

'What's it like exactly, that kind of a process?'

Van Kooten went over to his desk and rummaged in a drawer. 'The process of mourning involves a number of different phases. I've written a leaflet about it. I'll give you a copy. In here you can read about how the various phases generally go . . .'

He handed me a leaflet with a shiny, black-and-white front page.

Tonight I could Write the Saddest of Poems
Mourning, step by step
A practical guide
by Dr Beau van Kooten

'Wow, Mr van Kooten, I didn't know you were a specialist.'

'"Specialist" may be overstating it. I've made a thorough study of the subject, that's true. Grief is more common than you'd think. And not only when someone dies; people sometimes go through a grieving process after a divorce, even after moving house.'

'Really? I didn't know that.' I scratched my chin. 'I've been divorced once and I've moved house lots of times. Without finding myself grieving about it. Maybe I'm simply incapable of grieving. Are there people like that, who just don't have it in them?'

Van Kooten put his hand on my shoulder.

I trembled.

'Don't worry, Lea. Everyone can do it. You too.' He sat down. 'My dear Lea, what do you think, are you ready to start grieving?'

I flipped through the leaflet. I read the last paragraph.

Allow yourself time to find a path through your own emotions, to experience the entire process and finally to take leave of the dead in the way your instincts tell you to. It's a long, difficult process, but a necessary one. Death is a fact of life.

'Well, what can I say? If you really think it's necessary.'

'I don't think so, I know so.'

'Then I'll simply have to do it, right?'

Van Kooten clapped his hands together. 'Wonderful. Excellent. Then we'll start straight away.'

I looked at him, frightened.

My shrink stood up and started pacing the room again. 'I've

just thought of a little plan. It may sound strange to you, but I think it might be a very good way to start you off . . .' He stood still. His eyes had their old twinkle back. 'I want you to come to my mother's cremation.

chapter thirty-four

20th May 1969

The little girl Marny next door often comes to play with you, so you have a friend while Birgit is at school. You love it when school finishes for the day.

'What are you up to?'

I was wriggling into a simple black dress when Harry came in.

'I have to go to a cremation.' I bent down to get my patent leather shoes.

He yawned. 'Anyone I know?'

'No, I'd have told you if it was.'

Harry lay on his back on the bed. 'Do you realise I was up four times last night? Four times!'

'It was your turn, my love.'

'I know. I just thought I'd mention it. When does a baby start sleeping through the night?'

'No idea. One of Birgit's friends has been driving up and down the highway every night with her son for the past year and a half. If she doesn't, he screams the whole neighbourhood down.'

Harry groaned.

'Have you seen my black clutch bag anywhere?'

He turned over onto his stomach. 'I think it's on top of the coat stand.'

'I'm off then, darling. I'll be back for dinner.'

'Wait a moment.'

I already had one foot outside the door.

'Where did you say you were going?'

'To a cremation.'

'Whose?'

I bit my lip. 'Marie-Antoinette. Mother of . . .'

'Corine, right?' Harry yawned and shut his eyes. 'See, I do listen to all your stories about your tennis-club friends. Give her my condolences.'

'Bye, darling.' I went up to him and gave him a quick peck on the cheek. 'I really must go now, my love. Otherwise I'll be late.'

I'd arranged to meet my shrink at the crematorium. He had told me that attending the ceremony could trigger a break-through in my grieving process.

If you open yourself up to the grief of those present, you'll see that all the hidden pain will come to the surface of its own accord.
Think about your father. Think about the thirteen-year-old girl he abandoned, without even saying goodbye.

When Beau put it like that, I felt tears come to my eyes.

Let your tears fall freely, Lea. You won't be the only one. I'll be
there to stand by you. We'll grieve together. You for your father
and I for my mother . . .

I parked my car near the crematorium.

My psychiatrist wants to grieve with me. Not just a quick screw on
the desk, no, you must be kidding. With Lea you want to try
having a good grieve.

The hall was packed. Marie-Antoinette's coffin was covered in
white flowers. Next to the coffin stood a grand piano. My shrink
was sitting in the front row. The seat to his left was empty.

Hesitantly, I walked towards him.

When Van Kooten saw me, he winked. 'Ah, there you are.
I've saved you a seat.'

'Are you sure? I'd be just as happy sitting at the back.'

'No, out of the question.'

The man to his right mumbled something.

I nodded at him, but he didn't respond.

'That's my brother,' Van Kooten said, 'Pierre! This is Lea
Meyer, Lea, this is Pierre van Kooten.'

'Pleased to meet you,' I said.

Pierre van Kooten grabbed my hand and squeezed it almost
to a pulp. 'Glad you could come,' he said, in a husky voice.

My shrink's brother was wearing a pair of grey overalls torn
off at the knee and a black sweater with a pattern of snowdrops
on it. His grey hair was tangled, he had three days' growth of
beard and his eyes were bloodshot. Only his angular jaw
betrayed the fact that he was related to Beau.

I sat down.

'My brother's taking it hard,' Beau whispered in my ear. 'He's not eating, not sleeping, he's been going around in the same clothes for days on end. I tried to get him into a suit, but he refused.'

Pierre wiped his right sleeve across his cheek.

'My mother knitted that sweater for him last year. Wearing it gives Pierre the feeling he's close to her.'

'Is your brother further along in the grieving process than you are?' I asked.

Van Kooten nodded. 'He's always quicker. At everything. I'm still in the first phase.'

'You're numb, you still can't believe it.'

'Very good, Lea.'

'Whereas your brother is irritable and restless.'

'Exactly.'

'Which phase have I reached then exactly, do you think?'

An old woman with a Zimmer frame shuffled towards Van Kooten.

Beau stood up to receive her condolences.

Pierre followed his example. He spread his arms wide. 'Aunt Emily, that I should see you here, next to my mother's coffin.' He pulled the little old lady towards him over the top of the Zimmer frame and broke into sobs.

Beau sat down again. 'Actually, I think you've got stuck in the first phase. One can describe that phase as characterised by a complete lack of feeling . . .'

A man in a morning suit sat down at the piano. He laid his hands on the keyboard, waited a few moments and then began playing with his eyes closed.

When I looked to one side I saw that my shrink had his eyes closed too. I tried to open myself up to the music. I couldn't. Piano music always sets my nerves on edge.

My father was obsessed with classical music. A year before he died he developed a system of musical notation which was designed to make the existing method obsolete. He assigned combinations of letters to every note. A sort of doh-re-mi, but thoroughly comprehensive. Thanks to this invention, it would be much easier for people to read and play music. My father gave me piano lessons using his system, but I didn't get much further than the first few bars of *Für Elise*.

Night after night he worked on his invention. He laid books of music by Beethoven and Bach on the table, stuck long strips of paper over the staves and wrote out the music again on top, according to his own system of notation. To see if he'd got it right, he played the pieces through on the piano. The same phrases every time, until it drove my mother, Birgit and me completely round the bend.

Eventually, my father bought an electric piano. From then on he played to himself every evening with the head-phones on. You could see him, but you couldn't hear him. Actually, that was just as disturbing.

My father thought the system would make him world-famous. He sent it to publishers of sheet music all over Europe in the hope that they'd see what a brilliant mind was at work.

Unfortunately my father really was a genius – in the sense that he wasn't recognised. He got polite letters back from the publishers. *Sehr geehrte Herr, Dear Sir, monsieur, nous regrettons, nice effort, und so weiter, und so weiter*. Don't call us, we'll call you.

According to my mother, the rejections finished him off. Immediately before his death he received a *nein-danke*-letter from the German publisher in which he'd invested all his remaining hopes. After that he deposited the entire system at a public notary's office, so that at least no other lunatic could run off with the credit.

The pianist finished playing.

A thin old woman was standing on the podium. Her grey hair was wound into a tight bun and she was wearing a long skirt with a shiny black blouse and a string of pearls. Her reading glasses hung from a gold chain.

'Frederique van Ravensteyn, one of my mother's sisters . . .' whispered Beau.

The woman laid a sheet of paper on the lectern and put on her glasses. 'Dear family and friends. We are gathered here to pay our last respects to my darling sister, Marie-Antoinette. Her life was one of love. Love for everything that grows and flourishes. Love for those around her, especially for her husband Paul and her sons Pierre and Beau . . .' She looked in our direction for a moment.

The Van Kooten brothers bowed their heads in unison. Pierre put his hand over his eyes. A tear ran down my shrink's cheek.

Frederique went on praising her sister. Her voice had a metallic ring to it. '. . . you had good times and you had bad times. But you remained yourself to the very end'.

Pierre shook his head. 'No, not true,' he mumbled.

Beau laid his hand on Pierre's shoulder. He shook it off.

'. . . the final period of your life was a struggle. An uneven struggle which you lost . . .'

'They poisoned her,' Pierre mumbled. 'It didn't have to be that way. She was bald and nauseous on her deathbed. The scoundrels . . .'

'. . . Marie-Antoinette,' said Frederique loudly, 'I'll miss you terribly. I hope you're with Paul and Mum and Dad now . . .' She nodded towards a man waiting in the wings. He came forward and handed her a bouquet of white roses. Beau's aunt stepped carefully down from the podium. She walked slowly towards the coffin. '. . . Farewell my darling, I've got forty white roses here for you. I will lay them at your feet . . .' She placed the flowers at the very end of the coffin. '. . . Goodbye my darling sister, will you . . .' Her voice cracked.

All around me, people pulled handkerchiefs out of their bags. A man in the first row, who was recording the whole ceremony on his handycam, stood up to accompany Mrs van Ravensteyn back to her seat. Pierre sobbed uncontrollably.

Beau's shoulders were shaking, but he didn't make a sound.

Hesitantly I put my hand on his shoulder. 'You alright?'

He looked aside at me. His eyes were moist. 'I'm fine, Lea. This is fine. What about you?'

'I had a lump in my throat just now.'

'And?'

'I swallowed it.'

Beau shook his head. 'Let yourself go. That's why you're here, isn't it?'

I sighed. 'I know. I'm sorry. It was gone before I had time to think.'

'Shh!' said a woman behind us.

Pierre had gone over to stand next to the coffin. He took a chequered tea towel out of his trouser pocket and dabbed his eyes. 'Can everybody hear me from here?' he asked in a hoarse voice.

People on the front row nodded.

'Dear Mummy . . .' Pierre began.

'You'll have to speak up,' someone called out from the back.

Pierre cleared his throat. 'Is that better?'

'Fine!'

'Dear Mummy . . . You are a mother . . . You were a mother in a million . . .' Pierre stroked the flowers on the coffin. '. . . I know you wanted to go to Daddy . . . You missed him so much . . . He was the moon, you the sun . . . and Beau and I were the stars . . . That's what Daddy always said, remember, Mum . . .?'

Beau nodded. Tears were pouring down his cheeks.

'. . . I'm so glad I'm your son, Mummy . . . You made a man of me. I do so wish your final years had been better. Without pain, without hospitals, without doctors . . . It shouldn't have been this way . . .' Pierre fell to his knees. '. . . I want to read you a psalm, Mummy. Your God is not my God, but now, at this moment, there's nothing I'd like more.' He looked out into the hall.

Most of those present put their hands together.

Pierre laid the tea towel on the ground. He took a crumpled piece of paper out of his trouser pocket. 'I wanted to be able to recite it by heart, Mum, I really did . . .' He unfolded the piece of paper, coughed twice and read the text in an unexpectedly powerful voice.

Marie-Antoinette would have been proud, Pierre didn't stumble over it once.

The Lord is my shepherd, I shall not want;
He makes me lie down in green pastures.
He leads me beside still waters;
He restores my soul.
He leads me in paths of righteousness
For His name's sake.

Even though I walk through the valley of the shadow of death,
I fear no evil;
For Thou art with me;
Thy rod and Thy staff,
They comfort me.

Thou preparest a table before me
In the presence of my enemies;
Thou anointest my head with oil,
My cup overflows.
Surely goodness and mercy shall follow me
All the days of my life;
And I shall dwell in the house of the Lord
For ever.

'Are you coming to the buffet?' Beau asked.

We were standing in the hallway of the crematorium.

I shook my head.

He put his arm around me. 'Lea, dear Lea, I'm so happy for you.'

I swallowed and nodded. I couldn't speak.

'Your mascara has run.' Beau wiped my cheek clean. 'Shall I call you a taxi?'

Again I shook my head.

'Are you sure you'll be alright?'

I nodded.

'I just want to ask you one question. Just one. Why are you so sad now?'

When the answer came to me, my face crumpled. 'Because of my father,' I said. 'Because my father is dead.' As I looked at Beau, tears welled up in my eyes.

'Exactly,' he said. 'This is the start of it. You feel pain. Pain, because you have lost your father. It's quite wonderful, actually, that you can mourn so purely and so completely after such a long time.' He gave me a paper tissue. 'From now on you can expect to be overwhelmed by great waves of grief. You know that, don't you? I tell you so it doesn't come as a shock. You may become angry. That's part of the grieving process too.'

I let out a quivering sigh.

'Just go home now. Get some rest. Take it as it comes. I'll see you next week.'

chapter thirty-five

You're starting to want to go to school yourself, but you'll have to wait until you're four, which seems a long time off to you.

It was my Filipino girl who opened the door. She was holding Junior in one arm. 'Hello Mrs Meyer, you alright?'

Junior reached out his tiny arms towards me.

His little toothless mouth was irresistible. I laughed through my tears.

My Filipino asked if I'd eaten yet. She looked worried.

I grabbed Junior's little foot and bit it.

He shrieked with pleasure.

Harry was lying on the bed in the bedroom. His mouth was hanging open, his shirt was crumpled. I shook him by the shoulder. He didn't react.

'Harry! Wake up.'

He woke with a start. 'What time is it?'

'Four thirty. Have you been asleep all this time?'

'I don't know. What time did you say it was?'

'Half past four.'

He sat up. 'Shit, I was supposed to meet a client.' He blinked a few times. 'What happened to you? You look as if you've seen a ghost.'

I pulled off my skirt.

'What are you doing?'

'What does it look like? I'm going to bed. And for now at least, I'm not going to get up.'

'What do you mean, what's the matter with you?'

I slid down between the sheets. 'Just now, after the cremation, I had a terrible fit of crying. It was awful, I couldn't stop.'

Harry yawned. 'Yeah, that's how it goes, right? At funerals.'

'This was no ordinary crying fit. I'm in mourning. Beau says so.'

'Beau?' Harry frowned. 'When did you speak to him?'

'He was at the cremation. It was his mother.'

'I thought . . . What were you doing at Beau's mother's funeral?'

'Cremation. She was cremated. Beau asked me to come. To trigger off the grieving process.'

'Grieving process? What grieving process?'

'For my father, of course.'

'Hey, wait a minute, did you just say what I think you said? You go to the cremation of the your psychiatrist's mother to start a grieving process for your father?'

I smoothed out my pillow. 'It's a bit unorthodox, maybe, but I needed some kind of trigger in order to start mourning, right? And now I am.'

'Now you're what? Mourning?'

I nodded.

'For your father?'

'Yes.'

'Who's been dead for twenty years?'

'Go on, make fun of it, Harry. I've never mourned. You know that, don't you? But I have to.'

'Who says?'

'Nature. A grieving process is unavoidable.' I pulled open the drawer to my bedside table. 'Read this. It's all in here.'

Harry glanced at the leaflet Beau had given me. 'Jesus Christ, Lea, what have you fallen for this time?'

I felt angry. For a moment I wondered whether it was a normal kind of anger or whether this was the next phase of the grieving process already. 'I knew it! I knew you wouldn't take it seriously.'

'What am I expected to say, Lea? I thought you were going to see that idiot in order to get better.'

'In order to get better, I first have to grieve.'

'Now, just listen to yourself for a moment, darling. You're completely off your rocker. First all that bullshit you came up with after the baby was born, and now this . . .'

'Shut your face, Harry. I've a right to my grieving process. My father went and jumped in the lake when I was thirteen, for God's sake. Thirteen!'

'So what? You've always told me he was a bastard.'

'That's what my mother drummed into me, yes. And I believed her. I took her at her word. You don't grieve for a bastard. But that bastard was my father . . .' I started to cry.

Harry sighed. He came and sat next to me and took my hand.

'He's gone,' I sobbed. 'He didn't even say goodbye . . .'

'You don't know that, Lea.'

'What do you mean I don't know that? I know that perfectly well.'

Harry shrugged. 'Maybe he came and stood next to your bed for a moment before he left. Maybe he stroked your hair and spoke to you, while you slept.'

I cried even harder.

Harry put his arms around me. 'Did he actually leave a note?'

I shook my head. 'No. Nothing at all.'

It was silent for a moment.

'Maybe there was a note,' I said slowly, extricating myself from Harry's arms. 'Maybe my father left something for me. And my mother stole it . . .'

I could see it all happening. To think I hadn't thought of it before! Brooke did the same thing with Ridge's letter to Caroline. Ridge had put the letter on Caroline's pillow and that bitch Brooke, who had set her heart on Ridge, intercepted it. Unaware that Ridge loved her, Caroline married his brother. The wrong Forrester, because her heart really belonged to Ridge. The business with the letter only came to light much later. A good sixty episodes later.

I never got the letter, Ridge!

A fantastic scene, I've got it on video.

Harry rubbed my back. 'You're getting a bit carried away, my love.'

I lay down and pulled the sheets over me.

'Now, calm down and tell me what this grieving process is all about.'

'Have you got a handkerchief?'

Harry went to the bathroom and came back with a piece of toilet paper.

I blew my nose. 'Beau says it's like this . . .'

Harry made an impatient gesture. 'Please, let's leave Beau out of this, I can't stand to hear his name mentioned one more time.'

' . . . I keep thinking about my father. And that makes me feel very unhappy . . . About what happened and so on . . .'

'So what do you think about?'

' . . . his last evening . . .' Suddenly there was a lump in my throat. I didn't want to cry. Not again. I took a deep breath. ' . . . the thought that he was there at home with us and that he knew all along that those were his last hours. He was never going to see us again . . . Birgit said he acted a bit oddly, he was a bit giggly. Like when you're a kid and you have a secret . . .'

My father is sitting at the piano. Some time long after midnight he stops playing. He takes off the headphones and puts his glasses down on the table. He walks over to the coat stand, gets his bunch of keys out of his coat pocket and removes the door key from it. He opens the front door, steps out onto the walkway, pulls the door shut behind him quietly and turns the key in the lock. He takes the lift down to the ground floor. He walks out of the block of flats and turns right. It's warm outside. He walks to the Sloterplas, a quiet walk by the light of the streetlamps.

After about ten minutes he reaches the edge of the lake. He looks about him. He's alone. Then he gets into the water.

Does he take a run at it and leap in, hoping the water will swallow him up? Or does he wade calmly out into deep water? Does he swim?

My father is a good swimmer. I've never understood how he managed to do it. As a teenager I often tried to sit on the bottom of the swimming pool, but I never could. After a short time I'd feel I was about to burst. At that point I had to go back up to the surface, whether I wanted to or not.

A person is only capable of drowning himself if he has a strong desire to die. Beau.

My father's clothes and shoes are soaked through. He goes under. Perhaps he sucks in a few lungfuls of water. Water has enough oxygen in it for fish and water beetles. But not enough for my father. His lungs fill with water. The water gets into his blood. His muscles stiffen. He doesn't move any more. He becomes heavy. Heavier and heavier. He sinks to the bottom. His hair waves about, a wreath around his head. His life comes to an end. He ends up on the sandy bottom of the Sloterplas.

I looked at Harry with tears in my eyes. 'I keep trying to understand it. I think to myself, he was ill. You don't do a thing like that otherwise. But if he was ill, why didn't we help him?'

'Maybe he was beyond help. Your mother tried for twenty years. She gave up in the end too.' Harry tucked his shirt into his trousers. 'Don't get angry with me, but do you really think it's sensible to start mourning at this particular moment?'

'It's too late to stop now.'

'And how long is it going to take?' Harry looked at his watch.

'How nice of you to be so concerned all of a sudden. How should I know how long its going to take?' I picked up the leaflet.

> The time people need to take leave of the dead and straighten out their lives again varies. You usually need at least a year to recover from a drastic loss.

'A *year*?' Harry shouted. 'That's ridiculous! You know that's impossible right now. We have a child!'

'Just read what it says for a minute. I'm not doing this for fun.'

> The self-conscious process is by no means a way to escape any of this, nor to bypass any of the stages; it is a natural sequence of events which has to run its course. This is simply one of the things attachment to another person entails. We can speak of griefwork, which has to be completed to make it possible for us to go on.

'Well thank that Beau of yours very much from me . . .!' Harry got up, walked out of the room and pulled the door shut behind him with a bang.

I turned over and tried to sleep. I couldn't. Maybe I could get on with some griefwork. I reached for the telephone.

'Helma Cornelissen speaking.'

'Hello Mum, it's me.'

'What's wrong?'

'I'm unhappy.'

'Yes I can hear that. But why?'

'Because of Dad.' I blew my nose.

She laughed. 'What a row, you sound like an elephant!'

'My psychiatrist says I'm in mourning.'

'I could have told you that. You never really dealt with it. You didn't even go to the funeral.'

'Can you still remember Dad's last evening?'

'Of course I can, Lea. As if it were yesterday. We'd just got divorced, but your father flatly refused to move out of the house. The last few weeks of the school holidays I kept sleeping in different beds. In your bed when you were staying with friends and in Birgit's room while she was abroad. That Sunday evening everyone was back home, so I wanted to sleep in my own bed again. But not next to your father, that was the last thing I had in mind. I got a camp bed and put it in the living room. I told your father he'd have to sleep on it.'

'Jesus Christ, Mum, I didn't know that!' I whispered.

'The next morning the camp bed was still precisely where I'd left it, folded up and untouched. Your father had gone. I knew straight away that something terrible had happened.'

'Really?'

'Yes. That's why he did it, too. That was the first thing the neighbours said. *Now he's really got you*, they said. And that's exactly how it is. It was revenge, Lea, pure revenge. He did it to make me pay. And it worked.'

'But people don't commit suicide out of revenge!'

'You have to see it that way, Lea, I was married to that man for twenty years. In fact I kept him alive for twenty years. Without me he'd have finished himself off a lot sooner . . .'

I didn't say anything.

'. . . after they found him, he plagued me for a long time. You remember?'

'Yes, Mum.'

After they'd dredged up his body and the police had been round, my father's ghost visited my mother every night. At first he was more angry than anything else. He stabbed my mother in the back with a knife, until she woke up soaked with sweat. Or he came and stood next to her bed in a pair of pyjamas which my mother immediately recognised as his. 'Go away, you're dead,' she said, but Kees went on standing there. A few nights later he solemnly lay down next to her.

'Ah, Lea, he came to see me so many times. That time I was half asleep when I suddenly felt he was there again. I slid over towards the window, towards the side I always used to sleep on, so he could get in . . .'

'Didn't either of you say anything?'

'No. I wasn't going to start that.'

According to my mother, my father's ghost wandered the earth for a long time. That was because it was suicide and not a natural death. Apparently a soul that's shuffled off its own mortal coil has to stick around until the end of extra time.

Ten years after the death of my father my mother had a vivid dream.

The police are at the door. *Your husband's down at the station.*

He's asking if you want to come for him.

That's impossible, my husband's been dead for ten years.

He isn't dead, he's with us, in a cell. He wants you to come and fetch him.

I haven't got time now. Tell him I'll come tomorrow.

The following day the police come to the door again.

You no longer need to come, Mrs Cornelissen your husband died in the night.

'That was a sign to me that he'd really gone,' my mother said. 'I burned some incense and he never visited me again after that.'

chapter thirty-six

You and Birgit were always playing schools together. She taught you songs and did all the things she'd seen her teacher do. When you went to school, it was all very familiar to you, because you'd already been there so often in your games and in your imagination.

'Well, what a state of affairs . . .!' Corine stormed into my bedroom. Corine is my tennis partner. She still had her coat on. A stunningly beautiful coat. She threw her Alfa Romeo marque badges onto my bedside table with a dismissive gesture. 'Remind me to take those with me, would you? Ted hates me driving around without emblems.'

I nodded.

'Move over.' She flapped her hand in the air. Sometimes Corine is a little like Cruella de Ville.

'Don't you want to take your coat off?'

'This is a lightning visit, darling. You've no conception of what my schedule looks like for today.' She kicked off her shoes and lay down next to me on the bed. She sighed, turned onto her right side and winked at me. 'You've pulled off a pretty neat trick here, haven't you.'

I looked at her, mystified.

She jogged my shoulder playfully. 'Come on, love, you know you can be honest with me. I think it's a stroke of genius. I'm filled with admiration. The girls at the club too. They couldn't get over it when they heard . . .!'

'Would you like a drink?'

'No thanks. Shall I tell you how it went?'

I plumped up her pillow.

She slid back onto it. 'I ran into Harry last night in the Hotel Americain. An enormous tumbler of whisky in front of him. I said, "Has the little husband managed to slip out for a bit?" He didn't think that was funny. I said, "What's up with you?" The whole story came out in one go, about your father, about Beau, about the grieving process . . .'

I was shocked. 'Did Harry tell you all that?'

'Hey, you've got him by the balls, love. He's no bloody idea where to start. He's thinking about taking all the holiday he's owed.' Corine roared with laughter. 'He'd be free for at least a year! Count your gains.'

Harry under my feet for a year. What a horrifying thought.

'Didn't I *tell* you it was Beau you ought to see? Isn't he heavenly? He gives you exactly what you happen to need. In your case a . . .' Corine gave me a meaningful look and made two quotation marks with bent forefingers, '. . . grieving process.' She lit a cigar and took a drag. 'I'll tell you one thing. Any other stupid psychiatrist would send you straight home if depression was all you could come up with. Not Beau. He understands today's woman better than anyone else I know. If I were to say to

Ted, darling, I'm depressed, he'd say, honey, the Prozac's in the bathroom cabinet next to the Viagra. End of conversation.' She looked around. 'Have you got an ashtray?'

I shook my head.

She flicked her column of ash onto the parquet. 'Doesn't matter. That'll give that girl of yours something to sweep up. Isn't she neat, by the way, your house is spotless! It smells so fresh too. Of limes. I haven't the faintest idea what limes smell like, but I'm sure they must smell fresh like that. Where's she from?'

'The Philippines.'

'I knew it! I had a whole discussion with Loretta about it recently at the tennis club. She swears by her Polish cleaner, but I said to myself, you're crazy my girl, all she's interested in is getting her hands on your man.'

I yawned behind my hand.

'Anyhow, Harry orders one whisky after another, so I join in for a few rounds. I say to Harry, I say, "You know what you should do? You should go home to that darling little woman of yours and spoil her rotten for a change" . . .' She nattered on without pausing for breath.

I usually had a wonderful time listening to Corine's stories. But now I couldn't concentrate. My thoughts wandered. I wanted to tell Corine about the black-fringed water beetle and piano notation systems. I wanted to explain that it felt as if my father had only just died. And that I missed him. That perhaps it sounded strange after all these years, but that really was how I felt . . .

Corine is my tennis partner. I'm not a hundred per cent sure, but I'm eighty-five per cent certain we're friends too.

Friends have to be able to talk about things like that. It says so in *Libelle*.

'. . . well, you can imagine, Harry and I came staggering out of the Americain.' Corine got up and put her shoes on. 'I bundled him into a taxi. He couldn't drive any more, he really couldn't. When I got into my car, I thought, Lea's absolutely right. Absolutely! If she has to go into mourning to get Harry to wipe the baby's bum, then she has to go into mourning . . .' Her index fingers kept waggling up and down. She held the burning cigar clamped between her lips while she spoke. '. . . if I were you, I'd let him sweat until Junior's out of nappies . . .'

'Corine, do you have a good relationship with your father?' I asked cautiously.

She frowned. 'Depends which one you mean. The sperm squirter or the stepdad?'

'Your real father.'

'Well . . .' She took a long drag on her cigar. She was silent for a few seconds. '. . . I was five when he ran off with Currycunt . . .'

'Currycunt?'

'Myriam is of Indonesian extraction, so my mother always called her Currycunt. Still does, actually. You can picture us when I was six years old going to the Efteling funfair with my father and Myriam, and me walking around the whole day shouting, "Currycunt, come and look at this! Currycunt, have you got any sweets for me?" My father was furious and Myriam was in tears. I didn't know what was the matter. My mother had also said, 'Give Currycunt my *hate*felt greetings."

'Do you still see much of your father?'

'Mm, yeah, about twice a year. He always acts pleasant, you

know, as if he's really interested in me. Myriam too. She's quite nice, actually. But still, whenever I'm there drinking coffee with them, I can't help feeling I'm betraying my mother . . .'

'That's how I feel too,' I stammered, 'when I'm telling Beau all the things that were nice about my father. It feels as if I'm lying. You know what? My father used to tell me his own made-up stories before I went to sleep.'

'Really? How sweet.' Corine buttoned up her coat.

'They all had the same central character. Do you know what he was called?' I smiled.

'No idea, but I really do have to go now, Lea, otherwise I'll screw up my whole schedule.'

'Oh yes, of course, sorry.'

'Don't take our Beau too seriously, will you love? The dys-functional parent-child relationship is his core business, you need to remember that. Throw enough mud and some of it's bound to stick.' She blew me a kiss.

Two hours later, Ted came to pick up the car emblems. He gave me his condolences on the death of my father.

Next come waves of almost physical pain, tears, feelings of abandonment, loneliness and despair, mixed with a fear of the present and of the future. There's often a feeling of guilt about things we did or neglected to do. If our feelings towards the dead person were anything short of entirely positive, then the new freedom often brings a degree of relief with it, which can in its turn contribute to a grave sense of guilt.

chapter thirty-seven

3rd November 1970

The first day at nursery school you were given some rug-making to do. You had to go on with it the next day. You went to the teacher and said, 'I've had enough of this,' and she let you do something else.

Jopie Bamigas was a pain in the neck, a little chap who terrorised the neighbourhood with his practical jokes. The man next door usually got the blame. But that was his own fault, because he was a nasty neighbour. Jopie Bamigas had a dog. The nasty neighbour had kicked the dog when he thought Jopie wasn't looking. Jopie would pay him back for that. He'd play a trick on him.

The neighbour happened to have a new car. He was very proud of it. One evening, when no one was about, Jopie crawled under the neighbour's new car. He bored a hole in the floor. Then he put a garden hose in the hole, fixed the hose to the tap and filled the car with water. Ice-cold water! Not just ankle deep and not half full, but right up to the roof, so that it almost looked as though nothing was odd about it, because water is transparent. Jopie bunged up the hole nice and tight. No one could see that the car was full of water, only Jopie knew that.

'And we do too, right Dad? But we won't give Jopie away.'

It would be a very unpleasant surprise for the nasty neighbour! The next morning he came out all unsuspecting. Jopie was standing just around the corner. The neighbour went over to his car. He opened the door.

'I don't know any more than that, Mr van Kooten, because by then my father was laughing too much to say any more.'

While I was describing it, I could see him as clearly in my mind's eye. His face flushed red, the saliva in the corners of his mouth.

'Pierre! Cookie!'

Startled, I looked around. On a stool in the corner of Beau's office stood a cage with a large, white bird in it. *'Pierre! Cookie!'*, it screeched, hopping to and fro on its perch.

'What's that creature doing here?'

Van Kooten smiled. 'That's Ludo, my brother's cockatoo. Pierre's off travelling. Ludo's usually with him at his practice. When Pierre has to go away, he always brings him here to stay with me. Ludo finds it hard to be alone.'

'I didn't see him there at all.'

'You were deep in thought when you came in.' Beau always noticed everything.

'Cookie!'

Van Kooten stood up. 'If he doesn't get enough attention, he acts up. He starts destroying his cage and mutilating himself.' He went over to the creature. 'No more cookies, Ludo, you've had enough.' My shrink spoke to the bird as if it was a child.

'Have you ever seen it do that, mutilate itself?' I asked, curious.

'Oh yes, it pulls out its feathers with rage. A terrible sight, such an impressive bird with bald patches all over it.'

'Has your brother had it long?' I really don't know why I asked that.

Van Kooten stuck his finger into the cage and scratched Ludo on the top of the head. 'Two years. It belonged to one of Pierre's patients, a schizophrenic.'

Van Kooten went back to his chair and sat down. 'Fred was an exceptional man. Very intelligent, but unfortunately very ill too. He jumped in front of a train.'

I didn't know what to say.

'He left a note on the kitchen table. It said that he was leaving Ludo to my brother. He'd already taught Ludo the name of his new boss. Pierre discovered that when he came to pick him up.' Van Kooten looked at his feet.

'Do you have any pets?' I asked, to take his mind off Fred.

He sighed. 'Unfortunately not. I'm allergic to most animals. Otherwise I'd have liked cats. What about you, Lea?'

'I'd like a dog. Harry wouldn't, though. I think he's afraid of dogs.'

It was quiet for a moment.

My shrink picked up where we'd left off. 'You were telling me about your father and Jopie Bamigas . . .'

I nodded enthusiastically. 'We used to laugh together a lot. I had a comic book called *Jan, Jans and the Children*, it had a picture in it of a little girl called Catootje, she was pulling her trousers down and you could see a little bit of bottom. My father always pointed it out to me and it made us giggle like mad. Very childish, of course, but . . .' I took a deep breath. '. . . it's so good to be able to talk about this, Mr van Kooten . . .'

He gave me a friendly nod. 'It's as if you're unburdening yourself of a big family secret. I'm not surprised there were intimate moments between you and your father.'

'Is that what you do when you're in mourning, think back to that kind of thing?'

Van Kooten nodded.

'I don't like it at all.'

'Why not?'

'Because that little girl was me. And he was that father. And because that same father a few years later, well, you know . . .' I turned away. The tears were coming easily again today. 'Do you know what? I don't wear mascara at all any more.' I sniffed. 'There's just no point. I cry so much every day, I keep having to wipe it off my cheeks . . .'

'I see,' said Van Kooten. He ran his eyes over my body.

I was wearing pink leggings and a denim blouse. My mother had given it to me. It was too small for her and too big for me. 'I just grabbed any old thing out of the wardrobe this morning,' I said, feeling my ponytail. I hadn't even got around to washing my hair. I'd lain awake all night and nodded off some time towards morning.

'One of my ex-patients had the same problem,' said Van Kooten. He stroked his chin.

'Really? Did her father drown himself too?'

'No, no, it was just that she got upset so easily, and her mascara kept running. She had to look presentable for work so it was very awkward. In the end she found a particular brand of mascara that really was waterproof. I could ask her which one it was, if you like.'

'Call Harry and tell him, he's the only one who goes around complaining about it all the time.'

'I hear a lot of anger in your voice.'

'You're right about that. Harry doesn't take my grieving process seriously at all. Nobody takes it seriously . . .'

Ludo screeched.

'Nobody?'

'Well you do, of course, but no one else does.'

'What about your mother?'

'When I tell her about it she immediately starts going on about herself. She has a patent on suffering, know what I mean? She's the victim, the martyr who's never had a scrap of love from anyone, not from her own mother, not from her husband . . .'

'That's tough too, isn't it?'

'But what am I supposed to do about it? What's the point of giving me all that information? When her mother died, I lay in my bed every evening crying. Not because I missed my grandmother, but because I thought it was so dreadful for my mother. It seemed like such a terrible thing, to lose your mother. I was very fearful of that.'

'How old were you at the time?'

'Six. *Save your tears, wait until I die*, my mother always said, *then you'll have a reason to cry*. When I thought about that I cried even harder. Then she'd comfort me by saying, *I'm not going to die, Lea. For as long as you need me, I won't die.* She kept her word. Ever since I left home, she's wanted to die. She gets depressed every time she has a birthday, because she hasn't died yet. She's already announced a number of times that she wants to end it all. As soon as she becomes dependent on others, she'll do it. *Imagine if I become incontinent*, she says, *I couldn't stand that. If I have to wear nappies, you and Birgit will have to help me pass over — I want to die with dignity.* She's given her body to science. All the spotty lab assistants in the Netherlands will be able to use her intestines as a skipping rope.' I started to sob. 'My father committed suicide, my mother's been dreaming about doing it for years. I missed his funeral, she won't even have one. No amount of mourning is going to help, Mr van Kooten, I can assure you of that.'

He passed me a tissue. 'What are you doing about medication at the moment?'

I blew my nose. Van Kooten always did that. Whenever I really went to pieces he blithely changed the subject. 'I'm not taking anything any more.' I hadn't taken anything for weeks. My shrink knew that perfectly well.

'And is there still a lot of tension between you and Harry?' Van Kooten was working through his list.

'When he heard that the grieving process could last for as much as a year, he went completely off his head. We argued about it again last night.'

Harry can't stand the fact that I've been lying in bed for days not getting anything done. 'The house is going to the dogs. You're going to the dogs. You stink, did you know that? You can't have had a bath for days.'

'So? That's part of the process, Harry. You've no idea what I'm going through. Just you be glad I'm making a serious effort to sort myself out, for God's sake.'

'So you're going to rot in bed for a year?'

'No. This is going to be the shortest grieving process in history. I'll grieve hard and fast. Just don't keep fucking with me, it'll only last longer if you do . . .'

'Coffee?' Van Kooten was standing up already.

'Yes, please.'

He went over to his espresso machine.

I heaved a deep sigh. 'That Jopie Bamigas, do you think that was my father's alter ego, so to speak?'

'I'm not sure it was that simple, Lea. Maybe there was a bit of him in the nasty neighbour too.'

'That's possible. My father couldn't stand dogs. His favourite insult was 'stupid cur'. I once wrote a verse for St Nicholas' Eve* about it.'

'Was your father easily provoked?'

'That's putting it mildly, Mr van Kooten. No day was complete without a thorough scolding.'

Birgit and I knew how little it took to set him off. If our father started on any kind of do-it-yourself, we headed for cover immediately.

One time he had to fix a new piece of plate glass onto Koertje's pen. Koertje was our Turkish turtledove. He

---

* Small presents are given on St Nicholas' Eve, accompanied by a humorous verse containing mild criticism of the recipient.

lived on the balcony. He was a silver-grey dove, with a black collar around his neck. If you stuck your finger through the hole in his pen he'd bow his head and coo for you. *Coo-kerler-coo-oo-coo-kerler-coo-oo*. It was the kind of pet that needed hardly any attention. We were forever forgetting to give him anything to eat. Sometimes for weeks. He got increasingly good at going without.

Koertje got to be very old, he outlived my father by a long time. One day he was sitting very still in a corner of his pen. He used to sit there quite a lot, so I didn't think anything of it. Until I looked again a few days later and he was still sitting in exactly the same position. So I thought I'd just go over and feel him. He was stiff and cold. I thought birds always lay on their backs when they were dead. I felt slightly guilty, as the food tray was empty again. But I still think it was old age.

My father was going to cut the new plate of glass for Koertje's pen from an old piece. He had a special glass-cutter to do it with, it made a squealing noise as it cut through the glass.

The glasscutter made short work of my father's finger. He bled like an ox and swore like a trooper. The anger he was capable of! It always turned out to be our fault, or my mother's fault. It was never his fault. So he never cursed the hell out of himself, only other people.

Van Kooten put the coffee down in front of me. 'You were saying something about a verse?'

'It was part of a surprise I made for my father. We'd drawn straws for St Nicholas' Eve. I'd got my father.'

'How old were you?'
'About eight, I think.'

I made a big handkerchief out of a piece of white cloth. I sewed a seam around it neatly, using my mother's old hand-driven sewing machine, a gleaming black Pfaff. I embroidered a large K in the middle. I made an outsized sticking plaster out of a long piece of card. A day or two beforehand, I showed my mother the surprise presents and the verse that went with them.

'This doesn't seem very advisable to me, Lea. You know what your father's like. Let's keep it till last and see what state of mind he's in.'
My father was in a good mood when he got his surprise. While my mother and I looked on nervously, he read out the verse.

> *Dear Kees,*
> *Next time you want to curse and shout,*
> *Stuff this hankie in your mouth,*
> *And if the hankie doesn't do it,*
> *Stick this sticking plaster to it.*
> *St Nicholas*

He had a good laugh about it, because he did have a sense of humour. All the same, he never used the anti-swearing devices. That was a disappointment, I'd been hoping he really would find them useful. When he was in urgent need of them, I sometimes rushed up to him with the handkerchief. 'Here you are, Dad, quick, stuff it in your mouth!'

But at that point he didn't want to know. And he didn't laugh then.

'What do you feel when you think about that now?' asked Van Kooten.

I took a sip of coffee. 'Regret.'

Silence.

Van Kooten waited for an explanation.

'I have so few memories of my own. He died when I was thirteen. I know him mainly from my mother's stories. If you ask me what sticks in my mind, then pretty much all I can come up with is the water beetles, the ride around the room on his shoulders, Jopie Bamigas, the fits of temper, the piano notation system and the one time he asked me how I was doing at school.'

'Imagine he was still alive . . .'

I sat up. 'Then I'd want to talk to him. I'd want him to tell me in his own words why he was the way he was.'

'Is there any other way to find out?'

'What do you mean?'

'Some of your father's relatives are still alive, maybe they could help you.'

I put my empty cup down on the table. That was an idea.

'What would you want to say to your father, if he was here now?'

'That I . . . that I'm sorry . . .' I stared at my lap. There was a whitish stain on my leggings. Junior had probably thrown up on them. 'For the last few years of his life my father and I didn't really have any contact with each other. I ignored him. Out of solidarity with my mother.'

'Did he try to get closer to you?'

The buzzer went.

Van Kooten stood up and went to the door.

Reluctantly I picked up my bag. Time flew when I was with Beau. Sometimes I was in the middle of a sentence. My shrink was never so curious about what I was going to say that he ignored the buzzer. He never asked me if I wanted to stay a bit longer. He was patient. He assumed I'd show up again. And I did too. Week after week I came to him to hang out my dirty washing. Big, grubby sheets, black around the edges.

'Where were we?' Beau sat down again.

I quickly put my bag down again. 'You were asking me whether my father ever tried to get closer to me.'

'Right, yes.'

'No, not so far as I know.'

'Why do you think that was?'

'Birgit was the apple of his eye. All his hopes were riding on her. He was never particularly bothered about me. He wasn't expecting much from me.' I giggled. 'He had a point there, of course.'

Van Kooten's expression remained serious. 'No need to run yourself down, Lea. When I look at you I see a young, self-possessed woman with a good brain.'

Go on, go on! I wanted to shout, but I didn't dare. 'Don't you have to see your next patient?'

'That can wait a moment. How's it going with the grief-work?'

'I'm doing my best, I often ring my mother and my sister to talk about my father.'

'And how does that go?'

'It's difficult. Especially when I hear about things I didn't know before.' I told Beau how my father had been chased out of the marriage bed on his last evening. How everyone had looked down on him. 'We all wanted him to piss off. Birgit didn't even say goodnight to him when she got out of bed to pee . . .' Oops, there came the tears again. I pulled a tissue out of the box. 'She's not sorry either. Does that make any sense to you? I'd have liked to have said goodbye to him. But then, he didn't want to say anything to me, of course. He didn't want to see my photos either. Only hers.' I clenched my teeth hard. It hurt. It really hurt. *Waves of physical pain.*

'Let the sadness in. It's alright,' said Beau.

My body was shaking. I wanted to go on talking, I had to tell him everything now, even though my voice sounded as ridiculous as Ludo's. 'Do you know what my mother told me? My father took several weeks off work just before his death. He went out for little trips by himself a number of times.'

My father rides his bicycle, since we don't have a car. He cycles from Amsterdam West to Amsterdam East. He stops on the Plantage Middenlaan, locks his bicycle and walks through the tall gates of the Artis Zoo.

After standing in line for two minutes, he gets to the till. One ticket please; no, no wife, no child, not even a grandchild holding onto his hand. He is fifty-seven years old, so he doesn't qualify for a reduced price ticket. He gets his wallet out of his hip pocket and pays.

My father wanders into the zoo. The parrots squawk, the baboons scamper to and fro over their boulders. He visits the lions. They're asleep. He says hello to the leopard, which is pacing along next to the bars of its cage, exasperated. The giraffes look over the top of his head. He stands still to watch the polar bears, which are too big for their enclosure. The sea cow doesn't notice him, it's busy eating a lettuce. The flamingos make his eyes hurt. The penguins are smaller than he expected. He takes out his lunchbox and shares his sandwiches with the Przewalski horse.

My father is one of hundreds of people visiting the zoo on this particular afternoon. He passes unnoticed among the strolling crowds of people who lick their ice creams without a care in the world, thinking that the zoo will always be there, that they'll be able to come back every year.

He walks over to the aquarium. Inside he sits on a bench and watches the fish. He sits there for at least an hour. He thinks about the seasons. About the tides. About water and air. About everything that is and no longer will be. He's not going away, he's going to make the world go away. Like turning off the light. And the sound.

Waiting for death is for fools. They think it counts in their favour. That their patience will be rewarded. The Creator won't be able to take *him* by surprise any more. He is all-powerful. He will do away with life. Before it does away with him.

'Even his love of nature couldn't save him,' said Beau slowly. Then his eyes filled with tears.

I couldn't believe it.

I passed him a tissue and took one myself.

Beau took off his glasses and blew his nose.

Because he was crying like that, I had to laugh a little, through my tears. 'Does this often happen to you?' I asked.

'Not often,' he said hoarsely.

'It was the animals, right?' I guessed.

He nodded. Then he looked at his watch and jolted upright in dismay. The next patient was still sitting in the waiting room.

I stood up.

Van Kooten saw me to the door. In our hurry we forgot to make a new appointment. He took my hand and held it for at least three seconds. 'Thanks,' he said. He really was a bit confused, this shrink of mine.

'But you don't have anything to thank me for, do you?'

'Yes I do,' he said, his eternally lovely eyes searching for mine and finding them. 'Thanks for placing your trust in me.'

chapter thirty-eight

*The teacher told me later that she couldn't tell you were
new. Keep it up, little girl; adaptation is a key word in this
life.*

'Stefan de Wit speaking.'

'Hello Stefan, it's Lea.'

'Hi, Lea. How are things?'

'Fucked. Could I speak to Birgit for a moment?'

'I think she's in her study. I'll just call her.'

He put the receiver down. His footsteps died away. There
was silence for at least a minute.

'Lea?' It was Stefan again. 'She's got the headphones on. I told
her it was you, but she didn't want to come to the phone. Can
I give her a message?'

'I have to speak to her, Stefan. It's urgent.'

Stefan sighed and put the receiver down again. I clamped the
phone between my ear and my shoulder and went over to the
mirror. Harry was right. I really had to get my hair cut.

'Lea?'

'Yes, I'm still here.'

'Birgit's very tired. Could you call again tomorrow?'

'No. I have to talk to her now. You know what you could . . .'

'Lea?' Suddenly Birgit was on the line. 'I'll take it, Stefan, you can hang up now!' she called.

Stefan hung up.

'Lea, I'm knackered. I've been working very hard today.'

'I'll keep it short. It's about Dad.'

'What *now*?'

'I went to see my psychiatrist today and he started crying.'

'*What?*'

'Beau van Kooten, my psychiatrist, started crying. About our father. Because he thought it was so awful. What do you think of that? I go to a psychiatrist and what happens? The man starts crying.'

'What a softie.'

'He's not a softie. That guy's used to all kinds of stuff. But he's never heard anything as bad as this.'

'Yeah, yeah . . .'

'Do you know what I think? I think you've never grieved properly either. That's why you're so cold and unfeeling. You're stuck in phase one. Just like Mum.'

'What are you talking about?'

'Grief has several phases. If you don't grieve properly, you're in trouble.'

'Lea, I'm not in the mood for this.'

'Go on, deny it. Great. I did that for years too. Just go on pretending Dad was a monster. And Mum was a saint. Nice and simple.'

'Why can't you shut up about Dad. That man's been dead for twenty years. Let sleeping dogs lie.'

'A sleeping dog? Dad? I'm not going to shut up about him. I miss him.'

'Oh come on. You don't miss him at all. That stupid doctor of yours has been putting ideas in your head. Have you forgotten what he was like?'

'He had his good points too, Birgit.'

'Yes. And Hitler loved animals. Do you want to know what I think? Kees Cornelissen was a megalomaniac. When he saw that he was losing his power, he did away with himself. He was just a bigmouth. Like Hitler.'

'Don't talk about Dad like that. He doesn't deserve it.'

'Are you going to start crying now? Jesus Christ, Lea, do me a favour. He couldn't have cared less what happened to you. He didn't give a toss! He dropped you in the shit, for God's sake. He dropped all of us in it. And now you want to erect a monument to him?'

'I know he loved me. And I loved him.'

She laughed derisively. 'The way he loved me, I suppose. God, how that man loved me! Especially when I switched from science subjects to the humanities, remember? He gave me such a thrashing.'

'I'm talking about myself now. He never hit me.'

'Do you want to know what he thought of you? Just go and get your poetry album, you can read about it in there. Your dear father wrote a heart-warming poem for you.'

'A poem?'

'Yes. It's on page three. After Mum and your nursery school teacher.' Birgit always knew that kind of thing precisely. 'I'm going to hang up now, Lea.'

*

I ran up to the attic. So dad *had* left a note for me. I'd completely forgotten. The man had written me a poem. Specially for me. His youngest daughter.

Still panting from the two flights of stairs, I knelt down next to the boxes. I opened one of them and tipped out the contents. Old school diaries. Exercise books. No album. There were four more boxes. The album was dark blue. It must be here some- where. It must be. I opened the second box. My baby book. Envelopes with holiday snaps in them. Nothing else. The third box was only half full. I emptied it onto the floor. Letters from penfriends. Love letters. There was nothing blue in between the letters. I scratched my chin. Two more boxes to go. Two more chances. The fourth box was full of faded glory: LPs by Abba, Joe Jackson, U2, The Police. Damn, I couldn't find it anywhere! Surely I hadn't left it with Ed? I opened the last box. I was already running through the phone call to my ex in my head.

Suddenly I spotted it. My 'poetry album', as I used to call it. Dark blue. There was a picture of a cat on the front. I opened it with trembling hands. I turned to the third poem. I recognised my father's handwriting. 'Dad' it said at the bottom. *Dad. My father.*

See? I did have one. A dad. Tears splashed onto the page. I quickly wiped my face. I mustn't smudge the ink.

I lay down on my back.

> *On this dull day*
> *when the sun won't shine*
> *a happy song*
> *for a pretty little grub of mine*
> *this Lea of ours*

who is so good at getting her own way
that I've hurried off to write what she wants me to say.
How terribly sweet I find her
this is to remind her
the picture's here on show.
Be good, and know
that rhyming isn't something everyone can do
but many of us (sometimes) find we absolutely have to.

                                                      Dad

A pretty little grub. A terribly sweet, pretty little grub. That's what I was to him.

I hugged the poetry album close to my chest. The tears ran into my ears.

My father is dead. I'll never see him again. I'll never be able to tell him how much I love him. Our ways have parted for ever. No matter where I look, I won't ever be able to find him.

Nevertheless.

With the poetry album in my arms I ran downstairs.

chapter thirty-nine

25th November 1970

Last week you had a toothache, we went to the dentist and he filled two little cavities. You didn't mind at all. He put silver in your mouth, you thought that was wonderful. You were so proud that you showed it to everybody.

'Yes, madam?' The man in the doorway looked uncertainly at me. It was at least fifteen years since I'd last seen him. The older he got, the more my uncle looked like Toon Hermans[*]. It was unbelievable – the same twinkling eyes, the same grey moustache. His voice had that same mellifluous quality . . .

'Hello, it's me, Lea.'

'Lea?'

'Lea Cornelissen, your niece, Kees's youngest daughter.'

'Ah, Lea.' The penny dropped. 'How are you, Lea?'

'Fine, and you?'

'Fine.' He looked behind him for a moment. 'Aunt Mar isn't here. She's gone to a Women's Club meeting.'

_* Popular cabaret singer.

'Doesn't matter. It's you I came to see.'

'Me? Well, then come on in.' He stepped aside.

'Do you have some change, maybe?' I pointed to my car, which was parked across the street. 'I've forgotten my purse.'

'And your coat too, it would seem. My child, you're freezing.'

We went through the hall to the living room. The house was vaguely familiar.

Uncle Jan took an earthenware pot off the window ledge and turned it upside down. 'There should be a few guilders in here. It's outrageously expensive, that metered parking. Elise was clamped again two weeks ago when she came to bring the little one over. She can't have been here more than five minutes. I warned her, but there you go, she always knows better. How long are you thinking of staying?'

I studied the framed photos on the mantelpiece. As far as I could see my father wasn't among them.

'Lea?'

'Sorry, what was that?'

'How long are you staying.'

'Throw in an hour and a half's worth.'

'I can tell already, you're just as rude as ever.'

I giggled and gave Uncle Jan my car keys. He put a scarf on and went out.

'Shall I make you a cup of coffee?' he asked when he came back.

'Yes please.'

'It'll have to be instant, I'm afraid. Elise gave us an espresso machine, but there are so many twiddly bits on it, your Aunt

Mar spent three days studying the instructions. We're sticking to Nescafé for the time being . . .' He went to the kitchen.

I went with him.

The espresso machine took up half the available space on the terrazzo sink unit.

'Enormous thing, isn't it? We've put our old machine away in the cupboard. It still works fine, but there you go, Elise said we had to drink espresso from now on . . .'

I stroked the machine with one finger. It was precisely the same as the one Beau van Kooten had. That made sense. Everything made sense. I'd come to the right place. 'It's beautiful. Your daughter has taste,' I said softly.

'An expensive present, though. Aunt Mar went to the shop to find out how much it cost. It's shocking.' Uncle Jan put a kettle of water on. 'And how's life treating Lea? You were in the neighbourhood and you thought, I'll go and look up my old uncle. Are you aware that you're my godchild?'

Shit, that was true too.

Uncle Jan looked thoughtfully at me. 'Was it you who had a baby, or was that Birgit?'

'Birgit,' I lied. I didn't want to talk about Junior.

'A boy, right?'

'Yes.'

'Mother and child doing well?'

'She's on cloud nine.'

'Ah yes, so was Elise. She's gone back to work, though. My granddaughter goes to the crèche for two days a week and comes to us for one. It was a different story in the old days. Aunt Mar had to leave her job when she married. Your mother too, come to that. Is Birgit still working?'

The conversation was heading off in completely the wrong direction.

'I don't really know. I think she's got maternity leave.'

Uncle Jan poured the coffee.

'Shall I carry it into the living room?'

'It's alright, my dear.' Uncle Jan settled into a leatherette armchair.

He offered me the sofa.

The wall opposite me was one big bookcase. Left to right, top to bottom, the whole wall was covered in books. I wondered whether Uncle Jan had read them all or whether they were intended as decoration.

'Would you like a little treat?' He pointed towards the biscuit tin on the coffee table.

'No, thanks.'

'Dieting, no doubt.'

'No, I've just eaten.'

Uncle Jan took a shortcake biscuit out of the tin. As he ate, the crumbs rolled down over his clothes. He was wearing a red shirt, a check sleeveless jumper and a pair of grey rayon trousers.

There were several burn holes in his lap. 'Do you smoke a pipe?'

'Yes. You remember that?'

'No, I can tell from your trousers. My father's used to have little holes like that.'

Uncle Jan nodded. 'It drives your Aunt Mar crazy. She says she's going to sew me a great big bib and that she . . .'

'Do you ever think about my father?' I asked quickly.

He was silent for a moment. 'I visited his grave last month . . .'

His grave! So it's still there! They haven't cleared it!

'. . . once or twice a year. I burn a candle and think about him.'

'Was he a good brother?'

Uncle Jan took a sip of coffee. 'Your father was the brother I spent the most time with. When we got out of school we'd go and explore nature. We caught butterflies, looked for rare plants. We did all the things boys did in those days.'

'There were nine of you, right?'

'Seven brothers and two sisters. Your father was only a year older than me. The two of us slept in one big bed. During the war we were in Germany together. We saw the bombing of Dresden.'

I took a biscuit after all. Once these old folk start talking about the war . . . 'Birgit told me something about that once, about Dresden,' I said with my mouth full. 'That was quite something, wasn't it?'

Uncle Jan stuck his index finger in the air. 'On 13th February 1945 Dresden was bombed. A hundred and twenty thousand people met their deaths in one night. The whole city went up in flames. Your father and I were there. We witnessed the entire drama.'

'What do you mean, drama? They were all Germans, weren't they?'

My uncle frowned. 'They were citizens. Ordinary people, like you and me. There were a lot of refugees in Dresden too.'

'If you were there, and my father too, how come you survived?'

'Ha! Your father and I survived dozens of bombardments! We

knew better than anyone what to do, and above all what not to do.' His eyes began to shine. *Old soldiers never die.*

In 1943, Uncle Jan and my father are sent to Germany as forced labourers. They're in their early twenties and are put to work at the railway station in Heidebreck.

In January 1945 the two brothers desert. The Russian front is getting closer, they can already hear the gunfire. Hitler is losing the war. Jan and Kees put all their belongings onto an upturned table and set out on a gruelling journey across snow-covered plains. They are caught by a frustrated German officer. The man gives them a chilling look. 'Prepare a firing squad!' he growls to one of his subordinates.

At that moment, my uncle wets his pants.

'I started talking to the man, ad-libbing. Fortunately I spoke very fluent German. I told him we'd been sent West, that we were on our way to Dresden, that we certainly weren't deserters and that he should ring the railway station in Heidebreck if he didn't believe us.'

They put a call through to Heidebreck. With bombs coming in from all sides there, the phone is answered extremely promptly. Uncle Jan tells the officer on duty a very long and complicated story.

'I'm going to pass you over to someone else now, and all you have to do is to confirm that what I've told you is true,' he concludes his account. With a steely look, he hands the receiver to the officer.

'Yes, that's right,' the soldier says, having other things on his mind at the time.

The brothers are not executed; they are allowed to carry on to Dresden.

'We went by train. The heating wasn't working, it was ice-cold. I'll spare you the details, Lea, but they died in their droves on the train. Old people fell dead from their seats. Babies froze. It was dreadful . . .'

Kees and Jan end up at a guesthouse in the heart of Dresden. It's not safe even there. One of the heaviest bombardments of the Second World War is about to start.

'As soon as we arrived, your father and I worked out the best place to take cover. It was under the promenade next to the river Elbe. There were wine cellars under the terraces. You had three metres of earth above your head there.'

The city turns into a smoking heap of rubble. Jan flees further West. Kees stays on in Dresden. He wants to see the results of the bombing at first hand.

When he rejoins his brother later, he doesn't want to talk about it for quite a while. It seems he stood on the square where the guesthouse had been. There were enormous mounds of bodies piled up there, residents of the city. They were piled several metres high. There were so many that there was no way to bury them all. Petrol was thrown over the mounds. The petrol was lit. The corpses were all burned in one big fire. My father stood there and watched.

Uncle Jan heaved a deep sigh. He lit his pipe. 'I think that there in Dresden his darkest suspicions about life were confirmed. Kees got married, had children, he tried to do all the normal things, but I think deep down he was convinced from then on that no good would come of anything any more . . .'

It was so quiet. I could hear the clock on the mantelpiece ticking. The tears burned behind my eyes. It sounded so lovely, so final, so true, what Uncle Jan had said. But still. I looked at my uncle who was sucking on his pipe with his eyes shut. My father's brother. He was married too, he had children too. Grandchildren. He could make coffee. He smoked a pipe. Apparently he'd never felt the urge to do away with himself.

'If you were there with him,' I said after a while, 'how come you got over it?'

He opened his eyes. 'Your father and I were two very different people. Kees had a melancholic tendency. He didn't say much, didn't have many friends. After the war he threw himself into the works of the great philosophers. He made a radical break with the church, studied Kant, Nietzsche, Schopenhauer. He could quote whole pages by heart. His eyes would gleam when he did that. Whether it was books, poetry or music, he always went for the heavy fare. That's what he found beautiful.'

'Did he have many girlfriends?'

My uncle shook his head. 'He was a real man's man. He had no feeling for the feminine. Once during a walk he explained to me how he thought biological reproduction worked. He thought there were seeds that originated in a woman's womb and developed of their own accord. He was twenty-three, and he'd been through a war . . .'

I giggled. 'He was joking.'

'Absolutely not. I knew better by then and I told him he should go and talk to his father confessor.' Uncle Jan stood up. He took a book off the shelf.

A photograph album. A grainy black-and-white snapshot showed two boys in short trousers. Next to them stood a powerful-looking woman in an oversized black skirt that reached to her ankles. One of the boys was large and blond, he had rosy cheeks and a mischievous look. The other one was small and thin – he had dark hair and was wearing a serious expression. The second boy stood arm in arm with his mother.

'That little chap is your father,' Uncle Jan pointed. 'Even though I was younger, I very soon grew bigger than him. I went to the technical high school, whereas he was at the secondary modern. He was shy. Your father once said to me, *you dared to do anything, I was always scared*. I think deep down he was very sensitive. So sensitive that he had to armour himself like a tank.'

My shrink was right. I was right. My father was a sheep in wolf's clothing. He was a Christmas tree. Same as me. He wore a spiky cloak. He was like me. I am like him.

While all the Cornelissens carve out careers for themselves, my father chooses a simple existence as bookkeeper for a firm of masons in Amsterdam North. 'I work to live,' he says. 'I don't live to work.' In his spare time my father works single-mindedly on his experiments. On water beetles, on his gliding float – which gets a mention in *Het Visblad* – and finally his system of musical notation.

*

'He always sent me everything. Including his poetry. Asking what I thought of it. I'd have loved to be able to say, 'Yes, Kees, they're excellent, you must go on writing!' but I couldn't. The only authentic element they conveyed was his anger, the anger he felt towards the world. I showed his piano system to someone I knew who worked at the conservatorium. He said it was worthless. Said the same thing had been tried a hundred times. I didn't dare tell your father . . .' Uncle Jan closed the photograph album. His voice grew deeper. '. . . I didn't realise how serious the situation was by then. I didn't know that your parents had already got divorced. Of course I could see that your father's condition was deteriorating. We all saw that. He rambled, he sounded increasingly confused. When I came to visit you, I took care to stick to lightweight subjects. That was what your mother longed for. I spoke more and more to her too, rather than to him. He drifted away. He drifted away from us . . .' He winced with pain. He looked past me, towards the window. '. . . I used to think maybe it was an early form of Parkinson's disease. Shortly after the war Kees had a kidney infection. He was admitted to hospital. He was unconscious and had terrible fits, his arms and legs would thrash about uncontrollably. He looked really dreadful. Perhaps his brain was affected by that . . .'

No one has ever told me about a kidney infection. I don't know anything about Parkinson's. I've never seen bodies burning. No one has ever told me anything. I've been kept stupid by my mother's propaganda.

'Suicide is a form of indictment. I took it very badly. I've often thought, if only I'd written him a long letter. If only I'd made more of an effort.'

I laid my hand on Uncle Jan's arm. 'I don't think it would have helped, Uncle Jan.'

'I should make it clear to you that your father was never unpleasant towards me, Lea. On the contrary. When I wanted to continue my studies there wasn't any money. He, the lad from the secondary modern, offered me all his savings. He acknowledged my superior intellect. So you'll understand why I'll never say a word against my brother . . .'

I scratched my chin. I couldn't answer, because I'd start crying if I did.

'Your father had his difficult side. But then, don't we all? His misfortune was that there was no one to spur him on at the crucial moment. Ask any successful person. They can all point to someone who helped them get to where they are now. Your father never had that advantage.' He stood up. 'Excuse me, I have to go to the toilet.' He took a single step and then grabbed me by the shoulder. 'My knee's seized up.'

'That's okay. Take it easy.'

Uncle Jan breathed in and out a few times. 'One, two, there it goes.' As he tried to walk away on his stiff legs, he bumped into the coffee table. My cup fell to the floor. There was a dribble of coffee left in it, which spattered onto the beige carpet. Uncle Jan looked around, irritated.

'You carry on, I'll clean it up.' I got a tea towel from the kitchen to dab at the drips. Once I'd moved the coffee table slightly to one side you could barely see the stains.

Uncle Jan shuffled back into the room.

I helped him to his chair. 'Do you think anyone could have done anything to help my father?'

'What do you mean?'

'Well, I have a . . . I've heard there's a lot a good psychiatrist can do. If you're on a downward spiral, say.'

'As far as I know, your father never consulted a psychiatrist. And I can understand that perfectly well.'

'Really?'

'He only believed in the greats: Freud, Kant, Goethe, they were the men he regarded as his spiritual equals. What use did he have for some little man from Amsterdam who'd just got his diploma? He'd have laughed in his face. And a man like that would have brought up the subject of sexuality almost from the start. That was something he definitely didn't want to talk about.'

'Do you think he was queer?'

Uncle Jan drew back his chin. 'No. Absolutely not. Of course not.'

'It's possible though, isn't it? I've sometimes thought about it. It would explain an awful lot, his attitude towards the world in general and towards his family in particular . . .' My God, how beautifully I'd worded that. I could tell I'd spent a lot of time lately with men of a certain calibre.

Uncle Jan put his hand on my knee. 'I'm going to tell you something. This may be painful for you, but you're a grown-up woman now. You can face the truth.'

I stared hard at his wrinkled hand. *He's going to hurt me. I like the way he announces it beforehand.*

'Kees was actually a typical bachelor. A loner. He clung to his mother's apron strings for a long time. If it'd been up to him, he'd never have left the parental home. We – your father's brothers and sisters – often used to say, considering his last unhappy years . . .'

He left a short pause.

'Your father should never have married.'

chapter forty

23rd September 1971

*During the summer holidays we went camping for the first
time, in the Belgian Ardennes. We had a great time
together, especially you; there was a little stream behind
the tent and you spent the whole time in it with your
rubber ring.*

*Failure. He'd failed at everything. His career, his battle to save the
water beetle, his marriage, his notation system, fatherhood. He was
completely useless.*

I clamped my hands tight around the steering wheel.

*It's as clear as crystal. You're somebody. Or you're nobody. Kees, my
father, acknowledged the superiority of others. Not only of his brother.
Of the rest of his family too, of his wife, his children. Everyone looked
down on him. Full of disgust. Of pity. The one just as bad as the other.
With each passing day he diminished, and the madness grew.*

'*He drifted away from us,*' Uncle Jan had said.

*He didn't drift. He sank. Like a stone. Nine children, and it had to
be Kees who was the lame duck. The rest lived long and happily.*

I was crying so hard that I had to park at the side of the road.

Why in hell's name hadn't I got a mobile with me? I had to ring Beau. He had to comfort me. The pain was unbearable.

I drove on again.

Two hundred metres further on I saw a telephone box. I parked on the grass, got out and struggled through the little swing doors. I picked up the receiver.

Goddammit, it only accepted phonecards! I dropped the receiver and leaned against the glass wall.

If you find yourself in an unexpected situation, there's no need to panic straight away. First analyse the problem. Reduce it to its essentials.

Essentials, essentials, what were the fucking essentials? The essential thing was that I wanted to make a phone call. I was standing next to a telephone. But I didn't have a phonecard.

I stood facing the phone and studied it from top to bottom. Right at the bottom there was a slit I hadn't noticed before. Holy shit, I could stick a credit card in there. Eureka!

'This is Dr Beau van Kooten's practice. The practice is now . . .'
Cunt.

I looked at my watch. Five past five. My shrink had got away.

Or not. Maybe he was still there, even though the answering machine was on. If he heard my voice, he was bound to pick up the phone.

'This is Dr Beau van Kooten's practice. The practice is now closed. You can leave a message after the tone. In case of emergency please contact Dr Bent. His telephone number is . . .'

Shocked, I hung up. Dr Bent? Never heard of him. And there was Beau on the tape telling me that I should call him in case of emergency. But I wanted Beau. My very own Beau. To hell with Bent.

I rang for the third time and waited impatiently for the beep.
Beep.

'Hi there Beau . . . Mr van Kooten, it's Lea. I have to talk to you. We don't have another appointment and it's not going very well at all. With the grieving. I've been talking to my father's brother and I feel so terrible . . .' My voice cracked. 'Can you hear me? I'm in a box, a telephone box. I'm going home now, I hope you'll call me there. Bye Mr van Kooten, say hello to Ludo for me.'

As soon as I got home I ran to the phone. I got the tape again.
Beep.

'It's Lea here again. I'm home now. I just wanted to let you know. You've got my number, haven't you? Please call me, I really don't know what to do any more . . .'

Thumping noises on the line. 'Hello?' An unknown woman's voice.

'Who's that?' I asked suspiciously.

'Hello madam, I heard your message, I happened to be here at the practice and . . .'

'Who are you?'

'I'm a friend of Pierre van Kooten. He's the doctor's brother.'

'I know who Pierre is.'

'I thought so, since you mentioned Ludo. I've come here to fetch Ludo. Dr van Kooten has gone to Africa.'

Africa? Africa? Good God, this was a disaster. A complete disaster. Beau had fled. To Africa, to the wild animals. He'd gone back to work again too soon. He hadn't grieved properly. The life force was draining out of him. He'd set off on a final tour of all the beautiful things in creation. My shrink was in a dark tunnel. I had to save him.

'Is he . . . does his departure have anything to do with the death of his mother?'

'I think so, yes. He wanted to complete the grieving process in peace, he said. If you're one of his patients, then you'll know how important that is. Beau was a tremendous help to me when my daughter died.'

'How wonderful for you. Great. That's exactly what you need when you're in mourning. Someone to lean on. Beau is my rest and refuge too, you know. My father just died.'

'My condolences.'

'Thank you. When will the doctor be back?'

'I'm expecting him in about six weeks from now.'

A cold hand closed around my heart. *Six weeks, six weeks without Beau. Six endless weeks. Forty-two bleak and empty days. Forty-one lonely nights.*

'Madam? Are you still there?'

I made a confirmatory noise.

'I think I may be in touch with Van Kooten shortly. Shall I tell him you called?'

'Would you do that?'

'Of course. Just give me your number.'

I gave her my number.

'Anything else I should tell him?'

'Just say that I've reached stage three.'

'Oh Lord, that's the worst one.'

'I know,' I sniffed.

'I understand now why you want to talk to the doctor. I'll do my best, I promise. Take care of yourself, won't you.'

Harry put his head round the kitchen door. 'Any coffee going?'

'Make it yourself. Why are you so late?' It was the third evening in a row that I'd eaten alone with our Filipino girl. If you can call it eating. She was the only one who ate anything. Where she managed to put all that rice in that thin little body of hers was a complete mystery to me. She certainly must have a fast metabolism.

Harry went to make coffee. He was humming to himself.

'It doesn't interest you one scrap, does it?'

'Did she speak?' Harry said, without looking round.

'What I'm going through.'

He sighed. 'Lea, this household has been revolving around your suffering for months. What is it now?'

'I went to see my uncle. He told me about what my father did in the war. Dad was . . .' There was a catch in my voice. 'Dad was a victim. The horrific things he went through. Burning bodies, frozen babies . . .'

'Well well, dear oh dear. Do you want coffee?'

'No.'

He sat down at the kitchen table. 'I don't understand you. I've given you everything. Everything you've ever wanted. A house, clothes, a child, more shoes than Imelda Marcos. And all you do is whine on about your father.'

'I miss him.'

'Are you only capable of loving someone when they're

dead? You have a son to whom you devote two minutes a day—'

'Don't exaggerate.'

'Okay, four minutes.'

'I can only enjoy the present if I first come to terms with the past.'

Harry put his hands over his ears. 'I'm fed up to the fucking back teeth with hearing that sort of thing! The way you insist on talking like that psychiatrist of yours.'

'Beau predicted this, you know. Beau predicted I'd meet with incomprehension.'

'Does that Van Kooten only ever go on about your father, or does he talk about you once in a while?'

'What do you mean?'

'In my opinion you're the one who needs their head examined. Because of the great disappearing trick you played with our son, remember?'

'I'm not getting involved in this.' I stood up.

Harry grabbed my wrist. 'You can take that friend of yours for a ride but not me! I've been thinking. I know exactly how it is.'

I tried to pull free.

Harry got up, grabbed my shoulders and started screaming at me. He reeked of alcohol. 'You don't love me! And you don't love Junior at all! You only love yourself! Junior was in your way, so he had to die! You'd have loved to be able to mourn for him! Oh yes, how splendid that would have been, the pitiful young mother with her baby in a white coffin . . . But no, it didn't work out, did it?!' His breath made me retch. 'So what did the young mother do? She went off in search of another dead body. By chance she

had one in the closet already. That all worked out very nicely . . .
She was worthy of pity after all. She had an excuse after all . . .' He
gave me a shove. 'Say something, bitch! Don't just stand there
looking stupid! SAY SOMETHING!!'

Fuel to the fire.

I said nothing.

'You're utterly selfish. You want to know why I don't fuck
you any more? I'll tell you why. Because you disgust me. It's not
your body, as you seem to think, *you* disgust me!' He burped and
fell back into his chair.

Someone knocked at the bedroom door.

'Mrs Meyer?'

'Yes?'

'I have something for you.'

'What?'

'Open the door, please.'

I got up and opened the door.

My Filipina had a sheet of paper in her hand.

I could read it even upside down.

FAX MESSAGE FOR LEA MEYER
FROM BEAU VAN KOOTEN
CAPE OF GOOD HOPE

'I was cleaning your husband's room and then I heard the
machine and—'

I snatched it out of her hand and slammed the door shut.
Beau had sent me a fax. The angel. *He hasn't forgotten about me.*
He still loves me. My eyes sped across the page.

Lea,

As Martine has told you, I'll be in Africa for a few weeks.
Unfortunately I neglected to mention this the last time you came to see me.
Martine tells me you are in the third phase. I think the time is ripe for you to move on to the next phase. Namely, to become angry. With your father. You can read the details in the mourning leaflet.

Yours, Dr Beau van Kooten

P.S. If you need an appointment, you can get in touch with my highly respected colleague, Dr Bent. His telephone number is given in the answerphone message at the practice.

I read the letter three times. Perhaps I'd missed something. Perhaps there was a clue in it somewhere. An indication. An *I-miss-you-please-come-out-here-at-once*. Why was my shrink being so distant?

I pulled open the drawer of my bedside table and rummaged among the pairs of tights. I pulled the drawer all the way out and tipped it upside down. I did not find what I was looking for.

I walked out of the bedroom and ran down the stairs.

Harry was sitting on the sofa. He had a glass of whisky in his hand. The television was on.

'Have you seen my mourning leaflet?'

No reply.

I went over to the TV and switched it off. 'I asked you a question.'

'Turn that bloody TV on!'

'I need my mourning leaflet.'

Harry put his glass down with a bang, walked up to me and pushed me aside. He turned the TV on again.

It was an action movie. The sound was turned up full blast.

Harry plopped down onto the sofa.

I went over to the dresser and pulled open a drawer. There was the leaflet. On top of the Yellow Pages.

I took the leaflet with me to the toilet. I carefully locked the door.

Phase Four
And next comes anger. Directed at those who were involved with the death, at friends and family, possibly also at God, and finally at the dead person himself.

He/she has abandoned you. There is no avoiding this phase either.* Do not be afraid to become angry. Feel free to curse the dead. There's no harm in it. Regard it as part of your griefwork.

*In a certain sense the fourth phase is comparable to the anal phase. People who omit this phase can be recognised among the senile elderly who poke at their own faeces with sticks or other objects. An unpleasant sight, which only goes to emphasise the importance of working through all the above phases.

Suddenly my crotch was warm and wet. I'd wet my trousers. Just like Uncle Jan when the Germans were about to execute him. No doubt my father wet his trousers as well. And now I had too. Like father, like daughter.

Of course. I have to go through what he went through. That's not such a bad thing. It's good. I won't get angry with him. No way. I've been angry with him all my life.

I stood up and walked out of the toilet.

In the hall I picked up my keys.

From the living room I heard a gunshot. A woman screamed.

I softly pulled the front door shut behind me.

chapter forty-one

23rd September 1971

We had glorious weather this summer and everything went smoothly. After the holidays it was back to school; that was a bit difficult for you. You found it a bit hard to face the strictness of the everyday routine. But you got over that too within a week and school started to appeal to you again.

It was dark. The cobblestones gleamed. I got into my car.
  When I turned the key in the ignition the radio came on.

Christ suffered for our sake, to set an example to us, so that we would follow in His footsteps.

I quickly turned the radio off. There was the Message again. I scratched my chin. I didn't dare listen any longer. I put the windscreen wipers on the interval setting and drove off.
  Suddenly I had the feeling I wasn't alone. I looked in the mirror. The back seat was empty.
  AND SEE, I AM WITH YOU, ALL THE DAYS OF YOUR LIFE, UNTIL THE END OF TIME.
  That gentle male voice again. Who had turned the radio on?

I didn't want to hear it. Not now. I pulled the radio out of the dashboard and threw it onto the passenger seat.

DO NOT BE AFRAID.

It wasn't coming from the radio. Someone was talking to me.

Who are you?

WHO DO YOU THINK?

I don't know.

THINK ABOUT IT.

I frowned. Suddenly I laughed. *Beau, is that you, my love?*

For three seconds there was silence.

WRONG.

The voice sounded angry. Irritated. It wasn't Harry, was it? He wouldn't do that, he'd use the phone.

PRETTY LITTLE GRUB.

Goose bumps. They crept up my arms. He'd whispered it, but I'd heard it distinctly.

Daddy? Is that you? Is that really you?

YES, LEA.

Tears poured down my cheeks. I couldn't steer properly any longer.

Wait a moment, Dad, let me stop the car. Don't go away, will you?

He chuckled. I'd know his laugh anywhere. How wonderful it was to hear it again.

I've missed you so much, Daddy, so much has happened.

I KNOW.

What do you know?

EVERYTHING.

How can you know everything?

I WAS THERE.

What do you mean?

I'VE ALWAYS BEEN WITH YOU. I NEVER LEFT.

I wiped a tear from my cheek. It was too beautiful to be true.

So, you know everything? About Harry and about . . .

EDDIE-GIVE-'EM-ALL-YOU'VE-GOT ? AND HOW WHAT A SIGHT THAT WAS. I YELLED MY LUNGS OUT WHEN I SAW YOU STANDING THERE IN THE REGISTRY OFFICE. BUT YOU WOULDN'T LISTEN. PIG-HEADED, AREN'T YOU? JUST LIKE YOUR FATHER.

What did you think of my wedding dress?

THE FIRST ONE OR THE SECOND ONE?

The second one.

PRETTY AS A PICTURE. YOU COULD HAVE WORN A GARBAGE BAG, YOU'D STILL HAVE BEEN BEAUTIFUL.

I giggled. *That's what Harry always says. What do you think of him?*

ROUGH DIAMOND. YOU COULD HAVE DONE WORSE.

Daddy, listen, I've had a son. You have a grandson. A little boy.

YOU WERE SO BRAVE IN THE HOSPITAL. I WAS SO PROUD OF YOU. AND WE GOT A DELIGHTFUL LITTLE DUTCH BOY OUT OF IT. HE'LL GO FAR, LEA.

Have you seen him already?

OF COURSE. I WATCH OVER HIM. THE WAY I WATCH OVER YOU. ALWAYS.

I heaved a deep sigh.

Oh Dad, I'm so glad I can talk to you. There's so much I want to ask you. But what I'd really like . . . it's not possible of course, but I'd . . .

TELL ME.

I'd so like to see you. Really see you. Hold you. Maybe it sounds ridiculous, Dad, but if I shut my eyes, I know exactly what you smell like.

THERE IS ONE PLACE. ONLY I DON'T KNOW IF IT'S WISE.

Do tell me, Dad, do tell me. I found out from Uncle Jan that your grave is still there. Do you want to meet me there?

NO, I'D GET HOPELESSLY LOST.

What do you mean? That's where you are, isn't it?

I imagine my father shook his head.

THEY TOOK SOME BODILY REMAINS TO THAT PLACE. I'VE NEVER BEEN THERE MYSELF.

Neither have I.

I KNOW.

Do you mind?

OF COURSE NOT. I THINK IT'S VERY SENSIBLE OF YOU. A FUNERAL IS SUCH A PUPPET SHOW. WHEN YOU'RE DEAD YOU'LL SEE EXACTLY WHAT I MEAN.

You said something about there being one place.

THERE'S ONLY ONE PLACE WHERE I CAN APPEAR. WELL, TWO ACTUALLY. THE PLACE I WAS BORN AND THE PLACE I DIED. A TURKISH FAMILY IS LIVING IN THE HOUSE WHERE I WAS BORN.

They'll see us coming a mile away! They'd eat their headscarves with shock.

THAT'S WHAT I THOUGHT. SO THAT LEAVES . . .

The Sloterplas.

EXACTLY.

I started the car.

WHAT TIME SHALL WE SAY?

. . . mm . . . in half an hour?

GOOD. SEE YOU SOON.
Bye Dad. See you shortly.

When I got to the junction a penetrating smell hit me. A smell of urine. How was that possible? I sniffed again. Shit, it was my trousers. They were still wet from just now. I couldn't show myself to Daddy like that.

I turned the car around and drove back to the house.

Cautiously, I put the key in the lock. I carefully stuck my head in. The living room door was closed. Rambo was still at it. He was making an infernal row. Not everyone was dead yet.

I crept upstairs. I hesitated. What should I wear?

Ah, of course.

I went up the stairs to the attic. It was hanging there. Pretty as a picture, Daddy had said.

I pulled the ivory-coloured dress out of its plastic cover. It was a work of art. Fong Leng himself had sewn all the hundreds of little pearls on by hand.

I took off my clothes, pulled on the dress and struggled with the zip.

Now for the veil.

I crept down the stairs. I fetched the white court shoes from my bedroom and carried them down in one hand.

I left the house without being seen. I looked at my watch. Less than twenty-two minutes to go. I'd have to hurry.

In the driveway I put on my shoes. I ran to my car, got in and roared off.

*

I didn't drive to Amsterdam, I glided. All the lights turned green. What little traffic there was made plenty of room for me. Brides always have priority.

Oh Daddy, I don't know whether you can hear me. Even in my wildest dreams I never thought our reunion would be so festive.

I was overcome with emotion. I'd have to do something to stop myself from bursting with joy. I could try breaking into song. I cleared my throat.

> *Tonight, tonight, it all began tonight.*
> *I saw you and the world went away.*
> *Tonight, tonight, it's only you tonight*
> *In my arms, in my . . .*

> *I'd go down on my knees*
> *Kiss the ground that you walk on*
> *If I could just hold you again*

I sang all the way, until I was completely hoarse. Just like years ago when we went on school trips. The whole journey we sang about ten green bottles. When we got back, we had to lie down under the seats. The bus driver told the mothers he'd lost all the children. The mothers used to shout 'Oh no!' and put their hands over their mouths. At that moment we all jumped into view and all the mothers were overjoyed.

It was pitch-dark at the Sloterplas. I parked my car and walked across the grass to the edge of the water. The wind made my wedding dress billow out. I looked at my watch. Two minutes late. A lady was allowed that much.

'Daddy! Daddy, are you there?'

Silence.

'Dad! It's me, Lea. I've put on some different clothes, see?'

The Sloterplas lay there, desolate. There were slight waves on the surface of the water.

He's late. I should have known he would be. He hasn't got a watch.

I sat on the grass.

Ten minutes later he still hadn't shown up. I was starting to get pretty cold.

Suddenly I remembered what he had said. He could only appear at the place where he'd died. What an idiot I was! He hadn't drowned in the grass!

I took my shoes off and stuck my foot in the water. God almighty it was cold!

I took a run at it and dashed into the Sloterplas. After four paces I threw myself headlong into the water. Plunge straight in, that's always the best way.

Push, stretch, push, stretch . . . I had to get to the middle of the lake.

My dress weighed a ton. My veil came loose. I tried to catch hold of it but it floated out of reach. I let it go and swam on.

I was there. Treading water, I gazed out over the surface of the lake. Not a hint of a ghost to be seen. Nothing at all. Slowly it dawned on me once more. *Where did he die? Right!* Good God. It was going to be a short meeting. I wouldn't be able to last more than ninety seconds.

*

I took a deep breath. Then I dived down under the water. I swam to the bottom with my eyes wide open. Damn, it was far too dark – I couldn't see a blind thing!

I went back up to the surface, took another lungful of air and dived down again.

Nothing.

I felt around on the bottom with my hands.

Sand. Stones. No father.

My mouth filled with water. 'Fresh' water, they called it. Undrinkable.

The pressure on my chest increased. I couldn't hold out any longer. I came back to the surface gasping for breath. My nose was full of water. Fuck, it hurt! I was blue with cold. My muscles were stiff. And I still had to swim all the way back. I'd never make it.

I shut my eyes. *Come on, Lea, you can do it. Push, stretch, push, stretch . . . Just pretend it's a swimming pool. Pretend the water is warm. You're wearing a swimming costume, you're light as a feather. Push, stretch, push, stretch . . .*

Suddenly my toes touched the bottom. Damn, the water was only ankle deep, I could have walked the last few yards.

Panting, I fell onto the grass. I pulled a brown tendril out of my low-cut dress. Jesus, I stank!

I stood up. The wedding outfit clung to my body. I stripped off the dress, wrung it out and threw it over my shoulder. The little pearls tinkled against my buttocks.

*

And I saw
a new heaven
and a new earth
And God will wipe
all the tears from our eyes
and there will be no more death,
nor grief, nor crying, nor pain,
for the old order of things has passed away.

Revelation 21, verses 1 and 4

chapter forty-two

Hello Harry my little love, this is your mummy. The three of us went to the clinic together today. You weigh 8200 grams and you're already 71 centimetres long! Everything's going just fine, little man. I'm sitting at Daddy's desk. You're outside in the garden playing football with Daddy. Daddy races after the ball and you sit on the grass. I don't think you've much of a clue what Daddy's doing. Oh . . . now you're rolling over. You're going to cry. I'll go down straight away. I'll write again tomorrow.

With thanks to

My mother, for the baby book
My father, for the verse in my poetry album
Agaath, for her childbirth
Myrte Gay-Balmaz, for the lyrics of Birgit's song
Roland and Wilbert, for reading and re-reading
Liz, for the translation
Linda Michaels, for the sales
Oscar, Adriaan and Lex, for their confidence

> Some people believe in God
> I believe in Ton
> He really exists
> Ton is my husband

The following publications were used in the writing of this book:

Various authors, *Bevallen & Opstaan*, Uitgeverij Contact, Amsterdam 1980
Pablo Neruda, *De mooiste van Neruda*, Lannoo/Atlas, Amsterdam 1998
Various authors, *The Bible*
Ron Ramsey, *Rouw* (*Mourning*; leaflet)
Information leaflet, St Lucas Hospital, Amsterdam, Department N. (Psychiatry)

OMNIVORES

Lydia Millet

In the name of science, Bill Kraft has tortured animals, murdered an old woman and finally imprisoned his daughter Estée in her own home. As his remit moves from pushing back the frontiers of moth research to declaring his house an independent country, Esté comes to realise its time to head for womewhere more normal. So she moves to L.A.

'Reads like a cartoon with soul' –
Los Angeles Times Book Review

'With her adacious début novel . . . Millet proves herself one of the most fiercely intelligent young writers in recent years: a bold satirist with a wickedly unbridled imagination' – *Spectator*

'Has a barnstorming full-blooded craziness of invention . . . For sheer nasty, anarchic fun, *Omnivores* is a toothsome chunk of crab apple pie' *Herald*

£6.99 paperback

SWEET DESSERTS

Lucy Ellmann

Born in a middle-class, mid-Western family dominated by opera, art history and tuna fish sandwiches, Suzy Schwartz longs to be normal. In her opinion she eats too much and makes love too little, a lifestyle only slightly modified by marriage to one of her sister's ex-boyfriends. The birth of her daughter, Lily, prompts Suzy to set off, leaving husband and crosswords behing, to find the love of a good man.

'Lucy Ellmann does write a good novel. She knits the inner and outer worlds together with a natural grace: a kind of conversational elegance. An enviable skill, and an enchanting, enchanted book' – *Fay Weldon*

'Droll, drastically honest and deeply moving – the real thing' *Craig Raine*

£5.99 paperback

Now you can order superb titles directly from Virago

☐ Omnivores	Lydia Millett	£6.99
☐ Sweet Desserts	Lucy Ellmann	£5.99
☐ Going Down	Jennifer Belle	£9.99
☐ Lesbianism Made Easy	Helen Elsenbach	£6.99
☐ What Girls Learn	Karin Cook	£6.99
☐ Halfway Heaven	Melanie Thernstrom	£6.99
☐ Lady Moses	Lucinda Roy	£7.99
☐ Justine	Alice Thompson	£6.99
☐ Tipping the Velvet	Sarah Waters	£6.99
☐ The Girl with Brains in her Feet	Jo Hodges	£6.99

Please allow for postage and packing: **Free UK delivery.**
Europe: add 25% of retail price; Rest of World: 45% of retail price.

To order any of the above or any other Virago titles, please call our
credit card orderline or fill in this coupon and send/fax it to:

Virago, 250 Western Avenue, London, W3 6XZ, UK.
Fax 0208 324 5678   Telephone 0208 324 5516

☐ I enclose a UK bank cheque made payable to Virago for £ . . . .
☐ Please charge £ . . . . . . to my Access, Visa, Delta, Switch Card No.

Expiry Date ☐☐☐☐   Switch Issue No. ☐☐

NAME (Block letters please) . . . .

ADDRESS . . . .

Postcode . . . . Telephone . . . .

Signature . . . .

Please allow 28 days for delivery within the UK. Offer subject to price and availability.

Please do not send any further mailings from companies carefully selected by Virago ☐